The Anonymous Client

ALSO BY J.P. HAILEY

The Baxter Trust

The Anonymous Client

by

J. P. Hailey

DONALD I. FINE, INC.
NEW YORK

c.1

M

Library of Congress Cataloging-in-Publication Data

Hailey, J. P.
The anonymous client.

I. Title.
PS3558.A3275A84   1989   813'.54   88-45850
ISBN 1-55611-124-X

Manufactured in the United States of America
10 9 8 7 6 5 4 3 2 1

For Lynn,
Justin and Toby

1.

STEVE WINSLOW rode uptown in the back of a cab and thumbed through the casting calls in Backstage. They were, as he'd expected, much the same as in last week's issue. Most of the open auditions were for chorus work. Steve Winslow was neither a singer nor a dancer. Not that he hadn't done musical comedy in his time—in summer stock you did all the shows, and when a musical came along you faked it. Steve could carry a tune, and laboriously learn a dance step by rote if pressed, but no one was ever going to *hire* him to do it. Not with the wealth of legitimate singers and dancers New York City had to offer.

Steve sighed and flipped the page.

The cab pulled up in front of an office building on West 48th Street. Steve paid the fare, over-tipping as usual. After years of driving a cab himself, Steve had a soft spot for cab drivers.

Steve folded the paper under his arm, went into the lobby, took the elevator up to the seventh floor, got off and walked down the hall. It was a little after nine, and a mailman with a pushcart was making his morning rounds, sliding letters through the mail slots in the office doors. He had just stopped in front of a door and taken two letters from the cart when Steve walked up.

"I'll take those," Steve said.

The mailman gave him a funny look. Steve wasn't surprised. It was October, and Steve was seasonably dressed in brown corduroy pants, a blue T-shirt, and a tweed sports jacket. That, coupled with his shoulder-length dark hair, made him look somewhat younger than his thirty-five years.

The mailman glanced at the office door. On the frosted glass were the words, "STEVE WINSLOW, ATTORNEY-AT-LAW." The mailman looked back at Steve, hesitated a moment, then handed him the letters, and pushed his cart off down the hall.

Steve smiled. There was no way the mailman thought *he* was the lawyer. Probably some office boy *hired* by the attorney. Steve turned the knob, pushed open the office door.

Tracy Garvin was seated at her desk reading a book. Without looking at the cover, Steve knew it would be a murder mystery. It was all she ever read.

Tracy was about twenty-four, with long blonde hair that always seemed to be falling in her face, and large, round framed-glasses that had a habit of getting tangled in the hair. She was dressed in blue jeans and a sweater, her usual office attire. Steve didn't mind. How could he, the way he dressed? And it wasn't as if he had any clients he wanted to impress.

Tracy looked up from her book when Steve came in.

"Good morning, Tracy," Steve said. He held up the two letters. "Mail's here." He tossed the letters on her desk, smiled, and went into his inner office.

Steve sat down at his desk, tipped his chair back, and unfolded the Backstage.

"Mr. Winslow."

Steve looked up.

Tracy Garvin was standing in the doorway. The first thing he noticed was that her glasses were folded and in her hand. Steve frowned. In the little he'd seen of Tracy Garvin, one thing he had observed was that when she took off and folded her glasses it usually meant that she was upset about something.

"Yes," Steve said.

Tracy Garvin took a breath. She seemed to be controlling herself with an effort.

"Mr. Winslow, I haven't seen you in over two weeks."

"I know," Steve said.

"Then you come walking in here, toss the mail on my desk, and say, 'Good morning,' as if nothing had happened."

Steve looked at her. "What happened?"

"Nothing," Tracy said.

Steve frowned. This was not one of his days. But then, he reflected, not many of them were. "So what's wrong?"

Tracy took a breath, blew it out again. "Mr. Winslow, I sit at that desk eight hours a day, five days a week."

"I know. That's what I hired you for."

"Yes, but nothing happens. I open the mail and answer it. That takes a good fifteen minutes. And I answer the phone calls, a particularly demanding job, since most days there are none. I sit here all day long and I don't *do* anything."

"I know," Steve said. "I have no law practice. I have one client, Sheila Benton. Handling her affairs doesn't amount to much. She's in Europe now, so it amounts to even less. There's no work. I told you that when I hired you."

"I know that, but . . ."

"But what?"

"I don't know."

Steve smiled. "I do. You didn't believe me. You figured it was a law office, so something had to happen. Well, you're wrong. I have no clients, and I see no prospects of getting clients. But I still need someone to hold down the office. To hang out here and read books all day long. Some people would kill for the job."

"I'm not one of them."

"So what are you trying to say?"

Tracy took a breath. "I'm saying I can't take it. I need something to do. So . . . well, I'm giving two weeks' notice. I'll stay on till you get a replacement."

"I see," Steve said. "So where you gonna go?"

"I thought I'd try some of the larger law firms."

Steve nodded. "That's what I thought you'd say. You may have some trouble there."

"Oh?"

"Yeah. You're not a paralegal, you're just a secretary. You have no legal training or education."

"I know. But . . ."

"But what?"

"I hate to ask, but I need a recommendation."

"I'm afraid my recommendation won't cut much ice with the larger law firms. But you're welcome to it. But I'm afraid you're going to be disappointed."

"You think I won't get a job?"

"No, I think you might. But if you do, I think you'll be disappointed."

"Why do you say that?"

"Well, what do you think you'd do in one of those law firms?"

"I don't know. Assist the lawyer. Take notes. Look up things for him."

Steve frowned. "Yeah. That's the problem."

"What is?"

"It's those books you read. Those murder mysteries. Murders, clients, chases. Real life isn't like that. It isn't even like 'L.A. Law.' You might as well work for a business firm."

Tracy set her jaw, defensively. "Oh yeah?" she said. "You know that for a fact?"

"No, I'm just telling you what I think. And I think you'd be bored silly."

"Well, it couldn't be worse than here."

"Yeah. It could. Here you have no expectations. You sit and read your books all day. There you start off with high hopes, and wind up a bored file clerk." Steve sighed. "Look, I'm not trying to argue with you, and I don't want to disillusion you, but I don't want to send you out of here with false hopes, either. Cause you don't really want work. What you want is to play Della Street to my Perry Mason. And real life isn't like that. Now, if you want to leave, I can't stop you. You're welcome to my recommendation and I wish you good luck. I just think you're going to be disappointed."

Tracy stood looking at him for a moment. She frowned and went out, closing the door behind her.

Steve Winslow leaned back in his desk chair.

Damn. He really needed that. Now he'd have to find a new secretary. Not that that should be a problem—if worst came to worst, he could always call one of the temporary agencies. And it wasn't as if he knew Tracy Garvin well enough to really care if she left.

But still.

He'd started the day in a fairly good mood. After years of scratching out a living, of driving taxi cabs as an out-of-work actor, and then as an out-of-work lawyer, it was real nice to be on an annual retainer. To have enough money coming in to rent an office, hire a secretary, and draw a weekly salary himself. All right, so it wasn't that much. And all right, so all it really meant was he didn't have to drive a cab any more and had more free time to go to more disappointing auditions. And of course, it was galling to have no real law practice. To see his legal education go for nothing. To be washed up as a lawyer after handling just one case.

Particularly a case he had won. Steve smiled at the irony. Yeah, he'd won the case all right, but no one knew it. Not even Tracy Garvin. Oh, they knew his client got off. They just didn't know *he'd* got her off. And the things he'd had to do to win that case, playing the clown in court to take the heat off his client—well, after all that, there was no chance anyone was going to hire him to do anything else.

But he'd accepted that, and he was used to that, and he was living with it.

He just didn't need to have it flung in his face.

Steve picked up the Backstage, opened it to the casting calls. Shit. More of the same. He folded the paper over, ran his finger down the listings. "Off-Broadway showcase." Great. A chance to battle a hundred other actors for the chance to work for three months for nothing on the off chance some agent or producer might see his work. "Chorus work." "Chorus work." "Independent casting director accepting pix and résumés." Christ, had he registered with that one?

"All right, what the fuck is this?"

Steve looked up.

Tracy was standing in the doorway. Her folded glasses were in one hand. A letter was in the other.

Steve frowned. He'd never been an employer before. Never had an employee. Tracy Garvin was it. But he considered himself a liberal employer. He let her dress as she pleased, do what she liked. And she'd just given notice and he thought he'd taken it well.

But this was a little much.

He raised his eyebrows. "I beg your pardon?"

Tracy strode over to his desk and thrust the letter at him. From her action, it might have been a sword. "This!" she said.

Steve looked up at her. "And what is that?"

"A letter."

"I can see that. What about it?"

"Open it."

Steve frowned. After all, *she* was the one who had given notice. Had he offended her in some way? Perhaps the Della Street crack? Had she gone back to her desk, gotten pissed off, and typed up a formal letter of resignation? No, in that case, she wouldn't be asking him what it was. So what was it?"

Steve sighed, and took the letter from her. It was typewritten, postmarked, and addressed to him; in fact, it was one of the letters he had just set on her desk.

The letter had been slit open. Steve reached in and pulled out the contents.

It was ten one thousand dollar bills.

2.

THERE WAS also a letter.

> Mr. Winslow:
> I am in a desperate situation and require your ser-
> vices. The matter is extremely delicate and must be
> handled with the utmost discretion. Enclosed find a
> retainer of $10,000.

Steve Winslow read it out loud. He frowned, and looked at the
letter again. He looked up to find Tracy glaring at him accusingly.

"You did this, didn't you?" she said.

He stared at her. "What?"

"You did this. Because of the books I read. You did it as a joke.
Well, fine. You didn't know I was giving notice. But after I did,
not to tell me . . . well, it isn't funny."

Steve shook his head. "What, are you nuts?"

"No. You did this, right? You put the ten thousand dollars in
there."

"Are you kidding?" Steve said. "I don't *have* ten thousand dollars. If I did, I sure wouldn't put it in an envelope and give it to
you."

"You didn't?"

"No. Of course not."

Tracy stared at him. "You mean . . . ?"

"What?"

"You mean it's *real?*"

Steve shrugged. "I don't know. It could be counterfeit, but it looks real to me. Frankly, I've never seen a thousand dollar bill before."

"No, no. I mean, someone actually sent this to you."

"They sure did."

Tracy's jaw dropped open. "Holy shit!"

Steve smiled. "My sentiments exactly."

Tracy's face was struggling through a myriad of reactions. "But, Jesus Christ. I mean, hey look. I'm sorry. I just thought . . . I mean, seeing that letter, and—"

"Yeah," Steve said. "That's what I would have thought too. If I didn't know better, I'd think *you* put that ten grand in there to needle me."

Tracy could hardly contain herself. "So it's real. It happened. Someone just sent you ten thousand bucks!"

Steve frowned. "Yeah."

Tracy looked at him. "What's the matter?"

Steve shook his head. This was his day to disillusion her, all right. "I can't keep it."

Tracy's jaw dropped open again. "What?"

Steve held up the letter that had been in the envelope with the money. "Did you read this?" he said.

"Yes."

"It's typewritten and unsigned."

"I know. That's what makes it so interesting."

Steve shook his head. "That's the problem."

"What is?"

"This is an anonymous letter. An anonymous retainer."

"Yeah. So?"

"So I can't keep it."

"Why not?"

"I'm Sheila Benton's attorney. I handle her affairs. I can't take any other case unless I'm sure there won't be a conflict of interest."

"Why would there be?"

"I have no idea. But until I know for sure, I can't accept this retainer."

Tracy couldn't believe it. Or didn't want to believe it. "But that's ridiculous," she said. "There isn't the slightest chance in the world this has anything to do with Sheila Benton. It would be an incredible coincidence."

"Even if that were true, I couldn't discount the possibility. But it's not."

"Why not?"

"Think about it," Steve said. "I have no law practice what-so-ever. No one knows about me. The only people who know I'm practicing law at all are people connected with Sheila Benton."

Tracy's face clouded. "Oh. But . . ."

"But what?"

"Oh," she said in helpless frustration. "You can't give it back."

Steve smiled. "Now there you are absolutely right. I don't know who it came from, so I can't give it back. Which puts me in a hell of a position. I can't keep it, and I can't give it back."

"So what are you going to do?"

"Well," Steve said. "First thing, let's find out where it came from. Tell you what. Call the Taylor Detective Agency and see if you can get Mark Taylor on the phone for me."

"Right away," Tracy said. She turned and headed for the outer office.

"Hey, where you going?" Steve said.

She turned back in the doorway. "To look up the number on the Rolodex."

After the hard time Tracy had been giving him, Steve couldn't resist the shot. "Della Street never had to look up Paul Drake's number," he said.

Tracy made a face. "Hey, fuck you," she said.

"She never said that either."

3.

TRACY USHERED Mark Taylor into the inner office.

"Hi, Mark," Steve said. "Come in. Sit down. This is my secretary, Tracy Garvin. Mark Taylor."

Mark Taylor cast an appreciative eye over her. "Pleased to meet you," he said.

"Don't get too attached to her," Steve said. "She just gave two weeks' notice."

"I don't blame you," Taylor said to Tracy. "The guy's a slave driver. He's been overworking you, huh?"

"That's right," Steve said. "She can't stand the pace."

Taylor nodded, and slumped his bulk in the overstuffed clients' chair. Mark Taylor was Steve Winslow's age; in fact, they'd been roommates in college. But while Steve was tall and thin, Taylor was all beef. At six feet, 220 pounds, he had had professional football aspirations, before an injury cut short his career.

"So what's up?" Taylor said.

"I want you to locate a client."

"You have a client?"

"I will if you find him."

"Skipped out?"

"No."

"Police?"

16

Steve frowned. "No, but it's an idea."

"So who's the client?"

"I don't know."

Taylor looked at him. "You're kidding."

"I'm serious."

"You don't know your own client?"

"No."

Taylor ran his fingers through his curly red hair. "Now wait a minute. Let me make sure I've got this straight. You want me to find a client for you, but you can't tell me who the client is?"

"That's right."

"Could you give me a hint?"

Steve grinned and passed the envelope with the money over to him.

"What do you make of this?" Steve said.

Taylor opened the envelope and pulled out the thousand dollar bills. He riffled through them and whistled.

"Well?" Steve said.

"Well," Taylor said. "This seems to be ten thousand smackers of genuine U.S. currency. The bills are old and are not in sequence."

"That's right," Steve said. He handed him the note. "And what do you make of this?"

Taylor read it and looked it over.

"Well, this is your basic anonymous letter. It appears to have been written on a non-electric typewriter, with elite type. The *r* is slightly out of alignment."

"Not bad. I don't suppose you could tell me the make?"

"No, but I got an expert who could, if you want to pay the freight."

"O.K., send it along," Steve said. "And then start tracing the numbers on those bills. Cover all the banks. Today's Tuesday, so the withdrawal was probably made yesterday."

"Hell, Steve, you don't have to tell me how to do that. With a withdrawal of that size it should be a snap." Mark hefted the envelope. "I suppose you'd like me to take these along with me."

"I don't think so," Steve said, grinning. "Tracy?"

Tracy, who had been watching wide-eyed, was startled at being addressed. "Yes?"

"If you could type up a list of the serial numbers on these bills."

"Sure."

Tracy took the envelope from Taylor and hurried to her desk. Mark Taylor watched her go.

"Nice looking girl," he said.

"Yeah."

"Why's she really leaving?"

Steve shrugged. "Bored. Says I'm never here and there's nothing for her to do."

"Now where would she get an idea like that?" Mark Taylor said. He leaned back in his chair and yawned. "You know, when I got you an office in my building, I figured I might run into you now and then."

"Yeah. I know."

"So how come you never come in to work?"

Steve shrugged. "I just can't bring myself to come in here when there's nothing to do."

Taylor nodded. "Makes sense." He grinned and jerked his thumb over his shoulder toward the outer office. "But I suppose you find her attitude unreasonable."

Steve grinned. "Of course I do. She's young and impressionable. She wants everything to be exciting and fun. I, on the other hand, am a cynical old fogy—just on the near side of senile—and I happen to know that nothing is exciting and fun, and I'd be happy to settle for interesting."

"An anonymous ten thousand dollar retainer's rather interesting."

"It is for a fact. It's also a pain in the ass."

"Maybe for you," Taylor said. "I can always use the work."

"Things slow?"

"Not slow. Just dull. Lotta personal injury shit."

"You got some men on tap to put on this?"

"No problem."

Tracy returned from the outer office and handed a typewritten list to Mark Taylor and the bills to Steve Winslow.

"Thanks," Taylor said. He glanced at the list, folded it, and stuck it in his jacket pocket. "I'll get right on this. Anything else?"

"Yeah. When you find my client, put a tail on him. Don't let him out of your sight, but don't let him know he's being tailed."

"I like the sound of that."

"Why's that?"

"Sounds expensive."

"I'm sure it is. Just don't pad your bill too much, cause I may have to eat it."

"I'll pretend I didn't hear that particularly offensive remark. But for the sake of future argument, let's pin down exactly what you want."

"I want you to find my client. I want you to tail him. I don't want him to know he's being tailed."

"And you want to pay a buck ninety-five."

"Exactly."

Taylor nodded. "That gives me a pretty good idea. And how extensive do you want the surveillance?"

"Total. I want to know where he goes and who he sees."

"That's a problem."

"Why?"

Taylor shrugged. "Well, this may surprise you, but there's a lot of people still don't walk around with name tags on their chests. Which means I gotta tail the people he talks to in order to find out who *they* are."

"Of course."

"And I presume these people can't know they're being tailed."

"Naturally."

"I don't want to ruin your day, but if this guy has an active social life, this just could run more than a buck ninety-five."

"Just remember it's coming out of my own pocket."

"Well, it's a pretty deep pocket. I see a ten thousand dollar retainer in it."

"Yeah, well I can't keep it till I know whose it is. I can't even put it in the bank."

"You're kidding."

Steve shook his head. "Depositing it in my account might be considered tantamount to accepting employment."

"So what you gonna do with it?"

Steve jerked his thumb. In the corner was an old office safe he had inherited from the previous tenant. "Tracy, we got the combination to the safe somewhere?"

"I don't know," Tracy said. "If you did, it was before I started work."

"Yeah," Steve said. "The guy gave it to me, and I'm not sure what I did with it."

"Probably locked it in the safe," Taylor said.

"Yeah, right. Well, if I can find it, I'll put the money in there. Otherwise, I'll have to rent a safe deposit box. But the one thing I'm *not* going to do is deposit it in my account." Steve frowned. "O.K., Mark. Get me off the hook. Tell me who my client is."

"No problem," Taylor said, getting up. "I'll get right on it."

"How soon you think you'll have it for me?"

Taylor shrugged. "I should have it before lunch."

Tracy had been standing there, hanging on every word. She was obviously very excited, and was making a great effort not to show it. But this was too much. In spite of herself, she blurted, "You're kidding."

Mark Taylor looked at her and smiled. "No, I'll have it. It's just routine."

Mark Taylor meant his remark to be friendly and reassuring. And perhaps to impress this attractive young woman with his efficiency.

But the effect he achieved couldn't have been worse. Tracy looked as if he'd just told her there was no Santa Claus.

4.

IT WASN'T quite that easy. Actually, it was closer to two thirty when Mark Taylor finally got back with the information.

In the meantime, Tracy had been giving her best impression of someone who was not excited out of her mind. It was easy at first because she was occupied—the combination to the safe had to be found. An exhaustive search of the office had finally located it where Steve had shoved it, among the papers in one of his desk drawers. And it had been interesting to watch Steve try the numbers on the antique safe and see if the combination actually worked. But after it had, and the ten thousand dollars had been safely locked inside, Tracy had come full face up against her original problem—there was nothing to do. It had been boring before. In light of the anonymous letter, it was excruciating.

Steve was keyed up too, but on a different scale. Tracy was like a kid with a new toy. She accepted the letter as a matter of course. She was young enough and romantic enough and so conditioned by a steady diet of detective novels, that she *expected* anonymous cash retainers sent in the mail. Steve was old enough and cynical enough to realize such things were fantastic and totally unreal and therefore to be regarded with the utmost skepticism.

Which didn't stop from making them interesting as hell.

21

22 J. P. HAILEY

When the intercom buzzed at two thirty, Steve Winslow picked up the phone and Tracy Garvin in the outer office said, "Mark Taylor on 2."

"Thanks," Steve said. "Stay on the line and take notes." He pressed the blinking button. "Yes, Mark."

"Got him, Steve."

"Great. Who is he?"

"His name is David C. Bradshaw. He's around forty-five, short, wiry, dark hair. He lives in an apartment on East 3rd Street."

"Good work. How'd you find him?"

"Just routine. I covered the banks. The withdrawal was unusual enough that the teller took down the serial numbers. Fortunately, it was a bank I'd done a few favors for in the past, so they were most cooperative. Naturally they wouldn't tell me anything about the account, other than when it had been opened, which was about a month ago. But they did confirm the withdrawal and gave me a pretty good description to go on."

"Where is he now?"

"Apparently he's home."

"How do you know?"

"As soon as I got the address I sewed up the apartment building. Five minutes after my man got on the job, a young woman showed up, pressed the button for 2A, and was buzzed upstairs."

"Got a description of the girl?"

"I'll say. My man says she's a baby-faced blonde of about twenty-five with a hell of a nice ass."

"Miss Garvin is taking notes on the line, Mark. Let's not bog her down with too many details."

"Right."

"Where's the girl now?"

"Still up there."

"How many men you got covering the apartment?"

"Two."

"Put another one on. Two if you have to. Tail the girl when she leaves. Slap a tail on anyone else who calls on Bradshaw. Use as many men as you have to, but keep that apartment covered. When the girl leaves, let me know."

"No problem. You going to go see him?"

"Not just yet. I want to be a little more sure of my ground before I actually talk to him. You don't have anything else on him?"

"How could I, Steve? You said don't let the guy know he's being tailed."

"Yeah. I know."

"I'll get the dope, but it's gonna take some time."

"O.K. Call me as soon as something breaks."

Tracy was in the door practically before Steve hung up the phone.

"He got him," Tracy said.

"Yes."

"That's great."

"It's a start."

"It's more than a start. Now you know who the client is. Now you can keep the retainer."

"No I can't."

"Sure you can. The client's David C. Bradshaw. He has nothing whatever to do with Sheila Benton."

"How do you know?"

Her eyes were wide. "How do I know? I've been handling the business for months. There's been nothing even remotely connected with any David C. Bradshaw."

"I'm sure there hasn't. But that's not conclusive proof."

"But—"

"Look. As I said, it's a start. Mark Taylor's getting the dope on him. As soon as he does, I'll talk to the guy and we'll work something out. At least the situation will be clarified. In the meantime there's nothing to do but wait."

Tracy gave him a pout. "And what are we supposed to do while we wait?"

Steve shrugged. "Why don't you read your book?"

Tracy gave him a look and flounced out.

Mark Taylor called back a half an hour later.

"She left the apartment, Steve, and Bradshaw left right after her."

"Your men pick them up?"

"Uh huh. I had four men on the apartment. Two of them took Bradshaw, and two of them took the girl."

"Any idea where they're headed?"

"The girl hailed a taxi and started uptown. Bradshaw went to the corner drugstore and made a phone call."

"Your man listen in?"

"He couldn't get that close, Steve. You told me you didn't want Bradshaw to know he was being tailed, and my man couldn't take any chances. But he thinks the number Bradshaw called was busy."

"Why?"

"Because Bradshaw was only in there a minute. Then he came out and walked a block, and made another phone call from the booth on the corner. He got a busy signal again. He tried two more times before he got through. He talked on the phone a few minutes, then hailed a cab and headed uptown. So my man figures Bradshaw got a busy signal on the first call and knew his party was in, so he walked down to where he could get a cab, called his party again, made a date, and that's where he's going."

"O.K. Just keep him in sight and let me know where he goes."

"Will do."

Fifteen minutes later an apologetic Mark Taylor was back on the phone.

"They lost him, Steve."

"Shit."

"Yeah. I know. I'm sorry, but what can I say. He got out of the cab, walked into a hotel lobby, and disappeared."

"Was he wise?"

"I don't think so. The two guys I had on him were pros, and they had specific instructions not to tip their hands. I'm afraid it's just one of those unlucky flukes."

"What hotel?"

"42nd Street and Third Avenue. That was part of the problem. My guys were in a car. You know what parking's like midtown. There's none. So one guy stayed with the car, and the other hopped out and followed him into the hotel. When he got into the lobby, the guy was gone."

"Hell. Where are your men now?"

"One's gone back to cover the apartment in case Bradshaw shows up. The other's covering the hotel just in case."

Steve sighed. "O.K. I guess that's the best you can do under the circumstances. What about the girl?"

"She seems to be on a shopping spree. At the moment she's in Bloomingdale's trying on clothes."

"Got a line on her yet?"

"Are you kidding? You said you wanted this handled discreetly. I could have my men start shaking down salesgirls and maybe get a look at a charge card receipt, but then the cat would be out of the bag. I'm hoping the girl will go home, so I can get a line on her, but now she's shopping and there's nothing much I can do."

"O.K., Mark. Do the best you can."

Steve Winslow hung up the phone and rubbed his chin, thoughtfully. Tracy, who had been listening on the other line, came in the door.

"You heard?" Steve asked.

"Yeah. They lost him."

"Yeah. And Mark thinks it was an accident."

"And you don't?"

Steve shrugged. "I don't know. But here's a guy who sends an anonymous ten thousand dollar retainer. He obviously doesn't want to be found. But I hire detectives and find him. And as soon as I do, he gives the detectives the slip. Now am I supposed to believe that's just coincidence?"

Tracy shook her head. "It couldn't be. He has to be wise. But what's the point? If the detectives picked him up at his apartment, there's no way he can keep you from finding out who he is."

"Right."

"So what's the point?"

"He must want to keep me from finding out where he's going."

Tracy's eyes widened. "Of course. That's it." Her face fell. "And now you'll never know. He's done it."

Steve shook his head. "This is true."

"But—"

The sound of the outer office door opening and closing cut Tracy off.

"Someone in the outer office," she said.

"Our busy day," Steve said. "Better see who it is."

Tracy went out, closing the door behind her.

She was back moments later. She slipped in theatrically, closing the door behind her, and said, in an exaggerated stage whisper, *"He's here!"*

5.

DAVID C. BRADSHAW matched Mark Taylor's description—short, tough, scrappy. He also matched Tracy Garvin's description—pissed off. He had a thin moustache under a narrow, protruding nose, which gave him an insolent quality. He was wearing a gray suit that on someone else might have looked fine, but on him somehow looked cheap. Steve Winslow's first impression was sleaze.

Bradshaw's eyes flickered when they took in Steve Winslow—Steve was obviously not what he'd expected—and Steve thought he saw a flash of doubt. It was momentary, however. Bradshaw scowled, marched up to the desk, and stuck his finger in Steve's face.

"All right, what the hell do you think you're doing?"

Steve shrugged. "I think I'm running a law practice. What the hell do you think you're doing?"

Bradshaw frowned. "What are you, some sort of clown? I warn you, you better have a pretty good explanation."

"I assume if we talk long enough, you'll get around to telling me for what," Steve said. He glanced over to the doorway where Tracy, who was supposed to call Mark Taylor, was hovering, unable to tear herself away from the scene. "Miss Garvin," he said, "if you would take care of that other business."

27

"Don't bother," Bradshaw said. "I'm sure that other business is tipping off your detectives that I'm here. I'll save you the trouble. When I leave here, I'm going straight home. They can pick me up there. Or if you don't believe me, call them and have them pick me up here, it's all the same to me."

Steve nodded. "Under the circumstances, Tracy, you may as well stick around."

Bradshaw's eyes narrowed. "Then you admit you hired detectives to follow me?"

"I admit nothing of the sort."

"Do you deny it?"

"I'm not in the position to admit or deny anything."

"That's a hell of an attitude."

"After all, I didn't seek this interview."

"After all, I'm not having you shadowed."

"Can you prove it?" Steve asked.

That caught Bradshaw up short. He frowned. "What?"

"Do you have any proof of it?"

"Of what?"

"The fact that you're not having me shadowed."

"Don't be absurd."

"Why is that absurd?"

"I'm not having *you* shadowed. You're having *me* shadowed."

"How do I know you're not?"

"I told you!" Bradshaw screamed.

"That's a self-serving declaration," Steve said calmly. "It doesn't constitute proof. Can you prove you're not having me shadowed?"

"Why should I want to have you shadowed?"

"Why should I want to have *you* shadowed?"

"That's exactly what I came here to find out."

"Well now," Steve said. "As you have so aptly pointed out, there is no way that you can prove that you are not having me shadowed. You must realize that it follows that there is no way that I can prove that I'm not having you shadowed."

"Because you *are* doing it. You won't even deny it."

Steve frowned. "Look at it this way, Bradshaw. If I were having you shadowed, I would not be doing it on my own accord. I would be doing it for a client."

"Of course."

"And if I were doing it for a client, my duty to my client would prevent me from giving you any information on the subject. I would not be in a position to either confirm or deny it."

"Which is exactly what you are doing in this case."

"However," Steve went on, "if I were *not* shadowing you for a client, I would be forced to give you exactly the same answer. I could neither confirm nor deny."

"Why?"

"Because if my behavior wasn't uniform in either instance," Steve said dryly, "my attempts to divulge no information would be somewhat futile."

"Fuck that," Bradshaw said. "I didn't come here to listen to that. I say you're shadowing me. Now forget your lousy ethics for a minute and tell me why you're doing it."

Steve sighed. "I'm afraid this interview is not going to be very satisfactory. Now, you say you're being tailed by detectives?"

"You ought to know."

Steve picked up the phone and punched in a number. "Steve Winslow for Mark Taylor." Steve covered the mouthpiece and said to Bradshaw, "This agency handles all my detective work. Let's see what they say about it." He uncovered the mouthpiece. "Mark, Steve. Look, Mark, I have a fellow here in the office by the name of Bradshaw."

"What!?"

"That's right. A David C. Bradshaw. He claims detectives have been tailing him."

"Son of a bitch!"

"Do you admit you had operatives following him?"

"You mean he's there now?"

"Well then, do you deny it?"

"What's going on? Can he hear this?"

"I see. I hoped you could give me a little more help than that."

"What do you want me to say, Steve?"

"No. I understand. You have to protect your clients."

"Shit. Let me get off the phone and I'll get a tail on him."

"O.K., Mark. Sorry to bother you."

Steve hung up the phone. "I'm sorry, Bradshaw, but you're going about this all wrong. You can't get information from lawyers and detectives. They have to protect their clients."

Bradshaw scowled. "When I find your client, he's going to need protection."

Steve studied Bradshaw narrowly. "Now look here, you wouldn't be trying to kid me, would you?"

"What do you mean?"

"You seem to know more than you're letting on."

Bradshaw laughed. "That's a good one. I seem to know more than I'm letting on. You won't tell me a thing. Can you give me one good reason why I should spill my guts to you?"

"I could give you ten thousand reasons."

For a second there was a flicker of expression in Bradshaw's eyes. Then he controlled himself, put his hands on the desk, and leaned into Steve's face.

"You know something, Winslow, you're smart. But this time you've been a little too smart. Go ahead. Shadow me to your heart's content. See if I care. All you're gonna get for your trouble is a big fat detective bill. Now then, if your detectives have managed to get here in time, I'll pick them up in the corridor. If not, I'll pick them up at home. So long, wise guy."

With that, Bradshaw turned and stalked out of the office.

6.

MARK TAYLOR stuck his head in the door.

"Steve, this is getting screwy."

"You're telling me, Mark? Did you pick up Bradshaw?"

Taylor waved it away. "Yeah, yeah, he's covered. Never mind him. I just got a call from the guys tailing the girl. She left Bloomingdale's and they're tagging along. But get this. There's another agency on the job."

"What!?"

"That's right. There are two other guys tailing her."

"No shit! Any idea who it is?"

"My man didn't recognize them, but he got the license number. I'm running it down now."

The phone rang. Tracy was so fascinated with what she was hearing that it rang twice and Steve had to give her a look before she answered it. She listened, then handed the phone to Mark Taylor. "It's for you."

Taylor took the phone, listened, said, "Uh huh," and hung up. "Got it, Steve. It's the Miltner Detective Agency."

"Know anything about them?"

"I've heard of them. They're a fairly reputable small agency. They mainly handle routine stuff. You know. Divorce cases, accident claims, stuff like that."

Steve rubbed his head. "Jesus Christ."

"Yeah. Look, Steve, I don't like this at all. We were just looking to I.D. the girl and drop her. Then we run into this. It's crazy."

"Yeah."

"And if we spotted them, it's a cinch they spotted us. I just don't like it."

"Well, there's nothing we can do about it. If she's being tailed, she's important. We gotta tag along and find out why."

Taylor sighed. "That's what I thought you'd say."

"So what'd you get on Bradshaw?"

Taylor shook his head. "Nothing. There's nothing to get. He's got no driver's licence, Social Security number, credit cards, birth certificate, marriage license, or what have you. My man pulled the old credit rating line on Bradshaw's landlady and drew a blank. The guy moved in two months ago. He pays his rent in advance and in cash. That's all she knows and all she cares to know. The bank can't give us any more information than it already has."

"What I.D. did he use with the bank?"

"Cold hard cash. After he deposited it the bank made him up a nice little photo I.D. with his signature, but for our purposes it's not worth the paper it's printed on."

"And that's it?"

"That's it. So the odds are, David C. Bradshaw isn't your client's real name."

"That figures." Steve frowned. "Look, Mark. You got a finger-print kit in your office?"

Taylor stared at him. "We got one. We never use it, but we got it."

"But you know how to use it, right?"

"Hey, give me a break. That's TV stuff, and it never happens, but I can do it all right. Why?"

"When Bradshaw got mad, he leaned over the desk to tell me off. I think we might have a pretty good set of latent prints."

Taylor shook his head. "Jesus." He went out and came back ten minutes later with an old leather satchel.

"Found it. I had to turn the office upside down, but I got it. Where are the prints?"

Steve pointed. "Right here on the top of the desk."

Taylor opened the satchel. "O.K. The surface doesn't look bad, but I'm not promising anything."

Tracy was hardly able to contain herself. She kept quiet, but her eyes sparkled as Mark Taylor pulled powders, brushes, a magnifying glass and a fingerprint camera out of the bag. He dusted powder on the desktop, and whistled.

"Well, wrong again. I got ten beauties, Steve."

"Gonna lift 'em or photograph 'em?"

"I'll photograph 'em first, then I'll lift 'em."

Mark Taylor busied himself with the prints. He'd finished photographing them and begun lifting them and transferring them to fingerprint cards when the phone rang. Tracy reluctantly tore herself away to answer it.

It was for Mark Taylor. He took the phone, listened, and hung up.

"You're client's an honest man, Steve," he said.

"How so?"

"He went straight home, just like he said he would. He's there now."

"How many men you got on him?"

"Right now I've got four men and two cars. If he has any more visitors, I'll throw in two more men and another car. This time he's gonna stay put."

"Good. Can you trace those prints?"

Taylor sighed. "If he's got a record, we can trace them. It's a bitch, but I can do it. But it's gonna take time."

The phone rang again. Tracy picked it up, listened, said, "Just a minute," and handed it to Mark Taylor.

"Mark Taylor here . . . Uh huh . . . The Binghamton? . . . descriptions . . . Uh huh . . . O.K., if they leave separately, split up and tail 'em. I may send another man. Whatever you do, don't lose the girl. Stick with her and keep me posted."

Taylor hung up the phone.

"Is that our girlfriend?" Steve asked.

"Uh huh. She's at the Binghamton. It looks like she's gonna have dinner with a young couple who joined her in the cocktail lounge."

"What about the couple?"

"Best bet is they're married."

"To each other?"

"More than likely. The guy's about thirty, and the wife is a few years younger. They seem to know our young lady pretty well, and the meeting seems to have been arranged rather than accidental. The couple came in together, and I assume they'll leave together, so I told my men to split up and have one take the girl and the other take the couple. Now then, do you want another man on the job in case the couple splits up?"

Steve frowned thoughtfully. "If they're married, they'll probably go home together. Where is the Binghamton, anyway?"

"Oh, it's in Jersey. Right across the river. On the river, actually. It's a boat. An old ferry boat. It's permanently docked and outfitted as a restaurant. Kind of nice. You can sit and have dinner on the river."

"How'd the girl get there?"

"In a taxi."

"What about the couple?"

"I don't know. They were there first. The girl walked in and joined them. I would assume they came in a car, but until they leave, there's no way to find out."

"I see. Assuming they have a car, you would expect the girl to leave with them. But we can't count on it. All right. Let's assume the couple's gonna leave together. So we don't need another man. But what about cars? Are your two men in one car?"

"Yeah."

"I think you better get another car down there then. I don't want to take a chance on the couple getting away without our finding out who they are."

"Do you think it's that important?"

Steve shrugged. "That's the hell of it. I don't know. I'm in a very tricky position, ethically, and I'm being forced to do a lot of things I don't want to do."

"Why?"

"All right, look," Steve said, "Either David C. Bradshaw's my client or he isn't."

"And either I'm a detective or I'm not."

"I'm serious, Mark. Either Bradshaw sent me the money or he didn't."

"I thought we'd established he did."

Steve shook his head. "Yeah, but he wouldn't admit it. And I keep trying to convince myself that he didn't. Cause I don't want him for a client. Now, I can get around the bills by figuring that he gave them to someone else. But there's one thing I can't get around."

"What's that?"

"He came to my office. The minute he noticed he was being followed he came straight to my office. He must have realized I traced the bills and hired detectives to find out about him. That means he sent the bills and the letter. So, much as I hate it, I'm forced to assume that David C. Bradshaw is my client."

"Why does that put you in a shaky ethical position?"

"Because a lawyer is bound to protect the rights of his client. Now then, if David C. Bradshaw is a client, he's already stated in his letter that his situation is extremely delicate and must be handled with utmost discretion. Therefore, if I inadvertently do anything indiscreet to jeopardize his situation I am violating legal ethics by acting against the wishes of a client."

"Oh shit," Taylor said.

"Exactly," Steve said. "On my own initiative I decided to have Bradshaw followed. Not only was this not in accordance with his wishes, but as soon as he realized it he flew into a rage and came up here to cuss me out about it. And I'm still having him followed."

"I see."

"There's one saving grace. Tracy, you took shorthand notes, didn't you?"

Tracy had, but she hadn't thought he noticed. "Yeah."

"I thought you had. Good. Hang on to them. They may be important."

"Why?" Taylor said.

"That's the saving grace. Bradshaw came to tell me to stop following him. But I got him so pissed off he never got around to it. In fact, he finally said something like, "Go ahead and follow me, see if I care, you're just going to run up a big detective bill." So if worst came to worst, I could use that to show he'd O.K.'d the surveillance."

"I see."

"I don't like it much. It makes me look like a tricky shyster. But right now I got no choice."

Taylor nodded. "Shit."

"So what about that car? Can you get another car out to the boat?"

"Yeah. I'll probably have to bring it out myself. I got my men stretched out pretty thin."

"I'll go with you. I want to check out the girl anyway."

"O.K."

As they started for the door, Tracy said, "Hey, what about me?"

Steve stopped and thought a moment. "Close up at five as usual. If anything important comes in, call the Taylor Detective Agency and have 'em relay the message. Come on, Mark, let's go."

They went out the door.

Tracy stood there, staring after them. She took a breath and blew it out again. So. This was her reward for taking the short hand notes. When she hadn't even been asked. Great.

Tracy stalked into the outer office. Her book was lying on the desk. She snatched it up and looked at it for a moment.

Then she slammed it down on the desk.

7.

THEY TOOK two cars, seeing as how they had to get home again. Mark Taylor led the way in one, and Steve followed in the other. It was a short drive, up the West Side Highway to the George Washington Bridge, and then back down the river to the boat.

Steve Winslow had hoped to spot a likely car in the parking lot, but there was no hope of that. The Binghamton shared the huge parking lot with the Showboat Cinema and a racquetball club, and the place was jammed.

Steve found a parking space, got out, looked around, and joined Mark Taylor who had found a space in the next row. They walked up the covered gangplank to the boat. Inside were stairs leading up to the restaurant on the main deck.

Mark Taylor stopped at the bottom of the stairs. "They're gonna spot us, Steve. You know that."

"Who?"

"Miltner's men."

"That's all right. They don't know me," Steve said.

"Yeah, but they know me. And by now they've spotted my men, just like we spotted them. On a job like this, you can't help that."

"Yeah, I know."

37

"So they'll know my agency's on the job, and when I come in they'll spot me."

"I know, Mark. Right now I just don't care."

They went up the stairs. At the top was the cashier's booth. Taylor said, "Wait a minute," and went up to it. While Steve watched, Taylor conferred with the cashier, then extended a bill.

"What was that all about?" Steve asked, when Taylor came back.

Taylor jerked his thumb. "Phone's there. I left the number with my office. If anything breaks, they'll call me here."

"That's good."

"Yes and no. I'll wind up back in the office eating a soggy hamburger."

A waiter appeared to usher them to a table. "Party of two? Would you care to eat inside or on deck?"

"Inside," Taylor said.

The waiter led them to a table, seated them, gave them menus and took the drink order. Steve had scotch and Taylor bourbon.

When the waiter withdrew, Mark said, "You got them spotted, Steve?"

"Yeah. I spotted 'em on the way to the table. In the far corner. It's the only party of one man and two women that's even in the ballpark. Gotta be them."

"Gotta be. You spot the detectives?"

"No, and I don't want to look around for 'em. Where are they?"

"Look over my right shoulder. The two bored businessmen at the table by the wall—those are Miltner's men. And then the table to the left. The two rather drunk out-of-town buyer types, trying to talk the blonde into calling a friend—those are mine. The blonde's one of their wives. They brought her along for cover."

"And for dinner," Steve said. "You know, the more expenses I run up on this thing, the more tempting it's gonna be to keep that retainer." Steve picked up the menu. "So what's good here?"

"Well," Taylor said. "You can get a steak or a lobster if you want, but the best bet is a hamburger."

"You're kidding."

"Not at all."

Steve looked at him. "Here you are, so worried you're gonna get sent back to the office and wind up eating a hamburger, and then what do you want to order? A hamburger."

"Hey, there are hamburgers and there are hamburgers. The one in the paper bag is cold and soggy and small. The hamburger here is a half a pound of chopped meat served hot in a basket of fries with your choice of bacon, avocado, Swiss cheese or what have you on top. Trust me."

The waiter returned with the drinks, and they ordered hamburgers. As the waiter left with the order, Steve looked over Mark Taylor's shoulder and said, "One of Miltner's men is getting up."

Taylor watched as the man walked by, went out the door and down the stairs. "Pay phone's down there. Probably spotted us, and he's phoning in."

"Right," Steve said. "The report will read that, during dinner the surveillance of the subject was joined by Mark Taylor himself, in the company of a longhaired hippie freak."

Taylor grinned. "I would imagine that would piss off their client."

"It ought to," Steve said. "And wouldn't it be particularly nice if that client happened to be David C. Bradshaw?"

"You think it is?"

"It stands to reason. Bradshaw's scum. The girl's class. I can't imagine her associating with him unless he's got something on her. If he does, he probably hired detectives to get it."

"Probably right," Taylor said, He stood up. "Excuse me a minute. One of my men's heading for the bathroom. Time for me to slip him the car keys."

Taylor went out the door and down the stairs.

Left alone, Steve Winslow took the chance to size up the occupants of the far table. The girl who had called on Bradshaw was younger and prettier than the other woman. Steve placed her age at around twenty-three or twenty-four. The fact that she had called on Bradshaw in the afternoon, and then spent a leisurely day shopping, indicated that she was obviously not a working girl, but a woman of independent means.

The couple was different. The man was a nine-to-fiver. His suit, slightly wilted from a long day's work, indicated that he had come to dinner straight from the office. The purposeful aggressiveness in the man's demeanor led Steve to speculate that his occupation was insurance, advertising, or real estate.

His wife seemed older than the other girl. She was thinner, more angular, and seemed more sophisticated. Her makeup, though impeccable, seemed severe. The general impression Steve got was cold and catty.

Mark Taylor came back, sat down and took a slug of bourbon. "No food yet?" he said. "I'm starving."

"I think this is it coming now," Steve said.

The waiter stopped at their table and put the huge hamburgers in front of them. "You Mr. Taylor?" he said.

Taylor groaned. "Oh shit. That's timing. Phone call, right?"

"At the desk."

Taylor glanced ruefully at the basket of burger and fries, then pushed back his chair, got up and went to the cashier's booth, and took the phone.

He was back in a minute. He sat down, picked up his burger, and took a huge bite.

"What's up?" Steve said.

"Bradshaw went out."

"How?"

"In a taxi."

"Got him covered?"

"I'll say. I've got two cars on him this time. We've got him bracketed, one car in front of the taxi, and one car behind. He may know he's being followed, but there won't be anything he can do about it."

"I wouldn't be too sure of that, Mark. Bradshaw's tricky."

"Sure he's tricky, but this time we know it. He ditched my shadows this afternoon because it seemed like a routine job and no one suspected he was wise. My men are onto him now. They'll stick like glue."

"You sure of that?"

"Of course I am."

"Wanna bet?"

"What do you mean?"

"I'll bet you dinner Bradshaw walks away from your men again."

Taylor rubbed his hands together. "You're on, Steve. Shit, if I'd known that I'd have ordered steak."

"I thought you liked the burgers here."

"I do. But I love to gamble."

"Big deal. All we're really betting is whose expense account it goes on. So it'll come back to me anyway."

"I know, but what the hell. You want a side bet?"

"No. It's a bad bet for me anyway. If I win, I lose. But—" Steve broke off. "Son of a bitch!"

"What?"

"Don't look around, but there's a girl with blonde hair and big round glasses sitting at the end of the bar."

Taylor grinned. "No shit? Your secretary? Why don't you ask her to join us?"

"It's not funny, Mark. She's playing detective. I don't like it."

"She know you saw her?"

"I don't think so. Stay here and don't look at her. I'm gonna head for the men's room."

Steve got up, went out the door and down the stairs. Instead of continuing down to the men's room, he went up the stairs on the other side. He circled around the bar, came up on Tracy Garvin from the other side, and slid onto the bar stool next to her.

"You come here often?" he said.

Tracy turned to give him an exasperated are-you-really-trying-that-old-line look. Then she recognized him. For a second her eyes flashed embarrassment, then anger. Then she smiled and said, calmly, "No. First time. And you?"

Steve frowned. "Look. You're playing detective, and I don't like it."

Tracy's eyes flashed. "Oh, yeah," she said. "What are you gonna do, fire me? I already gave notice. And it's after hours, and what business is it of yours where I eat?"

Steve took a breath. "Look. This isn't a game. If the girl spotted you watching her, it could be serious."

"She won't."

"I spotted you."

"Bullshit. You *know* me. The girl doesn't."

Steve frowned again. She was right. Women who were right exasperated him. "All right." he said. "Since you're here, you might as well join us."

"Thanks for the invitation," Tracy said, pointedly.

They got up and went back to the table.

"Look what I found, Mark," Steve said.

Mark Taylor actually stood up, which Steve thought was overdoing it. "Hi, Tracy. Sit down. Join the fun."

"Go ahead and fill her in, Mark," Steve said. "She's gonna pump you for the information anyway."

"O.K.," Taylor said. "Now, if you promise not to turn and stare, I'll tell you who everyone is."

"I know that," Tracy said. "I just don't know who is who."

Taylor frowned. "What?"

"There's the two guys over by the wall, and the nitwits entertaining the blonde. I just don't know which pair is yours."

Taylor looked at her. "Son of a bitch," he said. "The nitwits happen to be mine. But how the hell'd you spot them?"

"The blonde pretending to be a pickup is one of their wives. She's wearing her wedding ring. If she were a real pickup, and she were married, she'd leave her ring off as a matter of course."

Mark Taylor stared at her.

Steve shook his head. Jesus Christ. A ridiculous, farfetched piece of deduction, that absurdly happened to be true. It was a little much.

The waiter came back. "You got another phone call."

Mark Taylor pushed his chair back. "Our bird must have lit somewhere. I'll find out where he went."

He went over to the cashier and took the phone.

"What's that all about?" Tracy asked.

"Bradshaw went out. We're tailing him."

"And Mark just got a report?"

"Maybe. I just bet Mark dinner Bradshaw's gonna ditch his men again."

"Why'd you do that?"

"Cause I think he will."

She stared at him. "Don't you care?"

"Sure, but there's nothing I can do about it. But I'm betting he will."

Tracy was interested. "Why do you think so?"

"Because he gave up trying to talk me into calling them off. That must mean he thinks he can handle them."

"Or that his heart is pure," Tracy said.

Steve grinned, in spite of himself. "Now there's a thought," he said.

Mark Taylor came back from the phone. He slumped into his chair, drained the last swallow from his drink, and sighed.

Steve Winslow shot Tracy Garvin a look. "What's the scoop, Mark?"

"You win, Steve."

"He lost 'em?"

"He sure did."

"How did he do it?"

Mark Taylor shook his head. "He did it so easy it makes me sick just to think about it."

"Gonna tell us how?"

"Yeah. Now get this, Steve, cause it's a new one on me. Bradshaw hails a taxi and my men pick him up. They've got him boxed in, with one car in front of the cab and one car behind. They've got the number of the cab and everything. O.K. They're going up Park Avenue, right? They hit 42nd Street, they go around the Pan Am building, you know? They continue up Park

Avenue, and you know what it's like—a two-way street with a median strip in the middle. So what happens? They come to 48th Street. That's a one-way street going east, a right-hand turn if you're going uptown. Now the cab slows down and gets in the right lane, but he doesn't signal, so the lead car has to play it by ear. He goes straight through, which turns out to be the right thing to do, because the cab goes through the intersection and pulls up at the far corner. Bradshaw gets out, pays off the cab, and starts across Park Avenue. The lead car sees this, so he beats it down to the end of the block and pulls a U-turn at 49th. The second car can't turn left because 48th is a one-way street, so he pulls up next to the cab to see what Bradshaw's gonna do. Bradshaw reaches the other side of Park Avenue, and starts trying to hail a cab going back downtown. When he sees this, the second car runs up to 49th Street and pulls a U-turn too. By this time, Bradshaw has walked halfway up the block toward 49th Street, still looking for a cab. So when the second car pulls up, the first car passes Bradshaw and waits on the corner of 48th, so when he gets a cab they'll have him bracketed again.

"O.K. A cab comes along. Bradshaw gets in. The first car pulls out ahead of the cab. He's right at the corner of 48th, so that takes him through the intersection. The cab cuts into the left hand lane and hangs a left onto 48th Street. That takes the first car out of the picture. His best bet is to beat it down to 46th, hang a left, run parallel, and try to spot the cab from two blocks away going through an intersection. That's what he does.

"Meanwhile, the second car is right on Bradshaw's tail. He makes the left hand turn onto 48th right behind the cab. Now get this. The cab goes twenty yards down 48th and stops dead in the middle of the street. He's blocking the whole street, there's no room to get by, and two cars have followed my man into the turn so he can't back up."

"So?"

"So," Taylor said, "Bradshaw gets out of the cab, walks calmly to the corner, hops back into the *first* cab that he's left waiting there, and goes off free as air, leaving my man caught in a traffic jam."

"I told you he was smart, Mark."

"Yeah."

Mark Taylor took a futile swig at his empty bourbon glass and lapsed into a moody silence.

The waiter reappeared. "Everything all right?"

"Just fine," Steve told him.

"Can I get you anything else?"

"Just the check," Steve said. "And you can give it to the gentleman who's been getting the phone calls."

8.

MARK TAYLOR slumped into the overstuffed chair, rubbed his bloodshot eyes, and said, "O.K., Steve, I've got the dope."

Steve Winslow, sitting at his desk, looked over to where Tracy Garvin sat with her shorthand book.

"O.K., shoot," he said.

Taylor flipped open his notebook. "The girl is Marilyn Harding. She's the daughter of Phillip T. Harding, the petroleum king. Harding passed away last month at the age of sixty-three. Harding married late. Marilyn is the daughter of his first wife, Martha. She died when Marilyn was born, twenty-five years ago. Ten years ago Harding remarried. His second wife was a woman named Gloria Conners. Rumor has it she married him for his money. She died three years ago. Gloria had a daughter by a previous marriage named Phyllis. Two years ago Phyllis married a young real estate broker named Douglas Kemper. Harding liked Kemper, wanted to take him into the business, but Kemper wanted to make it on his own, so he stuck with real estate. The Kempers have an apartment in Manhattan, but they also have a suite of rooms in the Harding mansion. They're your couple, by the way. Last night all three of them left together and stayed in the mansion, which is a big estate out in Glen Cove. Harding's will is yet to be probated, but the bulk of the estate should go to the natural daughter. She's an independent sort, never done a stick of work in her life, doesn't have to. She hangs around with the fast crowd, likes riding, swimming, tennis, golf, all that goes with being rich. She graduated from college three years ago, has several men on the line, nothing serious."

"What the hell would a girl like that want with the likes of Bradshaw?" Winslow said.

"What indeed?" Taylor said. "Our friend, Bradshaw, is the other side of the coin. David C. Bradshaw is actually Donald Blake, arrested three times on burglary, twice on extortion, served two years on one of the burglary counts. He just got out two months ago, which is when he came here. His background is all in Chicago. I've been tracing his movements, trying to find a tie-in with Marilyn Harding, and haven't come up with anything. Of course, she traveled with the jet-set crowd, so she may have run into him in Chicago. Still, I can't imagine what the connection is unless he's putting the bite on her."

Steve sighed and rubbed his head. "All right, Mark, I guess that does it. It's time Bradshaw and I had a showdown."

"You going to go see him?"

"If he's home."

"He's home. My men are watching the apartment. He was back by nine last night and he hasn't been out since."

"Any callers?"

"Not a peep. By the way, I got the report from the handwriting expert. The note was typed on a Smith Corona portable typewriter by someone using the hunt-and-peck method."

"That's fine, Mark, but I think we've pretty well established that Bradshaw's our man. However, I'll look around his apartment and see if he has a typewriter."

Steve walked over to the safe.

Tracy's face fell. "You taking the money?"

"Sorry," Steve said, spinning the combination. "I know it's going to break your heart, but I want nothing to do with this bird. I'm going to put it to him point blank and make him admit he sent me the money. Then I'm going to shove it in his face, walk out, and absorb the loss. If it's the kind of deal I think it is, I don't want any part of it."

Steve swung the safe door open. "What the hell!" he exclaimed.

"What's the matter?" Tracy said.

"It's gone!"

"What!?" Mark Taylor exclaimed.

Steve swung the safe door wide open so they could see. "The ten thousand dollars is gone. Look. It's empty."

Tracy and Mark crowded around the safe to look. Of course, there was nothing to see. The safe was empty.

"Son of a bitch!" Taylor said.

"Yeah," Steve said. "Mark, look. Run down and get your fingerprint kit, will you?"

Taylor looked at him. "You thinkin' what I'm thinkin'?"

"Yeah. Go on. Get the stuff."

Taylor returned with the kit and dusted powder on the combination of the safe.

"Christ, Steve, its lousy with prints."

"Most of them will be mine. You want to take my prints so you can eliminate them?"

"I don't think I need to. I've got Bradshaw's prints here. I figure one match is all we need."

Taylor busied himself with his work. Tracy stuck like glue, looking over his shoulder. Steve sat at his desk and buried his face in the drama section of the New York *Times*. As he read, he could hear Mark Taylor giving an impromptu lecture on the art of matching fingerprints.

Five minutes stretched to ten. Steve moved on to the Sports section. In the background, Tracy was now throwing around terms like "whorl" and "tented arch."

"Got it, Steve!"

Winslow folded the paper and stood up. "You sure?"

"Eighteen points of similarity. That's a positive identification. It's Bradshaw's right thumb."

"Well, thank god for that," Steve said. "I was certain it was

Bradshaw, but the way this case has been breaking, I wouldn't have been that surprised if it wasn't."

"Yeah, but what's up?" Taylor said. "Why would Bradshaw send you a retainer and then steal it back?"

"Beats me." Steve got up and started pacing. "Christ, what a goofy case. Yesterday I had a retainer and no client, and today I have a client and no retainer."

"Personally, I liked it better the first way," Taylor said.

Steve sighed. "All right, Mark. Call off your men. Bradshaw's given us a retainer and now he's taken it back. I don't know why he did it, but I don't care. The hell with him."

Mark Taylor nodded. He couldn't have agreed more.

But Tracy Garvin couldn't have agreed less.

9.

TRACY GARVIN sat and stewed. Wasn't that just her luck. The whole thing had been too good to be true. It figured that just when things got to be interesting, something would come up to spoil it. And didn't it just figure that that something would be named Steve Winslow?

Tracy could understand why he'd done it. It was frustrating that Bradshaw had taken his money back. And Tracy could understand Steve not wanting to work for nothing.

But still.

As she sat at her desk with nothing to do, Tracy's mind wandered away from Winslow and Bradshaw and her job, and back to the problems that had been obsessing her before the whole Bradshaw thing started. What to do now? She'd given notice, and she needed a job. When was she going to look, on her lunch hour? Damn. Why the hell'd she thrown out the Sunday *Times*. That was stupid. Didn't she want to get a job?

She realized, of course, the answer was no. Who likes looking for work? Getting a job was one of the worst experiences in the world.

But it was more than that. She didn't really want this job to end. She didn't really want to quit, to give up, to admit it was hopeless.

But there was no help for it. Two more weeks. She'd have to

find something fast. Her lease was up in three months, which meant a rent increase. And she was just getting by now. She couldn't afford to miss even a week of work. Then she'd really be in trouble. She might even have to take in a roommate. In a one-bedroom apartment, that meant giving up the living room. And sharing the bath. And the bathroom was off her bedroom, not off the hall. Which meant her roommate would have to come tromping through her room every time she wanted to use it. Jesus, what a nightmare. What a hell of a—

Tracy's thoughts were interrupted by the plop of the mail falling through the slot. She looked up. Two letters were lying on the floor by the door. Two. Wow. Big day. Tracy got up from her desk and plodded mechanically over to pick up the mail.

Steve Winslow looked up from his paper when Tracy Garvin appeared at the door. He figured that she was just reaffirming the fact that she had given notice, and was ready with some sarcastic comment, but the look on her face stopped him.

"What is it?" he said.

Tracy held out a letter. "Another one."

"Another letter?"

"Yes."

"Don't tell me there's another retainer."

"There is."

Tracy handed Steve the envelope. He reached in and pulled out the torn half of a dollar bill.

"Son of a bitch," Winslow said.

"There's a letter with it."

"Don't tell me," Steve said. "This is my change from the ten grand, right?"

"Not quite."

Steve pulled out the letter, opened it, and read it aloud.

"Dear Mr. Winslow: I realize that my first letter failed to establish any means by which I could prove my identity. Enclosed find half of a dollar bill. In the event that I am in need of your services, I will present you with the other half of the bill. In the meantime, please remember that this is a matter requiring the utmost tact and delicacy."

Steve looked at Tracy. "Jesus Christ."

Tracy eyes were gleaming. "Yeah. Why would Bradshaw send you that letter?"

Steve shook his head. "It doesn't make any sense. First Bradshaw sends me a retainer. Second, Bradshaw steals the retainer from my safe. Third, Bradshaw sends me the letter."

"Maybe it's the other way around."

"What do you mean?"

"Maybe he sent the letter before he took the money back."

"The letter is postmarked today."

"That's true, but he could have mailed it yesterday. He might have dropped it in a mailbox, and the mail wasn't picked up until today."

Steve shook his head. "He was in my office at three thirty in the afternoon. If he'd mailed the letter before then, it would have been picked up. And he wouldn't have mailed it *after* he'd been to see me."

Tracy frowned. "I see the point. But that's what he must have done."

"All right, then we come back to why."

Tracy shook her head. "You've got me. There's no reason on earth why he would send that letter."

"Exactly," Steve said. "If he stole the money, he wouldn't have sent the letter. And we *know* he stole the money."

"So who sent the letter?"

Steve sighed. "How the hell should I know? All right, Tracy, take this letter down to Mark Taylor and tell him pass it on to his expert to see if it was typed on the same machine."

Steve snatched up the phone and called Mark Taylor.

"Got your men pulled off the job yet, Mark?"

"Uh huh. You need them again?"

"I don't know, but I may. Be ready to go into action. In the meantime I'm sending Tracy down with another note for your expert."

"Bradshaw again?"

"That's what I want to find out. But it sure looks like the same typewriter."

"Well, I'll be damned. Don't tell me there's another retainer with it?"

"Uh huh."

"You're kidding. Don't tell me it's another ten grand."

"Not this time, Mark."

"No? What'd you get this time?"

"Half a dollar."

10.

STEVE WINSLOW took a cab home. For Steve, cabs were a luxury. After years of driving them himself, he loved riding in cabs instead of always taking the crowded subway. Even though, he had to admit, the trip from his midtown office to his Greenwich Village apartment was actually almost quicker by subway than it was by cab.

Particularly at rush hour. And it was rush hour now. Steve had stayed in his office the whole day waiting for something to happen. And nothing had. Except for Mark Taylor calling back to confirm that the two letters had been typed on the same machine, the place had been dead. And yet he'd stayed. And he realized, the reason he'd stayed was that, despite everything he'd said, his feelings about everything that had happened were just the same as those of Tracy Garvin: he found the whole thing fascinating and he couldn't wait to see what happened next.

And nothing had. And now he was stuck in a traffic jam on Seventh Avenue with a taxi driver who smoked like a chimney and who kept the radio blaring.

"Fire swept through a two-story building in Bedford Stuyvesant, Brooklyn, early this afternoon—"

Steve Winslow was sure one had. Fire swept through a building somewhere in New York City every day of the year. And it was tragic, of course, but Steve didn't want to hear about it. Not at that volume. And yet he didn't feel like telling the cabbie to turn it down. Because he sympathized with cab drivers, even obnoxious ones. He leaned his head out the window, away from the cigarette smoke and into the exhaust fumes of a bus.

The radio was still blaring. "In a surprise move, the Nassau County District Attorney's office secured an order for the exhumation of the body of Phillip T. Harding, the wealthy oil magnate, who died last month at the age of sixty-three. A preliminary report from the autopsy surgeon indicates that the cause of death, originally attributed to coronary thrombosis, was in fact due to arsenic poisoning. The D.A.'s office would issue no statement on the matter, but indicated that the police were making a thorough investigation and that the true facts would be forthcoming shortly."

"Cabbie!" Steve yelled over the radio. "Cabbie!"

"Yeah?" the cabbie yelled back.

"Turn the radio down. We're going to a new address."

It took nearly twenty minutes for them to get out of traffic and reach Bradshaw's apartment building.

Winslow got out of the cab a block away. As he hurried to the building, he kept a sharp eye out to see that the place wasn't being watched. He saw no one.

It was a four-story brownstone in the middle of the block. A narrow alley cut through the block to the right of the building, making the apartments on that side more desirable in terms of light and ventilation. Beside the front door of the building were a row of buttons and a call box, which Steve interpreted correctly as indicating that the front door was locked. Having no desire to talk to Bradshaw on the call box, Steve took a plastic credit card from his wallet and inserted it in the crack in the door. He couldn't help grinning—just like on television. The spring lock slid back easily, and Steve slipped in the door and climbed the flight of stairs. There were two apartments on the second floor. Steve located apartment 2A, knocked on the door, and waited. There was no answer. Steve tried again, louder this time, then put his ear to the door and listened. There was not a sound from the apartment. Cursing the fact that he didn't have a set of passkeys, Steve inspected the lock. He jiggled the doorknob, and to his surprise it clicked open. He hesitated a moment, then opened the door.

The body of David C. Bradshaw lay face down on the floor in a pool of blood. The handle of a large carving knife protruded from between his shoulder blades. Bradshaw's head was twisted sideways, and his eyes, in the glassy stare of death, seemed to be glancing over his shoulder, as if he were preparing to ditch one last shadow.

Steve couldn't help recoiling. It was, after all, his first dead body. He drew back, took a couple of deep breaths, and shook his head to clear it. Then he looked at the body again. No, it was something he'd never seen before, but something he'd visualized many times. The tableau, he realized, was exactly like the one Sheila Benton had described to him, in his other, his first, his one and only murder case—the dead man lying on the floor, the knife sticking out of his back. He knew now a little bit how Sheila must have felt. And this wasn't even his apartment, as it had been hers. God!

Steve snapped himself out of it. Time to think about it later. Right now, what do you do?

Steve stooped and checked for a pulse. As expected there was none. But the body was still warm, indicating that Bradshaw had been dead for a very short time.

Steve stood up and surveyed the apartment. Apparently there had been a terrific struggle. Chairs were overturned, a night table was smashed, and the phone was lying on the floor with the receiver off the hook.

On the desk in the corner that had not been touched was a small portable typewriter. Steve walked over and looked at it. It was a Smith Corona.

A police siren sounded outside in the street. Steve ran to the front window. A police car was pulling up in front of the building. Steve whirled, looking for a way out. Apartment 2A was the corner apartment, with windows on both East 3rd Street and the side alley. Steve raced to the side windows and looked out. There was no fire escape in the alley. Hell, it was too risky anyway. If they caught him trying to flee he'd be dead. Steve hurried back to the desk, grabbed a piece of paper, shoved it into the machine, and typed, "Now is the time for all good men to come to the aid of their party." He tore the page from the typewriter, then whipped out his handkerchief and polished the typewriter keys. He thrust the handkerchief back in his pocket, crumpled the paper into a ball, ran to the side window, opened it, and hurled the paper into the alley. As he did so, Steve heard footsteps coming up the stairs. Steve closed the window quietly, tiptoed across the room, and settled back on the couch just as an imperative knock sounded on the door.

"Come in," Steve called.

Two officers entered the room and stopped short as they saw the body on the floor.

A woman behind the officers said, "He may be quiet now, but when I called—" She broke off as she saw the body.

Then she screamed.

Then the officers spotted Steve Winslow. One officer drew his gun. The other officer followed suit.

"All right, buddy," said the first officer. "Hold it right there."

Steve Winslow smiled and put up his hands. "All right," he said. "You got me."

11.

FRANK SULLIVAN could have been at peace with the world. He had his collar—Steve Winslow; he had his paper—the *Daily News;* and he had a comfortable chair. The only thing intruding upon his tranquility was in the form of a 250-pound, fifty-five year old spinster named Miss Dobson, who happened to be the landlady of the building and who took exception to having her living room used as a holding cell.

"I don't see why you can't keep him in Bradshaw's apartment," she persisted.

"I told you, lady," Frank said, without glancing up from his paper. "We've sealed the place off. Nobody goes in there until homicide gets here."

"Why not?"

Frank grimaced as if he'd been stung by a bee. This time he looked up from the paper to give Miss Dobson the full effect of his sarcasm. "Homicide doesn't like to have murder suspects hanging around the scene of the crime. Homicide's funny that way. They have this theory that people who commit murder might also be so unscrupulous as to tamper with evidence if they were given an opportunity to do so. Of course, I don't believe that for a moment, but homicide seems to think so, so I try to humor them."

Frank returned to his paper.

Miss Dobson cast a sideways glance at Steve Winslow, who was seated on her couch. "I don't want a murderer in my apartment."

"I'm sorry to inconvenience you in this manner," Steve said.

"I wasn't talking to you," she snapped. "I was talking to the officer."

"He's trying to read the paper. Why don't you give him a break?"

"He's trying to read *my* paper. I haven't even seen it yet."

Frank sighed. "Sorry, ma'am. You want your paper?"

"No. What I want is for you to put it down and pay a little attention to your prisoner. You're supposed to be guarding him, aren't you?"

Frank merely grunted.

"That's right, read the paper. Leave me alone with a murderer to deal with."

"Lady, he's handcuffed. What could he possibly do to you?"

"I could kick her in the stomach, drop my shoulder, and slam her up against the wall," Steve said promptly.

Miss Dobson gave a little gasp. Her lips moved soundlessly, and she sank into a chair.

Frank looked at her, grinned at Winslow, and said, "Thanks."

"Don't mention it," Steve said.

There was a knock on the door. Miss Dobson started to get to her feet, but Frank beat her to it. He opened the door and ushered Sergeant Stams into the room.

"All right, where is he?" Stams said. "Where is—" He spotted Steve Winslow and stopped short. "Son of a bitch."

Sergeant Stams, a stolid, impassive, plodding and unimaginative homicide officer, knew Steve Winslow well. Stams had had the misfortune to arrest him once before. At the time, Stams had thought he'd cracked the Sheila Benton case. He'd taken a good deal of ribbing in the department when it had turned out he'd actually arrested Sheila's attorney.

Stams's eyes narrowed. "What the hell are you doing here?"

"I was just about to ask you the same thing," Steve said.

"I happen to be in charge of this investigation."

"Oh? I thought Lieutenant Farron was in charge of homicide."

"Farron's on vacation. I'm in charge."

"Congratulations," Steve said.

Stams snorted. "Yeah." He turned to Frank. "Why didn't you tell me it was Winslow?"

"Who's Winslow?"

Stams pointed. "Him."

Frank shrugged. "Means nothing to me."

"That's cause you don't know him. If he's here, it means something all right. Where'd you find him?"

"In the room with the corpse, sitting on the couch with his legs crossed. We knocked on the door and he called 'Come in.'"

"You're kidding."

"No."

Stams frowned. Thought a moment. "Did you search him?"

"Sure did."

"In my bedroom," Miss Dobson said indignantly.

Stams ignored her. "You make a good job of it?"

"Sure. Took his clothes off and searched him to the skin."

"Find anything?"

"Nothing. He's clean."

"Did he make any objection to being searched?"

"Not at all. In fact, he insisted on it."

"Insisted on it?"

"That's right."

Stams turned to Winslow. "You insisted on being searched?"

"You're damn right I did."

"Why?"

"Why do you think? So you couldn't claim I took anything out of that apartment."

Stams wheeled on Frank. "You sure he's clean?"

"Absolutely."

"Any chance he could have ditched something on his way down here?"

"Not a chance. We had him handcuffed."

Stams frowned. "I don't like it. I think he took something out of that apartment."

Steve smiled. "Thank you."

Stams eyed him suspiciously. "For what?"

"Not disappointing me."

Stams took a breath, blew it out again. "All right, Winslow. Let's have it straight. What were you doing in that apartment?"

"He told you. Sitting on the couch."

"I don't need any of your lip. This is a murder investigation. I want some answers. Why did you go there?"

"To see Bradshaw."

"What about?"

"I had a matter I wanted to discuss with him."

"What matter?"

"I can't tell you that."

"Why not?"

"It's privileged information."

"Involving a client?"

"Naturally."

"Who's the client?"

"I can't tell you."

"Was Bradshaw the client?"

"I can't tell you."

"If Bradshaw was the client, privileged information isn't going to help him now that he's dead."

"On the contrary," Steve said. "Many clients wish to have their rights protected even after they are dead. I believe that's the principle on which wills are drawn."

Stams pounced on the false scent. "Did Bradshaw consult you about a will?"

"I didn't say that."

"I know you didn't say that. I asked you if he did."

"My business with Bradshaw is confidential. I can't tell you about it."

"Do you deny it was about a will?"

"I don't deny it and I won't confirm it."

Stams changed his tack. "When you got there, where was Bradshaw?"

"Right where he is now."

"Did you move the body?"

"I felt for a pulse."

"So you did move the body."

"No. I just touched the wrist."

"Was there a pulse?"

"There was none."

"What time was it when you got here?"

"I didn't look at my watch."

"Approximately what time was it when you got here?"

"Somewhere around six. I tell you I didn't look at my watch."

"How long were you in the apartment before the police arrived?"

"Not more than a minute."

"And you claim he was dead when you got there?"

"Yes."

"And you only touched the body to feel his pulse?"

"Yes."

"You didn't remove anything from the body?"

"No, I did not."

"You didn't take anything out of the apartment?"

"No, I did not."

"And the police arrived a minute after you did?"

"Within approximately one minute."

"And yet you have no idea what time it was when you got to Bradshaw's apartment?"

"No."

"Then you didn't have a specific appointment with Bradshaw?"

"Congratulations, Sergeant."

"What for?"

"That's the first deduction you've made from my statements. I was beginning to think you were asking me questions just to keep in practice."

"So you had no appointment with Bradshaw?"

"That's right."

"You just decided to call on him?"

"That's right."

"Ever call on him before?"

"No."

"That right, lady?" Stams asked Miss Dobson.

"I think so. At least, I've never seen him. If you want my opinion—"

"I don't," Stams said. "So, Winslow, out of the clear blue sky you call on Bradshaw for the first time, and he just happens to be dead."

"I am rather unlucky," Steve said.

"It was just a coincidence?"

"Well, I would certainly hope that my calling on people had no effect on their longevity. Otherwise, I imagine my dinner invitations would be rather infrequent."

"You know what I'm getting at. You knew Bradshaw was dead before you got here, didn't you?"

"I did not."

"Can you prove it?"

"Of course not."

Stams blinked. "What?"

"Of course I can't prove it," Steve said. "I would have to prove a negative, which is next to impossible. If I knew he was dead, I could prove that I knew by divulging the source of information. To prove I *didn't* know he was dead, I would have to prove that I had no access to all sources of information. Since I don't know what the sources are, I obviously can't prove I didn't have access to them. It's an impossibility."

"Then you can't prove it?"

"No, I can't," Steve said, sarcastically. "Well, Sergeant, you've done it. Your skillful cross-examination has tripped me up, trapped me, backed me into a corner, and forced me into an admission. Now, are you ready to arrest me?"

Stams's face darkened. "I may at that. You're talking a lot, but you're not saying anything."

"Did it ever occur to you I might not know anything? You're wasting a lot of time down here, while there's a corpse upstairs screaming for attention."

"Bradshaw won't mind waiting a few minutes. I'm not done with you yet. I think you're hiding something."

"Think what you like."

"I will. You know what I think? I think a client called you and told you Bradshaw was dead. I think the client told you there was some incriminating bit of evidence in the apartment. I think you rushed up here and got the evidence."

"I'm glad to hear you say that, Sergeant. I was afraid you were about to charge me with the murder."

"Don't think that isn't a possibility. But for now, tell me about my theory."

"It's a fine theory, Sergeant. It's got class. I like it."

"Do you deny it?"

"I've already denied it several times. As I said, you're free to think what you like."

"Don't think I won't," Stams said. "I only put these questions to you so you could deny them. Now, if I can prove any part of my theory true, I can get you for obstructing justice, compounding a felony, and being an accessory after the fact to murder." Stams grinned. "And now, I think I'll go take a look at the corpse."

"I take it I'm free to go?" Steve said.

"Sure you are. Except before you do, you're going back in the bedroom and be searched again. And this time I mean searched. Search him good, Frank, and I want a complete inventory of everything he's got on him, no matter how trivial. I think he took something."

Stams started for the door.

"The murderer must have been really smart," Steve said. "I wonder how he knew."

Stams stopped in the doorway. "Knew what?"

"That Farron was on vacation."

12.

STEVE WINSLOW dropped a quarter in the pay phone on the corner and punched in the number.

A feminine voice at the end of the line said, "Taylor Detective Agency."

"This is Steve Winslow. Get me Taylor."

"He just left for dinner. If it's important, I might be able to catch him."

"Catch him."

There was no answer, but the rattle of the receiver and the clack of high heels told Steve the receptionist was doing her best. A minute later Mark Taylor's voice came on the line.

"Steve. Lucky you caught me. I was just going to dinner."

"Forget it. It's soggy hamburger time. I need information and I need it fast. Did you hear the evening news about Harding?"

"No, but my pipeline into police headquarters reported that they exhumed the body and found arsenic. I tried to call you but you'd left the office. But don't worry. I got men working on it. It's covered."

"Fine. Now you can cover something else. Our friend Bradshaw just became a corpse."

"What!"

"That's right. Someone stuck a large carving knife between his shoulder blades somewhere between five and six this evening."

"No shit!"

"None. So pull your men off Harding and get on it."

"Jesus Christ. How the hell'd you find out?"

"I heard the news on the radio about Harding. I went to see Bradshaw, walked in and found the body."

"You're kidding. You mean you're the one who called the cops?"

"It's worse than that. Someone else called the cops. They found me in the apartment."

"They what?"

"That's right. And here's the kicker. Lieutenant Farron's on vacation and Sergeant Stams is in charge."

"Oh shit."

"Yeah. Stams is ready to throw the book at me. He's so pissed off about the Sheila Benton case I think he'd frame me if he thought he could get away with it. Anyway, he's convinced some client called me, told me Bradshaw was dead, told me about some incriminating evidence in the apartment, and had me rush up there and pinch it just before the cops got there."

"Did you?"

"Fuck you, Mark. The thing is, if it sounds that good to you, think how it sounds to Stams. As a result, the murder has paled into insignificance. Stams is out to get me for tampering with evidence, obstructing justice, and being an accessory after the fact."

"Has he got anything?"

"No, he hasn't. Just the fact that he found me in the apartment. But his theory's so damn logical I'll have a devil of a time disproving it."

"Shit."

"So, get everything you can on the murder. Some woman, probably the one in the apartment across the hall, heard something she didn't like and called the cops. Get the dope on her, find out what she heard and what she knows. For the time being, forget the Harding thing and concentrate on Bradshaw. You won't be able to call me, so I'll call you."

"Where are you going?"

"You don't want to know that. But give me Marilyn Harding's address, will you?"

Taylor read out the address. Steve jotted it into his notebook.

"O.K.," Steve said. "I'll call you back."

"Just one thing, Steve."

"What's that?"

"Who's your client now?"

"I don't know. And I just got through telling Stams I couldn't answer questions because I was protecting his interests."

Steve hung up the phone, stepped out in the street, and hailed a cab.

13.

TRACY GARVIN couldn't concentrate on her book. And it wasn't that bad a book, either. It was a murder mystery, of course, and it was actually pretty exciting. There'd just been a second murder, and everything pointed to the client, and the detective was withholding evidence, and if the police found out there'd be hell to pay, and ordinarily Tracy would have been really into it.

But not tonight.

Tracy was stretched out on her living room couch, her shoes off, her feet up, a position in which she often read. She squirmed uncomfortably, scrunched up to a sitting position, pushed the hair back off her face, and adjusted her glasses.

The detective found a broken matchstick.

Tracy frowned. Shit. She knew that. She'd read the page twice.

Damn. She never should have come home. Never should have let Mark Taylor talk her into it. When he'd called to tell Steve about Philip Harding, she'd wanted to stay and keep the office open, but he'd convinced her there was nothing she could do. And he'd promised to call her at home if anything broke. And, of course, nothing had, and there was no point in her hanging out in an empty office.

But still.

Tracy sighed and returned to her book. The matchstick. What

was it about the matchstick? Probably something important, or it wouldn't be in the book. What did the detective think? Had she read that far?

One of the reasons Tracy couldn't concentrate was that she had the radio on. She'd been listening to 1010 WINS, hoping to get an update on the Phillip Harding murder. And, of course, there'd been none. And, she realized, realistically, there wasn't apt to be at that time of night. Every twenty minutes there was another report, but they were all the same. The body'd been exhumed, arsenic had been found, and the police were investigating. The end.

The news report came on again. Tracy put down her book and listened. Same thing. Exhumed, arsenic, investigating. The announcer moved on to the latest local political scandal.

Tracy picked up her book again and began reading.

The detective found a broken matchstick.

Shit.

The political corruption story ended. The newscaster then said, "The body of a man was discovered early this evening in his East Village apartment. He had been stabbed to death with a knife. The man has tentatively been identified as David C. Bradshaw, of 249 East 3rd Street. The motive for the crime is as yet unknown. Police are investigating."

Tracy sprang to her feet. Holy shit! Son of a bitch! Son of a bitch! Her mind was racing. Jesus Christ. How did this happen? What was going on? What should she do?

The announcer'd moved on to the weather. The radio was too loud. She couldn't hear herself think. She went over to the radio, clicked it off. There. That's better. Now . . .

Steve Winslow. Did she have Steve Winslow's home number? No. Would he be listed? And where did he live? Manhattan. Somewhere in the West Village. Or was it SoHo? Shit, what does it matter?

Tracy raced to the phone and dialed 411.

"May I help you?" the operator said.

"In Manhattan—a listing for Steve Winslow."

"One moment, please."

There was a click, and then the recorded message started giving the number. Tracy grabbed a pencil from her desk, jotted it down. She jiggled the receiver, breaking the connection, and punched Steve Winslow's number in.

No answer. She must have let it ring a dozen times.

Tracy slammed down the phone. She was really angry. Of course he wasn't there. Mark Taylor had a pipeline into police headquarters. He'd have gotten the news about Bradshaw way ahead of the media. He'd gotten it, and he'd called Steve Winslow, and that's why Steve wasn't there.

Tracy thought of calling Mark Taylor, but she didn't. In the first place, she was pissed off. In the second place, he wouldn't be there either. He'd have called Steve, and the two of them would be out there investigating the case, doing god knows what, and with never a thought of her. Son of a bitch! Son of a fucking bitch!

Tracy snatched up her apartment keys and slammed out the door.

14.

MARILYN HARDING had been crying. That was the first thing Steve Winslow noticed. She had combed her hair and put on makeup and composed her face, but nothing she could do was going to disguise the fact that she was distraught.

Of course, she had every right to be. After all, she'd just discovered that her father had been murdered. A tremendous shock for anyone, let alone a young girl.

But was that all?

They were in the library of the Harding mansion. Steve Winslow had taken a cab out to Glen Cove ("It's your money, buddy"), bullied his way past the Harding butler (Christ, did butlers really exist outside of British drama?), and been consigned to the library while the butler reluctantly delivered the message.

A few minutes later Marilyn Harding entered the room. She walked slowly, mechanically, and her eyes were dull and glassy. To Steve she looked stunned, as if she'd just been hit over the head with a hammer.

"Who are you?" she said.

"Didn't the butler tell you?"

"Yes, but I'm somewhat rattled. I'm sorry. What's your name?"

"Steve Winslow."

If the name meant anything to her, she didn't show it. "I'm Marilyn Harding. What is it you want?"

"I'm a lawyer."

"Oh?"

Steve looked closely at her. If she was bluffing, she was damn good. She wasn't giving anything away.

"I have something to tell you. It's important, and there isn't much time. Can you give me a few minutes?"

Marilyn rubbed her head. "Yes, I guess so. I'm just so confused. I've had a shock, you see, and—"

"I know. About your father. I hate to put you through it, but I have to have the details."

"Why?"

"So I can help you. Please."

She looked at him as if in a fog. Steve got the impression that it was all too much for her, that she wasn't really reluctant, just overwhelmed.

He was right.

"What do you want to know?" she said.

"Just tell me how it happened."

Marilyn walked over and settled into a chair. Steve pulled up a chair beside her.

"Well, there's not that much to tell. It's all such a shock, and I don't know anything."

"Of course."

"It was a Wednesday. Last month. After lunch my father felt queasy and lay down to rest. No one thought much of it. He'd had stomach trouble for years. Then he got worse. Started complaining of pains in his chest. So I called Dr. Westfield to come at once. By the time he got there, Dad was gone."

"Dr. Westfield was your father's regular physician?"

"Yes."

"And he diagnosed the cause of death as coronary thrombosis?"

"Yes. Dad had a history of heart trouble, and Dr. Westfield was not at all surprised. In fact, that's why Dad happened to be at home. Dr. Westfield had persuaded him to take a week off from the business to recuperate. He had always warned Dad someting would happen if he didn't take it easy."

"Who was in the house at the time?"

"Just myself and my father."

"From lunchtime on?"

"Yes. My stepsister, Phyllis, was here in the morning, but she left just before lunch."

"No one else in the house."

"No, except for John. The butler."

Steve had an absurd flash. The butler did it. Christ, this case was getting to him.

"Who served your father lunch?"

"I did."

"What did you serve him?"

"Soup, a sandwich, and coffee."

"Did he take cream and sugar in the coffee?"

"Yes."

"Did he put it in, or did you?"

"He did. You see, he liked a lot of coffee. I gave him a pot of coffee, a cup and saucer, a bowl of sugar, and a pitcher of cream. I put all those on his tray with the soup and sandwich and served it to him out on the terrace."

"What became of the sugar bowl?"

"I put it back in the kitchen."

"Have you used it since?"

"No."

"Why not?"

"I don't know. I guess I haven't done any cooking since Dad died."

"Where is the sugar bowl now?"

"The police have it."

"When were they here?"

"This afternoon."

"What did they do?"

"They searched the place from top to bottom."

"What did they find?"

"Nothing."

"But they took the sugar bowl?"

"Yes."

"Was it right where you left it?"

"It must have been."

"Don't you know?"

"Well, not really. I was out on the terrace. They brought out the sugar bowl and asked me if it was the one I'd put on the tray for my father."

"What did you tell them?"

"I told them it was."

"Did they ask you questions?"

"Yes."

"About the same questions I asked?"

"Yes."

"Who inherits under your father's will?"

"I don't know the exact terms of the will. The bulk of the estate goes to me."

"And your stepsister?"

"A specified sum. I don't know the exact amount."

"The police ask you *those* questions?"

"Yes."

"It's a wonder you're still here."

Marilyn just looked at him with a dull stare.

"Now then, we have another matter to discuss, and there isn't much time."

"You keep saying that. Why isn't there much time?"

"Because, unless I'm very much mistaken, you're about to have company."

"Who?"

"The police."

Marilyn frowned. "I don't think so. The police were quite thorough. The officer in charge said he was sure they wouldn't have to disturb me again."

"I assume he was polite and sympathetic and courteous?"

"He certainly was. He kept apologizing for the inconvenience he was putting me through."

"That's because they didn't have enough on you to charge you. When they come back tonight you'll find they've changed their tune."

"And why would the police come back tonight?"

"They'll want to question you about another matter."

"What other matter?"

"David C. Bradshaw."

Marilyn recoiled as if she'd been slapped. For a second sheer surprise contorted her face. Then she controlled herself. "Who?"

"David C. Bradshaw," Steve repeated.

"I'm afraid I've never heard of him."

"Then you couldn't know he was dead."

"What!"

Steve looked at her closely. The shock at his name had been genuine, he was sure of it. But her shock at hearing he was dead— Steve just didn't know. It could have been real, or she could have been acting.

"Then you couldn't know he was dead. For your information, Donald Blake, alias David C. Bradshaw, was murdered this evening, sometime between five and six. His apartment had been ransacked. A large carving knife had been stuck in his back."

Marilyn Harding had gone white as a sheet. "That can't be true."

"Why not? You don't know him."

Marilyn bit her lip.

"Beginning to place the name now?" Steve said, dryly.

"No. The name means nothing to me."

Steve shook his head. "It's no good, Marilyn. You can't get away with it. You called on Bradshaw Tuesday afternoon. You were shadowed by private detectives. Those detectives have a license to protect. As soon as they find out about the murder, they'll report to the police. I don't know how many other visits you made to Bradshaw's apartment, and I don't know if you were there today, but if you were it's ten to one the detectives know it and will so inform the police.

"You see where that leaves you. The cops will figure you poisoned your father—that Bradshaw found out about it and tried to blackmail you—that when you realized that this was only the first bite and you would have to keep on paying forever, you killed him.

"Now then, before the police get here, why don't you come down to earth and start talking sense?"

For a long moment, Marilyn just stared at him. Steve sat calmly, waiting for her to talk. He knew she would now. He had her boxed in a corner, and there was nothing else she could do.

She didn't. Instead she got up, walked over to the telephone, and dialed an number.

"Hello," she said. "Mr. Fitzpatrick? . . . This is Marilyn Harding . . . I'm sorry to call you at home, but I have a problem . . . There's a lawyer here, a Mr. Steve Winslow . . . That's right. He feels I'm going to be interrogated by the police concerning the murder of a blackmailer named David C. Bradshaw . . . No, I haven't . . . That's what I thought you'd say . . . That's fine. Goodbye."

Marilyn hung up the phone. "That was my lawyer, Harold Fitzpatrick. He's on his way over. He lives right up the road. He says I should have nothing to do with you and I should ask you to leave."

Steve looked at her for a moment. Then he laughed sardonically and shook his head. "Well, that's just fine. I should have known. Why the devil didn't you tell me you'd consulted a lawyer?"

"You didn't ask me."

"No, I don't suppose I did. Well, if that don't beat all."

Steve got to his feet. "All right. You have the information I wanted you to have. The only ethical thing for me to do at the moment is to wish you a good evening."

Steve turned to leave just as Phyllis Kemper swept into the room, followed by her husband.

"Marilyn," Phyllis said. "Why, I didn't know you had company."

Marilyn turned, saw them, and Steve saw a momentary flash of panic in her eyes. It's all too much for her, Steve thought. Her mind's going to give way.

"Oh. Oh," she said. "Phyllis. Doug. Oh dear. This is Mr. Winslow. he's leaving."

"I should hope so," Phyllis said. "I thought we left orders to let no one in. No offense,' she added, with a glance at Steve, "but our family's had a bit of a shock."

Steve pounced on the opening. "I know," he said. "That's why I'm here. My name is Steve Winslow and I'm an attorney."

."Oh?"

Up close, Steve revised his initial impression of the Kempers. Phyllis Kemper was a catty woman, yes, but it was a curious mixture of cat *and* mouse. Underneath the eyebrows that were plucked a little too fine and the lips painted a little too thin, was a rather plain, mousey face. A mouse dressed up as a cat.

But it was a good act. There was an almost feline, predatory quality to her. Steve actually felt uncomfortable under her gaze.

Her husband was the opposite. Douglas Kemper was a broadfaced, open, friendly sort of man. He had a young, puppyish quality about him, which, though necessarily subdued, under the circumstances of the tragedy, was nonetheless there.

In his wife's presence, though, he seemed to take on a secondary role. As if she were the master. As if she might have had a leash on him.

The cat walking the dog.

"Yes," Steve said. "But I have no wish to intrude on you at this time, and I really must be going."

"A lawyer?" Phyllis said. "But we have a lawyer. Did Marilyn consult you, Mr. Winslow?"

."No."

"Don't tell me you're suing us?"

"No, he's not," Marilyn interrupted irritably. "And he really had to go. Mr. Fitzpatrick is on his way over, and I'm going to have to talk to him alone."

"Mr. Fitzpatrick?" Phyllis said. "But he was just here this afternoon."

"Phyllis," Douglas Kemper said, "I don't think Marilyn wants to talk about it."

Marilyn Harding seemed on the verge of hysteria. "I don't," she said. "And I just heard a car in the driveway. That will be Fitzpatrick. I don't want him to find Mr. Winslow here, so would you please—"

She was interrupted by the entrance of the butler. "Excuse me, Miss Harding," he said, "but the police are here again and—Oh!"

The butler broke off as Sergeant Stams pushed by him into the room.

"All right," Stams said. "Which one is Marilyn Harding?"

Steve Winslow, who had been watching Marilyn's face, turned to face Stams.

Stams saw him. Blinked. "Winslow!" he said. His usually impassive face broke into a grin. "Well, well, well. Isn't that interesting. You know, I was hoping to find you here, but I didn't think you'd be that dumb."

"Apparently I'm that dumb," Steve said.

"Apparently you are. So," Stams said sarcastically. "You didn't have a client who tipped you off to the murder. Oh no. You didn't go to the apartment to get any evidence. Not you. Why, you didn't even know he was dead, did you? And yet, when we follow the clues out here, who do we find but poor, innocent Steve Winslow, closeted with his client. Now isn't that an interesting coincidence?"

"I'm sorry to disappoint you," Steve said, "but Miss Harding is not my client. Her attorney is a Mr. Harold Fitzpatrick, who is probably in the car I hear coming up the driveway now. It's been a wonderful evening, but unless you'd like to have me searched again, I really must be going."

With that, Steve nodded to the astonished Sergeant, and walked out.

15.

STEVE WINSLOW glanced over his shoulder to make sure Sergeant Stams wasn't following him, and then hurried through the spacious front hallway, looking for a telephone. He spotted one on a desk near the window and was making for it when a corpulent gentleman in his mid-fifties came bustling through the front door. The man saw Steve and stopped dead. "Who are you?" he demanded.

Steve looked at him. Despite the lateness of the hour, the man had on a custom-tailored three-piece suit. Short-cropped curly white hair framed a chubby face that, when smiling, probably looked as benign as that of a vaudeville comedian. At the moment, however, the cheeks were flushed, the jaw was set, and the eyes were narrowed in a suspicious stare.

Steve smiled. "For that matter, who are you?"

"Is your name Winslow?"

"That's right."

For a moment the man stared at him as if he could hardly believe the answer. "Then I demand to know what you're doing here," he said. "I told Marilyn to ask you to leave. I consider your failure to do so highly unethical and indicative of sharp practice."

"I take it you are Mr. Fitzpatrick?"

"That's right. And I demand an explanation."

"I see," Steve said. "You want me to leave, and you want me to explain. I'm afraid the two are mutually exclusive. Would you care to pick one?"

Fitzpatrick's cheeks grew redder. "I don't need any smart remarks either. You're tampering with a client. Do I have to file a complaint with the Grievance Committee or would you like to tell me why?"

"Don't hand me that shit," Steve said. "I have a perfect right to talk to anyone I want as long as I'm not soliciting employment. Now if Marilyn wants to tell you what we were talking about, she's free to do so, but as far as I'm concerned, it's none of your damn business.

"However, it might interest you to know that Sergeant Stams has just arrived, and he happens to be just as curious as you are about my conference with your client. The fact that he didn't follow me when I walked out of there indicates that he considered his business with Miss Harding far more pressing. I believe it involves a murder. Now, I wouldn't presume to advise you, but if I were Marilyn's attorney, I would have no doubt where my primary duty lay. Now, what was your question again?"

Fitzpatrick glared at Steve Winslow, then hurried into the library.

Steve grabbed the phone and called Mark Taylor. After the second ring, the detective's voice came on the line.

"Taylor here."

"Mark, Steve. I got a rush job, and I mean rush."

"Yeah? What?"

"I want you to get both of the Bradshaw letters and the list of bills and bring them to the corner of 59th Street and Third Avenue. The southeast corner. I'll meet you there."

"When?"

"Now."

"Can't I send someone? I got a lot of shit coming in."

"No. I need you. Leave an operative on the phone, grab the stuff, and get out there. And I mean now."

"I'll have to—"

"Now, Mark."

"Right."

"You'll probably get there ahead of me. Just wait."

"O.K."

"And don't let anyone know where you're going."

"The operative will have to know, so he can relay information."

"No way. It's important. You can call and get reports, but no one is to know where you are. Got that?"

"Yeah."

"O.K. Stop gabbing and get going."

Steve slammed down the phone, raced out the door, and jumped into the cab. The cabbie made good time back to Manhattan, going through the Queens Midtown Tunnel and up Third Avenue. Steve paid off the cab a couple of blocks away and walked on up Third.

Mark Taylor was waiting on the corner. Steve hurried up to him.

"You got the letters?"

"And the list of bills," Taylor said, tapping his pocket.

"Good. Give them to me."

Taylor handed them over. "There you are. Now what?"

Steve looked around and spotted a restaurant down the block.

"See that restaurant? Go inside and get us a table. I'll be with you in a minute."

Mark Taylor went inside. Steve waited thirty seconds, then followed him into the lobby. Taylor had already been escorted into the dining room. Steve took out his wallet, walked over to the cashier, and smiled.

The cashier, a young blonde, smiled back. "Can I help you?"

"You certainly can," Steve said. "I need an envelope and a stamp."

"I'm terribly sorry. We don't sell stamps or envelopes."

"I know you don't," Steve said, producing a bill from his wallet. "That's why I'll pay you five bucks for them."

The cashier grinned. "You're kidding."

"Not at all."

The blonde reached down under the counter and pulled out her purse. "Just a sec," she said. She rummaged through her purse and fished out a postage stamp and a pink, perfumed envelope. "I hope the color doesn't matter," she said.

Steve handed her the money. "Under the circumstances," he said, "it couldn't be better."

Steve took the envelope and stamp to a table in the corner of the lobby. He put the list of bills in his wallet. He put the Bradshaw letters in the pink envelope, then stamped and sealed it. He addressed the envelope to himself at his office. He hurried outside, found a mailbox, and dropped the letter in.

Steve heaved a sigh of relief. Well, one down and a lot more to go. And the first was the worst. Mark Taylor. Steve hated what he had to do, but he really had no choice.

Steve returned to the restaurant, where he found Mark Taylor sipping a bourbon at a table for two in the far corner of the dining room.

"O.K., Steve," he said. "What's the pitch?"

Steve glanced at the drink.

"I had to order it," Taylor said. "The waiter was getting impatient, and I didn't know what to tell him."

"That's fine, Mark," Steve said. "I'll have one too. It's been quite an evening."

"Hasn't it? All right, Steve. We can talk now. What did you drag me down here for?"

"To have dinner."

Taylor stared at him. "What?"

"Sure," Steve said. "You haven't eaten yet, have you?"

"I had some hamburgers sent up. Look, Steve—"

"But that was a while ago, wasn't it?"

"Around seven, but—"

"And it's eleven now. You could eat a nice steak couldn't you?"

"Sure, but—"

"Then let's have dinner," Steve said. He summoned the waiter. "I'll have a scotch, and this man could probably use another bourbon. Then we'd like a couple of steaks, medium rare. The kitchen's still open, isn't it?"

"Sure," the waiter said. "We serve food till midnight."

The waiter wrote down the order and left.

Mark Taylor turned to Steve Winslow. "Steve, please. Don't do this to me. I don't know what you're up to, but you know how I hate to be out of touch with the office. What the hell's going on?"

Steve took a sip of scotch. "I'm afraid your office isn't a very safe place for you right now."

"Why not?"

"You're going to have visitors."

"You man cops?"

"Yeah."

"Oh shit. How do you know?"

Steve shook his head. "I can't tell you that right now. But the way things are breaking, sooner or later Sergeant Stams is going to come down on you like a ton of bricks. When he does, you're going to have to answer questions. The less you know, the less you have to tell him."

"I know too much already."

Steve shook his head. "No you don't, Mark. Actually, you know very little. The rest you just infer. Any conclusions you may have drawn are incompetent, irrelevant, and immaterial, and you can't be forced to testify about them."

"Testify!" Taylor was alarmed. "Am I going to have to testify?"

"It's possible," Steve said. "Which is why it's important to differentiate between what you know and what you merely surmise. I'm going to tell you what you know."

Mark Taylor blinked. "Steve. I got a license."

"Just do what I tell you, and you won't lose your license," Steve said. "Now listen. This is what you know: On Tuesday I gave you a list of serial numbers of ten one thousand dollar bills. You traced the bills and discovered that they had been withdrawn from the bank by one David C. Bradshaw. On my instructions, you placed Bradshaw's apartment under surveillance Tuesday afternoon. Your operatives reported to you that a young woman called on Bradshaw that afternoon. Immediately after her departure, Bradshaw also left the apartment. Your operatives followed both parties. The young woman was eventually followed to her home and identified as Marilyn Harding. Your men reported that Miss Harding was also being followed by operatives from the Miltner Detective Agency. Bradshaw ditched his shadow. Later, I informed you that Bradshaw was in my office. Your shadows picked up Bradshaw when he left my office and followed him home. You lifted fingerprints from my desk and had them traced. You found them to be the prints of one Donald Blake, a convicted felon with a history of arrests for larceny and extortion. On Tuesday evening at around six thirty, Bradshaw left his apartment, ditched his shadows, and returned to his apartment at around nine thirty. The following morning you dusted the combination of my office safe for fingerprints and found one that matched the right thumb of David C. Bradshaw. At that point I instructed you to call off your operatives and drop your investigation."

Mark Taylor squirmed uncomfortably.

The waiter returned, set the drinks on the table, and departed.

Mark Taylor downed the rest of his first drink, and picked up his second. He swirled the ice around in the glass. He looked at the ice, rather than at Steve.

"Well, what's the matter?" Steve said.

"I can't get away with it."

"Why not?"

"Well, in the first place, you haven't said anything about the letters."

"But no one is going to ask you about any letters."

"They're going to ask me to tell them everything I know about the case."

"Exactly. That's just the point I was trying to make. They're going to ask you what you *know* about the case. What I've just told you is all you *know*."

"I know about the letters."

"What letters?"

"You know what letters," Taylor said, irritably. "The Bradshaw letters."

"See, that's just what I mean," Steve said. "You don't *know* those letters came from Bradshaw. As a matter of fact, there is fairly good evidence they did not."

"That's not the point. The police are going to ask where I got that list of numbers."

"And you'll tell them you got it from me."

"And then they'll want to know where you got them."

"And you'll tell them you don't know."

"But I *do* know," Taylor said. "Tracy copied them off the ten one thousand dollar bills that came in the first letter."

"And how do you know that?"

"You told me so yourself."

"Exactly. That's hearsay. You don't know where the list of numbers came from. What I told you is of no evidential value, and they can't force you to testify to it."

"Aren't there some cases where they can?"

"Yes," Steve said. "If they indict me and proceed against me on a criminal charge, anything I may have told you regarding the case could be received in evidence as an admission against interest."

"Indict you!" Taylor said. "You're kidding, of course?"

"Only half. I'm sure Stams would love to get me, if he could just figure out what to charge me with. But the point I'm making is, you don't *know* that the letters have anything to do with the list, so you don't need to say anything about them. It won't be that hard because nobody knows about the letters, so nobody's going to ask you."

"Aren't you forgetting something?"

"What?" ·

"I saw that ten thousand dollars with my own eyes."

"Did you compare the numbers on the bills with the list?"

"No."

"There you are. Ah, here are our salads."

"I'm rapidly losing my appetite," Taylor grumbled.

The waiter served them and withdrew.

"Snap out of it, Mark," Steve said. "You got nothing to worry about."

"I don't like it, Steve."

"I'm not asking you to like it. I'm asking you to do it."

Taylor sighed. He took a big pull of bourbon. "O.K. You win. But you're going to have to protect me on this."

"Of course," Steve said. "No problem. Now that we got that settled, what have you got on the murder?"

Taylor shook his head. "Not much. You pulled me out of the office before I could get a line into headquarters. All I know is the desk sergeant got a complaint from a woman in the building that there was a fight going on next door. A patrol car went out to investigate, and the officers were the *second* ones to discover the body." Taylor frowned. "I wish to hell you hadn't found that body."

"You and me both. So what about your line into police headquarters?"

"I got a friendly reporter feeding me stuff. Most of it is just routine, but this guy is friendly with one of the sergeants, so he gets the inside track on the police report."

"Think he'd have anything yet?"

"Hell, he's overdue now."

"Might be a good time for you to check in with your office."

"It might for a fact," Taylor said.

The food arrived while Mark Taylor was still on the phone. He returned to the table, sat down, cut off a huge slice of steak, and popped it in his mouth.

"O.K., Steve I got the dope."

"From the reporter?"

"Yeah."

"Any visitors in your office?"

"You mean cops?"

"Yeah."

"No."

"That's strange. Well, what's the dope?"

"The police place the time of the murder at 5:30 P.M."

"5:30! How can they do that?"

"The desk segeant got a call from Margaret Millburn, the woman across the hall, reporting an altercation in Bradshaw's apartment. That call was logged at 5:28. Now the desk sergeant didn't want to send a radio patrol car if it was just a family row or something like that. You know how it is with these 911 calls. Over half of them are just cranks. So the sergeant got the guy's name and address from her. When he hung up, instead of dispatching a cruiser, he called information, got Bradshaw's number, and called him up."

"And got a busy signal?"

"Exactly. The desk sergeant called him at 5:31 by the police clock. That clock is accurate. Bradshaw's phone was found on the floor with the receiver off the hook. The police theory is that the phone was knocked off the table during the struggle in which Bradshaw was killed. That fixes the time of death rather neatly. Bradshaw was alive at 5:28, because one obviously doesn't have a fight with a dead man. He was dead at 5:31 because the phone was knocked off the hook. There's no word from the medical examiner's office, but it's a good bet the autopsy surgeon will fix the time of death between 5:15 and 5:45."

"I see," Steve said, thoughtfully.

"Now then," Taylor went on. "The police have picked up Marilyn Harding and are holding her for questioning. Her lawyer, a Mr. Fitzpatrick, is down there causing quite a stir, and has apparently advised her not to say anything. At any rate, she's clammed up and won't give the police the time of day."

Taylor sawed off another bite of steak. "Now, here's the strange thing. The police have uncovered something that's making them absolutely ecstatic. I have no idea what it is. Even my reporter can't get a line on it. But whatever it is, Sergeant Stams is prancing around like his wife just had a baby, and Harry Dirkson himself has been called in. That's got the reporters puzzled. If Marilyn Harding isn't going to sing, they don't need the District Attorney to listen to her lawyer's solo. So they must have something else they're working on that clinches the case against the Harding girl, or is somehow of more importance."

Steve's eyes narrowed as he digested that information.

"So," Mark Taylor said, "even though you can't tell me certain things about the case, I can still make certain deductions."

"Such as?"

"Such as," Taylor said, watching Steve narrowly, "after you called me to tell me Bradshaw was dead, you raced out to the Harding mansion to talk to Marilyn. I don't know whether she told you anything or not, but after you were there a little while, Sergeant Stams showed up to question Miss Harding. That was probably just before you called me the second time to send me out here, which would be around ten thirty. The first report of Bradshaw's murder was on the nine o'clock news. Someone gave Sergeant Stams the tip-off to pick up Marilyn Harding. Marilyn Harding was being followed by Miltner's men. Now, if Miltner or one of his men saw the nine o'clock news broadcast, and if he knew that Marilyn had been to Bradshaw's apartment sometime this afternoon, and if he felt he had to report that information to the police in order to keep from losing his license, it would place Sergeant Stams's arrival at the Harding mansion somewhere around ten thirty."

Steve frowned. "You're making a lot of deductions, Mark."

"I'm not through yet. Let's go a little further. If Stams got a tip from Miltner and went to see Marilyn Harding, and if you were there when he arrived, and if shortly after he arrived a Mr. Fitzpatrick showed up claiming to be Marilyn Harding's attorney—and if Stams suspected you of having a client who had asked you to remove evidence from Bradshaw's apartment and whose identity you were attempting to conceal—then Stams would probably assume that Marilyn was the client, that after you left Bradshaw's apartment you dashed out to talk to her, that you advised her that under the circumstances the fact that you were her attorney would absolutely crucify her, and that therefore on your suggestion she immediately called in Fitzpatrick to act as a cat's-paw so that you could fade into the woodwork."

Steve Winslow said nothing.

"Well," Taylor said, cutting off another piece of steak, "look who's lost his appetite now."

Steve picked up his knife and fork and began mechanicaly slicing off a piece of steak.

"I'll tell you one thing," Mark said. "If they can ever prove that you took anything out of that apartment, Dirkson will throw the book at you."

"Don't worry, Mark. They can't prove it."

"You mean you didn't do it, or they can't prove it?"

"I told you there were certain things I couldn't tell you."

Mark Taylor's fork stopped halfway to his mouth. "Jesus Christ, Steve, don't even suggest you did that. If you did, I don't want to know it."

"Then stop asking questions I have to refuse to answer on the grounds that an answer might tend to incriminate me. For a guy who doesn't want to know the answers, you do ask the damnedest questions."

"It's the detective in me. I can't help it." Taylor wolfed down the last bite of steak. "All right. It's been a fun dinner and all that, but being out of touch is getting me a little crazy. When can I get back to the office?"

"You could go back now if it weren't for that new evidence. That's got me worried. I'd like to know what it is before the cops talk to you."

"Let me call in again. Maybe the reporter's managed to turn up something."

"Do that. And while you're at it, call information and see if Tracy Garvin's number is listed."

"Her home number?"

"Yeah."

"No problem. I got it."

Steve grinned. "Oh? Like that, eh?"

Taylor chuckled, shook his head. "No. Not like that. When I got the news about the Harding autopsy, I called your office trying to catch you. You'd already left, but Tracy was still there.

When I told her she got all excited. Said she'd stay there, keep the office open, wait for more reports." Taylor stopped and looked at Steve. "I don't know what your problem is with that girl, but in my book she's quite something, you know?"

"Yeah, yeah," Steve said impatiently. "So?"

"So, I knew you didn't want her doing that, so I tried to talk her out of it. It took some doing. Finally, she agreed, but only after she gave me her home number and made me promise if anything broke I'd call her, so she could come back and reopen the office." Taylor chuckled. "This case may be a big pain in the ass for us, but for her it's like she won a trip to Disneyland."

"And you didn't call?"

"I forgot."

"She's gonna be pissed. Well, call her now, tell her to hop in a cab, and come join us."

"Not the worst idea I've ever heard," Taylor said. "But I'm sure the only reason you're doing it is so you can tell her what *she* knows."

Taylor pushed back his chair and went off to telephone. Steve sat and looked at the half-eaten steak in front of him. He'd missed dinner, but he wasn't a bit hungry. Christ, what a fucking mess. All right, he had to admit he'd been bored. Tracy was quite right in complaining that nothing ever happened. But he'd liked that, at least at first. After a whole life of scratching out a living, first as an actor, then as a lawyer, it had been nice to sit back, not worry about the rent, and watch the monthly check from Sheila Benton roll in. Yeah, it was a little monotonous. And yeah, after three months of leisure he could have stood a case of some kind.

But not this.

Not two homicides, the cops on his case, and him not knowing who the fuck his client was.

No, not this.

Mark Taylor came back and sat down.

"Well?"

Taylor shrugged his shoulders. "Nothing," he said. "Everything at the station is very hush-hush. Dirkson is closeted with someone, apparently either a witness or a suspect, but no one on the force seems to know who it is."

"Well, the officers who made the arrest know," Steve said impatiently.

"Sure, and Sergeant Stams knows too. But the officers who made the arrest are nowhere to be found. In fact, no one seems to know who the arresting officers are. Of course, Sergeant Stams is taking the credit. Stams is very much in evidence, and about as helpful as you would expect. He's willing to pose for pictures, and he modestly admits that it was his investigative brilliance that cracked the case, but that's about it." Taylor sighed. "So I guess I'm stuck here for a while. You gonna finish that steak?"

"No."

"Then pass it over. If I gotta sit here, I might as well eat."

Steve shoved his plate toward the center of the table, and Taylor speared the piece of meat.

"So, what about Tracy?" Steve asked.

Taylor shook his head. "I struck out there too."

Steve's head snapped up. "What?"

Taylor shrugged. "No answer. I let it ring ten times, just in case she was asleep."

"Oh shit!" Steve jumped to his feet. He whipped out his wallet, flung money on the table. "Let's go!"

"What?" Mark Taylor said, but Steve was already halfway to the door. Taylor lurched his 220 pounds into gear and followed.

By the time Taylor caught up, Steve was out in the street trying to hail a cab.

"Steve! What the hell's going on?"

"It's Tracy, damn it! Where the hell's a fucking cab?"

"What?"

"Stams set a trap. No wonder he's so happy. He must figure I sent her back to get the evidence I ditched."

"What evidence? What are you talking about?"

"Tracy said she'd be waiting for your call."

"So? Maybe she had a date."

"Not that girl. She wouldn't have missed your call for the world.

No, she heard it on the radio and went out there. Damn it, where the hell's a cab?"

"Steve. What the hell are you talking about?"

"There's one. Taxi!" Steve turned back to Taylor as the cab swerved in to the curb. "Don't you get it? Shit, Mark. She's the mystery witness!"

16.

DISTRICT ATTORNEY Harry Dirkson shifted his bulk in his chair, ran his hand over his bald head, and frowned. Jesus Christ, what a fucking mess. First Phillip Harding getting murdered, and now Marilyn Harding mixed up in the murder of a blackmailer. The media always loved to see rich and powerful people in trouble, but not Dirkson. Rich and powerful people had connections. They could stir things up, make waves, put pressure on you. And you always had to step lightly. If you let someone big off the hook, the press and the public would scream bloody murder. And if you went after them, and they were big enough, there was no telling who you might offend.

Still, Phillip Harding was dead, and Marilyn was just a kid, too young to have any significant political connections. So the situation shouldn't have been that bad. Except for one thing. Steve Winslow.

Steve Winslow. The name haunted Dirkson like a death knell. Steve Winslow. Dirkson had had only one case against Steve Winslow, but that had been enough. Steve Winslow was young and inexperienced, probably didn't even know that much law, but Jesus Christ. The man was a clown, that was the problem. An actor, a showman, a jury-grandstander. After the things Winslow had done in court, Dirkson had been lucky to escape with his political career. And here he was, popping up again to taunt him. Steve Winslow discovered in the dead man's apartment. Steve Winslow interviewing Marilyn Harding at her mansion.

And now this. Now this young woman sitting before him. The young woman who had been apprehended attempting to enter the dead man's building. The young woman who'd told a few unconvincing lies to the police and then clammed, refusing to talk and demanding to call her attorney. And who was that attorney?

Steve Winslow.

Dirkson glanced over at Sergeant Stams, stolid and impassive as ever. Then at the stenographer, waiting, pen poised, for something to take down. And finally at the young woman, the girl, really, who might well be a college student for all he knew, sitting there in blue jeans, sweater, and glasses, her jaw set in an angry pout as if she'd just been called into the Dean's office and was refusing to name the names of the students to whom she'd slipped answers on the final exam.

Dirkson sighed. "Now, Miss Garvin, let's try this one more time. What were you doing at that apartment building?"

Tracy said nothing.

"There's no reason to keep you here," Dirkson said. "If you would just tell us what you were doing, I'm sure you could go home."

"I have nothing to say. I want to call my lawyer."

"We called your lawyer. He's not home." A fact for which Dirkson was grateful.

Tracy set her jaw again.

"You must understand, Miss Garvin," Dirkson said. "I don't think you had anything to do with this murder. I think the whole idea's absurd. But you must see, your refusal to answer questions and demanding to see a lawyer is suspicious. It's more suspicious than your going to that building. So you're really only making trouble for yourself.

"Now then," Dirkson said, with a glance at the stenographer, "I would certainly not want to violate your constitutional rights, and I would be the first person to suggest that you are entitled to a lawyer should you want one. But as a reasonable man, I have to ask myself, why in the world would a decent young woman such as yourself want a lawyer?"

The door opened. Dirkson frowned. The sergeant who had been standing guard in the outer office came in.

"Excuse me, sir," he said to Dirkson. "But there's a man here says you sent for him."

"What?" Dirkson said.

"Yes, sir. He says he's a witness and you called him in. He says you want to question him and—Hey!"

Steve Winslow stepped in front of the sergeant, took in the scene at a glance, and said, "Hello, Dirkson."

Tracy Garvin gasped and relief flooded over her features like a drowning person who's just been thrown a lifeline. Sergeant Stams's jaw dropped open, and his face darkened, murderously.

Only Dirkson kept his cool. Dozens of thoughts flashed through his head—my god, he hasn't changed a bit; he's still a clown; same hair, same clothes who the hell would dress that way? how the hell'd he find us?; who's this damn sergeant, and how stupid can he be, and who the hell assigned him, anyway? some heads are going to roll for this—but his face reflected none of them. Instead he matched Steve's smile and said, calmly, "Mr. Winslow. And how did you get in here?"

Steve smiled. "Being a private citizen, I just walked in. You, I believe, had to be elected."

The sergeant, fearful he was in deep shit, said, "He's not a witness? He said you sent for him, and—"

"I'm sure he did," Dirkson said. "Don't worry about it. But if you would just go see that no one else gets in here."

"There's another man out there," the sergeant said.

Dirkson looked at Steve. "Oh? You brought reinforcements? And who might he be?"

"Mark Taylor."

"Of the Taylor Detective Agency?"

"That's right."

Dirkson exchanged a glance with Stams. "Well, that's mighty interesting." Dirkson turned to the sergeant. "Tell the gentleman to stick around."

"Yes, sir." The sergeant gave Steve Winslow an aggrieved look, and went out, closing the door.

Dirkson turned back to Steve. "Well, Mr. Winslow. I wasn't expecting you, but I'm sort of glad you're here. We have a little situation here."

"And what is that?"

"This young woman," Dirkson said, indicating Tracy Garvin, "was apprehended attempting to enter the scene of a crime. We've been trying to question her about it, but she's being most uncooperative. At first she tried to give the cops some song and dance about visiting some friend in the building. When she saw they weren't buying it, she clammed. I haven't been able to get a word out of her."

"That's not true," Tracy said. "All I said was I wouldn't answer any questions except in the presence of my attorney."

Steve Winslow grinned. "And did you tell them I was your attorney?"

"Of course."

Steve's grin grew broader. He looked at Dirkson. "I see. And the minute she told you that, you and Stams figured you'd hit the jackpot, and instead of letting her contact me, you've been grilling her ever since."

Dirkson stole a look at the stenographer. "Not at all. We let her call you right away. You weren't there."

Steve grinned. "I'm sure that broke your heart."

"And I don't see why this young woman needs a lawyer to begin with. She's not a suspect, she's a witness."

"A witness? Witness to what?"

"I don't know. She won't talk."

Steve laughed. "You're really going about this ass-backwards, aren't you?"

"Not at all. But your being here simplifies things. She says she won't talk except in the presence of her attorney. All right, young lady, now your attorney's here. You can talk. Unless, of course, you're going to advise her not to answer questions."

Steve Winslow shook his head. "I'm not going to do that."

Dirkson smiled. "Well, that's a refreshing change. All right, Miss Garvin, your attorney's here and he's not advising you not to answer questions. So let's have it. What were you doing in that apartment house?"

"The reason I'm not advising her not to answer questions," Steve put in, "is because she's not my client. Miss Garvin happens to be my confidential secretary, and as such, all matters regarding my clients are considered to be confidential communications, and she is under no obligation to discuss them."

Dirkson blinked. "This woman is your secretary?"

"That's what I just said."

Dirkson turned to Tracy. "Why didn't you tell me you were his secretary?"

"You didn't ask."

"Yes, but—"

"Come on, Dirkson," Steve said. "I'd drop it if I were you. She told you she wanted to consult me before answering your questions. She couldn't reach me, and you kept questioning her, so she kept quiet. Now you're crabbing because she didn't tell you something?"

Dirkson took a breath and blew it out again. "All right, Winslow. I'll ask the questions of you."

"I may not be of much help either."

"I know. But if it's going to be like that, I'd like to have your refusal to answer in the record."

"Put it in the record, then. I'm not answering any questions."

"I can take you before the grand jury, you know."

"You still can't make me testify."

"About confidential communications, no. But this is something else. You yourself are actively involved. You're a witness. More than that, you're a suspect. At least with regard to tampering with evidence. I must tell you frankly, Sergeant Stams thinks you took something out of that apartment."

Steve gave Stams a look. "Sergeant Stams is entitled to his opinion."

"He is also of the opinion that Marilyn Harding is your client, and that she told you Bradshaw was dead and asked you to remove some incriminating evidence from that apartment."

Steve shook his head. "That's the trouble with Sergeant Stams. He's the type of cop who jumps to a conclusion, and then won't listen to anything else."

"It's funny you should say that."

"Oh?"

"I just happened to be thinking the same thing."

"About Sergeant Stams?"

"No, no," Dirkson said quickly, before Stams could protest. "No, about jumping to conclusions. Now take our present case, for instance. Stams, here, finds you in Bradshaw's apartment. He has you searched and finds nothing. From this he concludes that you managed to ditch the evidence."

"And you don't?"

"I don't rule out the possibility. But to my mind, an equally logical explanation is that instead of removing evidence, you were actually *planting* evidence."

"May I quote you on that? I may have a cause for action here. You consider planting evidence to be an activity I would logically be engaged in?"

"Let's not quibble," Dirkson said. "I'm making no accusations. I'm exploring possibilities. Now, I have no idea how long you were actually in that room with the body before the police arrived. And I don't know what you did in that room. And," Dirkson said, casting a look at the stenographer, "I am certainly not accusing you of searching Bradshaw's body. However, I wonder if you are aware that a rather large sum of money was found on the body."

Steve carefully avoided looking at Tracy. "A sum of money?"

"Yes. Ten thousand dollars in one thousand dollar bills."

"That's rather a large sum of money for a person to be carrying around with him."

"Isn't it? Now, without making any accusations, I'm just wondering if there is any chance you planted that money on the body?"

"Why in the world would I do that?"

"I don't know. But if you did, and I can prove it, I promise you that you will fine yourself disbarred."

"Thanks for the warning."

"Don't take it lightly. There's a good chance you could find yourself indicted as an accessory to murder."

Steve yawned.

"All right," Dirkson said. "I'm through playing games. I've told you what the score is, so you're completely aware of the seriousness of the situation. This is a murder case. I want the name of your client."

Steve shook his head. "I'm sorry. I can't help you."

Dirkson took a breath. "I could have you charged with obstruction of justice."

"Make up your mind. A minute ago you were going to charge me as an accessory. If you do, you could hardly charge me with obstructing justice for refusing to answer questions. In fact, it would be your duty to inform me I didn't have to answer questions and anything I said might be used against me."

With that, Steve Winslow pulled up a chair next to Tracy Garvin, sat down, and said, "How's it going?"

Tracy looked at him, blinked, found herself unable to speak.

Dirkson turned to Stams. "Bring in Taylor."

Stams nodded, went out, and returned escorting Mark Taylor into the room.

Dirkson rose to meet him.

"Mr. Taylor, is it? Please sit down."

Dirkson indicated a chair. Taylor sat in it. He did not look happy.

Dirkson sat down again, settled in. "Well now, your name is Mark Taylor?"

"That's right."

"Of the Taylor Detective Agency?"

"Yes."

"What brings you down here at this late hour, Mr. Taylor? Come to renew your license?"

Mark Taylor shifted uncomfortably in his chair.

"You heard him, Mark," Steve said. "He's threatening to go after your license. Go ahead. Talk. Tell him everything you *know.*"

Mark Taylor took a breath. "Well, Tuesday morning Steve Winslow called me into his office—"

"This Tuesday?"

"Yes."

"What time?"

"Around ten thirty."

"Go on."

"He gave me a list of serial numbers he wanted traced."

Dirkson sat up in his chair. "He what?"

"He gave me a list of serial numbers to trace."

"What kind of serial numbers?"

"The serial numbers off of thousand dollar bills."

Dirkson looked at Stams. Neither man could quite believe what he'd just heard.

"How many bills?" Dirkson said.

"Ten."

"And you traced the bills and located the bank from which they had been withdrawn?"

"That's right. The bills had been withdrawn from the First National Bank on Monday morning. The withdrawal was unuaual enough that the teller took the precaution of writing down the numbers."

"And you learned the identity of the person who made the withdrawal?"

"Yes," Taylor said, looking at the floor.

"Who was it?"

"David C. Bradshaw."

"Well, now, isn't that interesting. Do you by any chance still happen to have that list of numbers?"

"No."

"What did you do with it?"

"I gave it back to Steve Winslow."

"Is that so? And just *when* did you give it back to Mr. Winslow?"

"This evening."

"This evening? And how did you come to give it back to him this evening."

"Well, Steve called me, and—"

"What time?"

"Around ten thirty."

"And asked you about the list?"

"Well, he asked me to meet him for dinner."

"And did he ask you specifically to bring the list with you?"

"Yes."

"And you met him for dinner and gave him the list?"

"Yes."

"And that was just before you came here?"

"That's right."

"So, to the best of your knowledge, Winslow still has the list on him?"

Taylor hesitated.

"Well?"

"Yes, I guess so."

"That's purely a conclusion on his part," Steve said.

"You keep out of this," Dirkson said. "I'll get to you in a minute. All right, Taylor. Let's go back a little. What did you do after you traced the money to Bradshaw?"

"I placed Bradshaw's apartment under surveillance."

"Why?"

"I wanted to find out all I could about Bradshaw. I hadn't had much success with the normal routine lines of inquiry."

"What had you found out?"

"Not much. I learned he rented his apartment two months ago, that he paid his rent in cash, but that no one seemed to know where he came from or what he did for a living."

"So you put his apartment under surveillance?"

"That's right."

"And you did this purely of your own initiative?"

"Well, not exactly."

"Were you specifically instructed to put his apartment under surveillance?"

"Yes."

"Who instructed you to do so?"

"Steve Winslow."

"Ah. So Steve Winslow instructed you to put Bradshaw's apartment under surveillance?"

"Yes."

"Did he tell you why he wanted this done?"

"He wanted to get a line on Bradshaw."

"I could have assumed that. *Why* did he want to get a line on Bradshaw?"

"Because Bradshaw was the person who withdrew the ten thousand dollars."

"And why was he interested in the person who withdrew the ten thousand dollars?"

"I don't know," Taylor said, choosing his words carefully. "I presume it was because he was retained in the matter."

Dirkson pounced on that. "He told you he was retained by a client?"

"Yes."

"Who was the client?"

"I don't know."

"Winslow didn't tell you the name of the client?"

"No."

"You expect me to believe Winslow instructed you to trace the list of bills, and to put Bradshaw's apartment under surveillance, and yet he never once mentioned the name of his client?"

"That's right."

Dirkson frowned. "Mr. Taylor, I'd like to remind you that this is a murder investigation. Now, you're not under oath, so there is no question of perjury here. However, I am asking these questions in my official capacity as District Attorney, and a stenographer is taking down your answers. If those answers should be incorrect in any way, you would be in a position of obstructing justice, compounding a felony, and conspiring to conceal a crime."

"Oh, bullshit," Steve said. "Come on, Dirkson, we know the law for Christ's sake. You don't have to threaten us. Just ask your questions. The guy's telling the truth."

Dirkson wheeled around to confront Steve, about to start an argument. He glanced at the stenographer and thought better of it. He turned back to Taylor.

"All right, we'll let that pass. At any rate, you put Bradshaw's apartment under surveillance on Tuesday afternoon?"

"Yes."

"How many operatives?"

"Four."

"Four? Wasn't that a bit excessive?"

Steve grinned. "I hope the stenographer got that Mark. He asked you that in front of a cash customer. You may have cause for action."

Dirkson paid no attention, "Why four operatives."

"I wanted to tail anyone who called on Bradshaw."

"Why?"

"I told you. I was drawing a blank. I couldn't get any information the easy way, so I was trying the hard way."

"At any rate, you used four men?"

"Yes."

"And what did they report?"

"A young woman called on Bradshaw early Tuesday afternoon. She was in there approximately fifteen minutes. She was shadowed when she left, and later identified as Marilyn Harding."

"How long was she followed?"

"Only until she was identified."

"How long was that?"

"Actually, quite a while. First she went shopping. Then she went to dinner and was joined by a couple who turned out to be Douglas and Phyllis Kemper. Phyllis is Marilyn's stepsister. They all left together and drove to the Harding mansion. By that time my men had an identification so they dropped them."

"Is that the only time you've had Marilyn Harding under surveillance?"

"Yes."

"And the only significant thing your men learned from following her was her name?"

"No."

"No? What else?"

"They discovered that Marilyn Harding was being followed by two operatives from the Miltner Detective Agency."

Dirkson and Stams exchanged glances.

"All right," Dirkson said. "So much for Marilyn Harding. What about Bradshaw?"

"Bradshaw left his apartment immediately after Miss Harding. He took a cab uptown and proceeded to ditch my shadows."

"How?"

"Fairly routinely. Walked into a hotel and out another door." Taylor shrugged. "It happens."

"Did they pick him up again?"

"Yes."

"Where?"

"In Steve Winslow's office."

"What?!"

"They picked him up in Steve Winslow's office."

"When?"

"About a half hour later."

Dirkson was staring at Taylor with great suspicion. "And just how did this happen?"

"Winslow called me and told me Bradshaw was in his office. My men picked him up there and followed him home."

"Then what?"

"Then Winslow called me into his office and had me dust his desk for fingerprints. I found a perfect set where someone had leaned heavily on the desktop. I ran them down and identified them as belonging to one Donald Blake, a convicted felon with a history of larceny and extortion."

Dirkson prided himself on having a good poker face, but he couldn't conceal his surprise. He frowned and thought that over. "I see. So what happened then?"

"Bradshaw left his apartment shortly after six."

"Where did he go?"

"I don't know."

"Why not?"

"He ditched my shadows."

"Again?"

"It was not one of my better days."

Dirkson's face darkened. "Look here, are you giving me a run around?"

Before Taylor could reply, Steve jumped in. "No he's not, Dirkson. I told you. This man is telling you the simple truth. Just ask your questions."

Dirkson took a breath and blew it out again. "All right. Did you pick up Bradshaw again?"

"Yes."

"When and where?"

"At his apartment. My men staked it out, and Bradshaw returned about nine."

"That evening?"

"Yes."

"Then what?"

"After that, Bradshaw stayed put and had no further visitors."

"Until when?"

"Until Wednesday morning when I pulled my men off the job."

"Why did you do that?"

"Steve Winslow called me into his office on Wednesday and

had me dust the combination of his safe for fingerprints. I found a thumbprint that matched the right thumbprint of Donald Blake. At that point, Winslow instructed me to pull my men off the case."

Dirkson digested that information. "All right. What did you do next?"

"Nothing. I'd been ordered off the case."

"What about tonight?"

Taylor shrugged. "Winslow called me and asked me to meet him for dinner."

"And told you to bring the list?"

"Yes."

"I suppose he just casually asked you to bring it along?"

Taylor frowned. "You're asking me for my opinion of his tone of voice?"

"No. We'll let it pass. The fact is he asked you to bring it?"

"Yes."

"The same list you received from him Tuesday and traced to Bradshaw?"

"Yes. The same list."

Dirkson nodded grimly. He turned to Steve Winslow. "All right, Winslow. You've refused to answer questions. That's one thing. Concealing evidence is another. Now, I want to know right now if you have that list."

"Yes, I have the list," Steve said. "But as far as I know, it has nothing to do with the murder."

"Well, I'm telling you that it does," Dirkson said. "I am hereby informing you that that list of numbers is a valuable piece of evidence in a murder case, and I am asking you in my official capacity as District Attorney to turn it over to the police. Now then, do you intend to do so?"

"Certainly," Steve said. He produced the list and passed it over to Stams. "I'd hate to make Sergeant Stams go to the trouble of having me frisked again."

Sergeant Stams whipped a notebook from his pocket and began comparing numbers.

"Now then," Steve said. "You've got what you wanted. Tracy

and I aren't talking, and Taylor's made his statement. I think this is where we came in."

Dirkson shook his head. "I'm afraid not, Winslow. I warned you what would happen if I connected you with those thousand dollar bills."

"You can't hold me without a warrant," Steve said.

Dirkson shook his head sadly. "I'm trying to give you a break. If you cooperate, I might be able to save you the embarrassment of a formal arrest. But if you want me to swear out a warrant, I will."

"You don't have the grounds to issue a warrant."

"I didn't before, but I sure do now. Those serial numbers clinch the case. Bradshaw withdraws the bills from the bank Monday. You get the numbers Tuesday. Bradshaw gets bumped off Wednesday. The bills are found in his pocket, and you're found in his apartment. Now put all that together and tell me if I can get a warrant."

Sergeant Stams cleared his throat. "Excuse me, but—"

"Just a minute," Dirkson said. "I just want to make sure Winslow knows where he stands. Now then, Winslow, you're not leaving here until you answer some questions. We can do it the easy way or the hard way. It's entirely up to you."

Stams cleared his throat again.

"Yes, what is it?" Dirkson snapped.

"I'm sorry," Stams said. "But there's been some kind of flimflam here. The numbers on the list don't match."

"What!?"

Stams shook his head. "That's right. None of the numbers match. Winslow must have switched lists."

Dirkson's face began to purple. "Son of a bitch!" he hissed. "By god, Winslow, if you switched lists—"

"You'll have a hell of a time proving that," Steve said, "after the bank teller gets through testifying that the numbers are genuine."

Dirkson hesitated a second, trying to gauge if Winslow was bluffing. He figured he couldn't be. Not if he expected the bank teller to back him up. "Damn it," Dirkson said, "if you didn't switch lists, then you switched the bills themselves."

"That's a fine theory," Steve said, "if you can find any way to prove it, be sure to let me know. In the meantime, I've done all I can here. Tracy, Mark. I think we've taken up enough of these gentlemen's time. After all, they have a murder to solve."

Steve bowed to Stams and Dirkson, and ushered Tracy and Mark Taylor out.

17.

TRACY GARVIN could hardly contain herself. She was seated across the table from Steve Winslow in a small diner three blocks from the courthouse. Steve had brushed aside all her questions, even after Mark Taylor, who didn't want to hear the answers, had hailed a cab and beat a hasty retreat back to his office. Now she waited in mounting frustration while a tired waitress plodded over and slid cups of coffee in front of them.

As the waitress departed, Tracy looked up at Steve and said, "Now?"

Steve dumped cream in his coffee. "Yeah, now."

"What happened?"

"You first. You heard it on the news, right?"

Tracy gave him an exasperated look, but realized argument would be futile. He wasn't going to talk till she did. "Yeah. I'd gone home, and I told Mark Taylor to call me if anything happened, but he hadn't called, and I was listening to the radio, you know, in case they had more details about the Harding thing. Then the news came on about Bradshaw. I called information and your number was listed, so I tried to call you. Of course, you weren't there. So I figured he'd called you and you'd beat it to Bradshaw's apartment. So I hopped a cab and went over there."

"And what happened?"

"You know what happened. I walked into a trap."

"How?"

"I was stupid. When I got to the building there were no cop cars, nothing. I couldn't understand it. I mean, this was a murder site. I thought maybe I got the address wrong. I went to a pay phone on the corner and called information, asked them if they had a David C. Bradshaw at that address. They did. I went back to the building. I went up the steps. And I tried to get in."

"How?"

"What do you mean?"

"What did you do?"

"I rang the bell."

"Good."

"What do you mean, good."

"Dirkson is going to try to prove you were trying to break into that apartment. If the cops have to testify you were ringing the doorbell, it weakens their case."

"What case?" Tracy cried. "Look. Please. I can't take it anymore. Just tell me what is going on."

He did. He told her all of it. From finding Bradshaw's body to his interview with Marilyn Harding to his dinner with Mark Taylor. The only thing he left out was the part about typing the note on Bradshaw's typewriter and throwing it out the window. He wasn't about to make her an accessory to concealing evidence.

She listened, fascinated, till he was finished. "So that's why Mark Taylor didn't mention the letters."

"Yeah. He wasn't happy about it, but he did it."

"Why are the letters so important?"

"They're the key to the whole thing. I'm withholding evidence from the police. So are you. We're doing it by relying on the law of privileged communications. Well, you can't have a privileged communication without a client. Those letters show I haven't got a client."

Tracy frowned. "Right. We're right back where we started. Who the hell's the client?"

Steve shrugged. "You got me. I was all but convinced it was

Marilyn Harding. I went out there and started questioning her. She could have told me to go to hell, but she didn't. She answered all my questions, and some of them were pretty damn impertinent. The way I saw it, the only way that made sense was if she sent me the letters.

"So I sprung the Bradshaw murder on her. That hit her hard. But she tried to pull an innocent act. Then I told her about Miltner's detectives. I figured that would break her. I was all set for her to reach down the front of her dress and pull out the torn half of a dollar bill. Instead, she went to the phone and called her lawyer, who advised her to throw me out of the house. You could have knocked me down with a feather."

"Is it true what you said? That as your secretary, I don't have to testify?"

Steve shrugged. "It's fine line. They can't make you testify as to confidential communications. Going to Bradshaw's apartment is something else. You are an active participant. You did something, and they can question you about it."

"Then eventually I'll have to talk?"

He shook his head. "No. That's why it's a fine line. I'll argue that the *reason* you went to Bradshaw's apartment was because of something you learned from a confidential communication from a client, and therefore asking you why you went there is the same thing as asking you to reveal that confidential communication."

"But there's no client."

"Right."

"So what's going to happen now?"

Steve took a sip of coffee. "Now we wait."

"For what?"

"I don't know. But I wouldn't be too surprised if Dirkson drags me in front of the grand jury and tries to get me indicted as an accessory."

"How could he do that?"

"He's going to claim I took some evidence out of Bradshaw's apartment and managed to ditch it somewhere in the building. He'll claim I sent you to get it."

Tracy's face fell. "Shit. It's all my fault."

To a certain extent it was. And Steve had uncharitably been thinking that very thing. But faced with Tracy's distress, he wasn't about to say so. And she had clammed up on Dirkson.

"Don't be silly," he said. "That's what he's going to *try* to do. He can't prove it, and I think he knows it."

"Oh."

Steve pushed back his coffee cup. "Come on. Let's go."

Tracy looked at him. "Where?"

Steve looked at his watch. "I'm putting you in a cab. It's nearly two, and I need you to open up the office tomorrow morning." He smiled. "After all, I still have twelve days left of your services."

18.

MARK TAYLOR, showing the ill effects of a sleepless night, slouched in Steve Winslow's clients' chair and folded open his notebook.

"O.K., Steve, here's the pitch. The police are still holding Marilyn Harding. She won't talk, but her lawyer's talking plenty. He's filing a writ of habeas corpus, and demanding they either charge her or release her. So far they haven't done either, but talk is they'll charge her by this afternoon. Rumor has it the only reason Dirkson's hanging back is he can't decide which case he'd rather try her on first."

"It'll be the Bradshaw case," Steve said.

"How do you know that?"

"Because that way he can drag in the Harding murder to prove motive. If he tried her on the Harding murder first, he'd have a devil of a time trying to tie the Bradshaw murder in with it. The minute he mentioned Bradshaw, Fitzpatrick would start screaming prejudicial misconduct, and Dirkson would find himself in a nasty predicament. Fitzpatrick might even get a mistrial out of it. But by trying her for the Bradshaw murder, Dirkson can prejudice the jury by dragging in the Harding business. And to top it off, he doesn't even have to get a second-degree murder verdict. If he can convict her of anything at all, even manslaughter or criminally

113

negligent homicide, he's home free. Cause then he'll turn around and try her for the murder of her father, and when he does, he can impeach her testimony by showing she's been convicted of a felony. After that she won't stand a chance. The jury will decide she's a habitual killer, and they'll return a guilty verdict without even thinking. Dirkson's smart enough to realize that, so that's what he'll do."

Taylor shrugged. "Well, either way the case sure looks black for her. The money they found on Bradshaw's body turned out to be hers."

"You sure?"

"Got it from the horse's mouth."

"Shit. That doesn't look too good, does it?"

"You don't know the half of it. Miltner's men have spilled every-- thing. I don't know what they said, and I don't know what time Marilyn called on Bradshaw last night, but from the way the cops are acting, you can bet it was right around 5:30."

Steve frowned. "Did the autopsy surgeon fix the time of death?"

"Sure. Between 5:15 and 5:45."

Steve whistled. "That's sticking his neck out."

"Sure is. Fitzpatrick should have a field day getting him to admit that he's basing his testimony on non-medical factors."

"Sure," Steve said. "That'll make Fitzpatrick look good, but in the long run all it will serve to do is to point up to the jury how conclusive those non-medical factors are."

Mark shrugged. "Well, that's your department."

"Wrong. That's Mr. Fitzpatrick's department. I have nothing to do with the case."

"I wish you'd told me that before I stayed up all night getting you this information."

"It's good practice for you, Mark. Keeps you on your toes. So what else? What about the murder weapon?"

"Apparently it was Bradshaw's. It's a large carving knife from a set of six. The other five are in a drawer in Bradshaw's kitchen. Dirkson isn't too happy about that."

"Why not?"

"The way I get it, he figures it'll be hard to prove premeditation if Marilyn killed him with his own knife."

Steve frowned. He thought that over. "No, that's not right. If she killed him in cold blood, it doesn't matter when she decided to do it. See, most people think premeditation means the crime was thought out and planned well in advance. It doesn't. All it means is that the crime was committed deliberately and not in the heat of passion. If Marilyn went into the kitchen to make a drink, opened the drawer, saw those knives, and couldn't resist the temptation to use one, that's still premeditated murder, and Dirkson can get her on it."

"In that case, I can't see what Dirkson is so worried about."

"Neither can I. Especially since all he really needs to do is convict her of manslaughter."

"Then how do you account for it?"

Steve thought a moment. He smiled. "I have one theory that you probably won't care for."

"What's that?"

"That Dirkson isn't worried at all. That he deduced from our finding Tracy Garvin in his office last night that there must be a leak at headquarters, and therefore he's handing out this crock of shit so your man won't find out what he's really up to."

Taylor made a face. "You're right."

"About my theory?"

"About my not caring for it. I've been up all night listening to this crock of shit." Taylor's eyes widened. "Jesus, Steve, do you suppose the bit about the bills being traced to Marilyn is phony too?"

"I would tend to doubt it," Steve said. "Since it's on the front page of the *Daily News.*"

Taylor shook his head. "Aw, fuck. Not only do I stay up all night listening to the shit put out by the D.A.'s office, but the only real information I come up with I could have got by buying the morning paper."

"Yeah, but I wouldn't pay you overtime to buy the morning paper."

"Hell, I'm not doing this for the money. I'm doing this so you'll keep me out of jail."

"You're not in there yet."

"Right. Thanks to my lucky stars and ten serial numbers that conveniently failed to match. You didn't by any chance switch those numbers around, did you Steve?"

"If I had, would you want to know?"

"Fuck no!" Taylor said. "Never mind. I withdraw the question."

Steve grinned. "It's all right. Just for your peace of mind, I didn't tamper with the list."

"You didn't?"

"Of course not. You saw the list yourself."

"Sure. Just like a volunteer from the audience sees the magician's ordinary deck of cards."

"The bank teller can vouch for the list, Mark. By now even the cops will have to admit it's genuine. What Dirkson's going to accuse me of is switching the money."

"You mean taking ten thousand dollars of Marilyn Harding's money and planting it on the corpse in place of Bradshaw's ten grand?"

"That's right."

"Shit, Steve, what the hell could you expect to gain by that?"

"Fortunately, I don't have to answer that question. Dirkson does, and that undoubtedly is one of the things he's really worried about."

"Gonna sit back and make him prove you guilty beyond a reasonable doubt?"

"No joke. That's exactly what I may wind up doing." Steve rubbed his head. "All right. What about the witness?"

"What witness?"

"The woman who called the police."

"Oh. Margaret Millburn. Well, there you know as much as anyone. She heard an altercation and called the cops."

"What kind of altercation."

"What do you mean?"

"Physical or verbal?"

"I gather both."

"Then she must have heard the assailant's voice."

"That's right, but not well enough to identify it."

"How do you know that?"

"Because the police haven't arranged for her to hear Marilyn's voice."

"You sure?"

"Positive. The police finished with the Millburn woman and put her back in circulation before Marilyn Harding was picked up. She hasn't been near the police station since. That confirms my report that Miss Millburn didn't actually see Marilyn Harding, and indicates she didn't hear the argument distinctly enough to recognize voices."

"Could she hear them well enough to tell if the other party was a man or a woman?"

"If the cops know, they're not letting on."

"What about Miss Millburn?"

"What about her?"

"You said the cops put her back in circulation?"

"That's right."

"What's to stop you from having a little chat with her?"

"Just one thing, Steve. You're forgetting she lives next door to Bradshaw's apartment. I wouldn't go near the place right now if my life depended on it."

"Right," Steve said. "They'd figure you were after the evidence I ditched."

"I got the dope on her anyway," Taylor said. He referred to his notebook. "She's twenty-eight and she's a divorcée. Millburn is her maiden name. She was married to a used car salesman named Buckley. Apparently he tried to trade her in on a new model, so she went to Reno, established a six months' residence, and got a divorce. That was three years ago. She moved here three months ago. She does nothing in the line of work, and seems to be living off her alimony."

"And how the hell did you get all that?"

"From the landlady, who, I'll save you the trouble of asking, was out shopping at the time of the murder and didn't see or hear a thing."

Steve leaned back in his chair and rubbed his head. "See, Mark, your evening wasn't wasted after all."

"What do you mean?"

"None of that stuff was in the morning paper."

There was a knock on the door and Tracy Garvin slipped in, closing the door behind her. She seemed excited and her actions were furtive.

"What is it?" Steve said.

She practically put her finger to her lips. "There's a man in the outer office," she hissed.

"So?"

"I'm not sure, but he looks like a process server."

"Oh."

"I didn't tell him you were here," Tracy said. "You want to duck out the back?"

Steve shook his head. "I'm not ducking service. Show the gentleman in."

Tracy obviously didn't agree, but she nodded and went out.

"Maybe I should get out of here," Taylor said.

"No. Stick around, Mark. I want to see if he serves you too."

Tracy returned with a rather apologetic looking individual with a briefcase."

"Mr. Winslow?" he said.

"I'm Winslow. This is Mark Taylor."

The man handed Steve a paper. "Mr. Winslow, there is a subpoena to appear before the grand jury at two this afternoon and to answer questions arising from the death of one David C. Bradshaw. I'm sorry to trouble you. Please understand, I mean no offense. I'm merely doing my job."

The process server bowed himself out of the door.

Steve eyed the subpoena thoughtfully.

"Well, that's quick work," Taylor said.

"Yes it is," Steve said. He looked up from the subpoena. "All right, Mark. At least they don't want you. Get out of here and get some sleep."

"You're kidding."

"No. There's nothing much you can do now. Put a man on the phones and go home."

Taylor heaved himself out of the chair. "That's a break," he said. He nodded to Tracy and went out.

The minute he was gone, Tracy turned on Steve. Her eyes were flashing.

"All right," she said. "I've had enough."

Steve held up his hand. "Whoa. Back up. What do you mean, you had enough?"

"You can't do this. It's not right."

"What?"

Tracy was going for righteous indignation, but she was bordering dangerously on schoolgirl pout. "You know what. I'm supposed to be your confidential secretary. That's what you told the D.A. That's why I'm not answering questions for the police. All right. Your detective just gave you a rundown on the case. Did you have me sit in and take notes? No. You kept me in the outer office and wouldn't let me hear a thing."

Steve rubbed his head. "Right. And that isn't fair, is that it? Well, I'm sorry. But I told you. We have a delicate situation here. You're my secretary, but you're also a participant. The D.A. may come after you. In fact, you can consider it a lucky break that process server wasn't after you."

"You said they couldn't make me testify."

"I said it was a fine line. And it is. Maybe they can, maybe they can't. But they can damn well try."

"So?"

"So while you're in the position of being a potential witness, there may be some things you're better off not knowing."

"Such as?"

Steve threw up his arms. "The hell of it is, I don't know. Now I'll tell you everything Mark told me. There was nothing you couldn't hear. But I didn't know that until I heard it. So I had to hear it first. See?"

"Yeah, I see. And I don't like it at all."

"You think I do?" Steve waved the subpoena. "You think this is my idea of a good time?" He sighed. "Well, at least now I know what we're up against."

"What do you mean?"

"You see this subpoena?"

"Yeah. What about it?"

"It's just an ordinary subpoena."

"What's wrong with that?"

"Everything. I was expecting a subpoena duces tecum. You know what that is?"

"Isn't that an order to produce a piece of evidence?"

"Right. I expected a subpoena ordering me to bring into court any or all bills in my possession bearing the serial numbers on the list I gave Stams. Since Dirkson suspects me of having taken the bills, it's only logical for him to order me to produce them. But he didn't do that."

Tracy frowned. "Why not?"

"Only one reason I can think of."

"What's that?"

"He's already got them. And if he has, it's ten to one he found them in Bradshaw's apartment."

Tracy's eyes widened. "Oh shit. What are you going to do?"

Steve shrugged. "That's the thing. I really don't know."

"I see."

"You do? Good. So get the chip off your shoulder and let me bring you up to date, and then with all due respect get the hell out of here cause I've got some thinking to do."

After he'd told Tracy everything he felt she needed to know and she'd departed for the outer office, Steve leaned back in his chair, rubbed his forehead, and blew out a breath of air. Yeah, he had some thinking to do, but there was one thing he'd already thought out. One thing he knew he had to do. He just didn't really want to do it.

Steve tipped the chair forward and picked up the phone. When he did so, the light on the receiver went on, to indicate that the line was in use. Steve frowned. He realized the light on Tracy's phone would have gone on too. He didn't like that. He wondered if Tracy would be curious enough to try to listen in on his calls. He wasn't sure. But he figured if she picked up, he'd hear a click on the line.

Steve shook his head. Shit, what was he doing. Tracy wasn't the problem. He was just thinking all that because he didn't want to make the call. He leaned forward and punched in the number of Judy Meyers.

Steve Winslow and Judy Meyers had an off-again on-again relationship. Usually it was off-again, and usually, Steve realized, that was his fault. Steve shied away from close relationships, and had a paranoid fear of being tied down. For him, two dates in a row seemed something like a commitment. So his relationship with Judy Meyers could at best be described as arm's length. For the present, to the best of his recollection, he hadn't called her in over a month.

Which was why he felt like such a shit for calling her now.

"Hello?" Judy said.

"Judy. Steve."

There was pause, then, "The man lives. How you doing?"

"Pretty good."

"I'll bet."

"What is that supposed to mean?"

"Is this social, sexual, or business?"

Steve sighed. "I need a favor."

"You in a jam?"

"Yeah. Kind of."

"You want to talk about it?"

"Not really."

"Figures. What do you need?"

"Got a pencil and paper?"

"Always. You could have been my agent with an audition."

"Fine. Take this down."

Steve gave her Bradshaw's address.

"O.K. What about it?"

"It's an apartment building with a side alley. I'm interested in the side alley."

"You want me to go prowling around in some alley?"

"Not at all. In fact, I don't want you to go near the place."

Judy laughed. "You'll pardon me if I'm not quite following this."

"Good. It's better if you don't."

"Are you serious?"

"Absolutely."

"This is fascinating. So what am I supposed to do about this address that I'm not to go to?"

"I want you to go to the neighborhood. Maybe a block or so away. Just so you don't go near the building."

"Then what?"

"Then I want you to find a couple of young boys playing in the street."

"Steve, have you been drinking?"

"No. Find some young boys. If you can't find any, you may have to look around. But again, don't go near the address."

"How young would you like these boys?" Judy asked facetiously.

"Young enough they don't rape you, but old enough you hold their interest."

"Great. I love the buildup. Say I find these boys. Then what?"

"Then you ask them if they'd like to play a game."

"Is there a point to all this? If so, I wish you'd tell me, cause I'd like to get on with my life."

"O.K. Here's the point. You tell 'em you'll give the winner ten bucks and the loser five bucks. Tell 'em the game is a treasure hunt. Give 'em the address I gave you, and tell 'em the treasure is in the alley next to that building."

"Son of a bitch," Judy said. "Did you get another murder case?"

"I didn't get it. It got me. I'm sorry to ask you, but I don't know who else to trust, and I happen to be in a lot of trouble."

"Shit. Don't tell me. The treasure's a bullet, right?"

"No."

"Well, you gonna tell me what it is?"

"The treasure is a crumpled piece of paper with the words, 'Now is the time for all good men to come to the aid of their party,' on it."

There was a pause. "Is this some kind of joke?"

"Not at all."

"There really is such a paper?"

"Yes."

"And it really is important?"

"You wouldn't believe. If you get it don't let anyone, and I mean anyone, know you've got it. Just bring it to me."

"And if I get the paper?"

"I'll buy you dinner."

"What a prince. And what if I don't get the paper?"

"I'll pay your bail."

19.

STEVE WINSLOW raised his right hand, took the oath, and seated himself on the witness stand.

Harry Dirkson, ever the politician, smiled at the grand jury before turning to Steve. It was not a broad, triumphant smile, even though Dirkson must have relished the thought of having his adversary on the witness stand where he could give him a good going over. No, the smile was just a quick acknowledgment of the grand jury's presence before Dirkson turned crisply to the matter at hand. This was serious business, Dirkson's manner seemed to say This was murder.

"Mr. Winslow, what is your occupation?"

"I am an attorney-at-law."

"Mr. Winslow, we are inquiring into events relating to the death of David C. Bradshaw, who was murdered on Wednesday, the ninth of this month. As an attorney-at-law, you have certain rights and privileges on which we do not wish to intrude. But this is a murder case, and you are privy to certain information that is vital to that case, so therefore it is necessary to ask you certain questions.

"Therefore I will ask you this: on Wednesday, October ninth, did you have occasion to go to 249 East 3rd Street?"

"Yes, I did."

"Why did you go there?"

"Now," Steve said, "you are inquiring into matters as to which I cannot help you. I am afraid that question calls for information of a privileged nature between client and attorney. Therefore I must decline to answer."

"What the client *told* you is privileged information. What you *did* is not."

Steve smiled. "Aren't you splitting hairs here, Dirkson? You're asking me, in effect, if a client told me to go to Bradshaw's apartment. If that were the case, it would be a privileged communication, and you can't inquire into it."

"Are you stating that such is the case?"

"Certainly not. I am stating a hypothetical point of law."

"We are not here to discuss hypothetical points of law."

"I agree. Why don't you move on to something else?"

Dirkson frowned. "It is not your place to tell me what questions I should ask."

"Quite right. You can ask any questions you want. I'm only telling you which ones I choose to answer."

That sally brought grins to the faces of some of the grand jurors.

Dirkson bit his lip. The cross-examination was not going as planned. Winslow wasn't supposed to be scoring any points. Dirkson needed to get him on the run.

"All right," Dirkson said. "We'll play in your ballpark. Let's talk about what you did. The fact is, you went to that apartment."

"That's right."

"What did you do when you got there?"

This was the part Steve wanted to skip over. He certainly didn't want to have to admit he'd opened the foyer door with a credit card. In the hope of getting around it, he threw Dirkson a crumb.

"I knocked on the door. When I got no answer, I tried the knob."

Dirkson pounced on it. "You tried the *knob?*" Dirkson said. His manner was the same as if Winslow had just confessed to murder.

"And why did you try the knob? Or was *that* the result of a confidential communication?"

"No, it wasn't."

"Well, what was it then?"

"Just a reflex action."

Dirkson put his skepticism in his voice. "A reflex action?"

"That's right. I knocked on the door. I jiggled the knob. The knob turned."

"Just like that?"

"Just like that."

Dirkson shook his head. "You knew that door was unlocked, didn't you?"

"No, I didn't."

"You suspected it."

Steve smiled. "You want to interrogate me on what I suspected?"

"Now *you're* splitting hairs," Dirkson said. "You had reason to believe that door was unlocked, didn't you?"

"No, I did not."

"Then why did you try the knob?"

"I told you why. I can't make any better answer than I already have."

Dirkson gave the grand jury a look. That look was a work of art. In one glance he managed to convey the idea that his work was being impeded by having to deal with a slippery, lying shyster.

Dirkson turned back to Steve. "The door opened and you entered the apartment?"

"That's correct."

"And what did you find?"

"I found the body of David C. Bradshaw lying on the floor. He'd been stabbed in the back with a knife."

"You recognized him as David C. Bradshaw?"

"That's right."

"Then you'd seen him before?"

"That's correct."

"Where did you see him?"

"In my office."

"When?"

"The previous day."

"What was Bradshaw doing in your office?"

"I can't tell you that."

"Why not?"

"It's privileged information."

"Regarding what client?"

"I can't tell you that."

"I'm not asking you what the client told you. I'm asking you the name of the client."

"I can't help you there."

"What business did you have with David C. Bradshaw?"

"I can't tell you that either. You know that. Look, Dirkson, I'm here as a witness. If you want to ask me about what I did, fine. If you want to ask me about my business, go roll a hoop. You know the law."

Dirkson took a breath. "All right. You found the body of Bradshaw?"

"That's right."

"What did you do when you found the body?"

"First I made sure he was dead."

"How?"

"I felt for a pulse."

"Where?"

"On his wrist."

"So you touched the body?"

"I touched the wrist, yes."

"Is that the only place you touched the body?"

"That's right."

"You didn't move the body in any way?"

"No."

"What about the clothing on the body?"

"What about it?"

"Did you touch the clothing?"

"My hand may have brushed his shirt feeling for the pulse."

"That's not what I'm asking. You know what I'm getting at. Did you search the body in any way?"

"No, I did not."

"Put your hands in any of the pockets?"

"No."

"None of the pockets?"

"No."

"Did you take anything out of any of the pockets?"

"No."

"You certain?"

"Absolutely."

"I see. Then let me ask you this: did you put anything *in* any of the pockets?"

"No, I did not."

"You did not?"

"That is correct."

"You understand you're under oath?"

"I object to that question."

Dirkson looked at him. "What?"

"I object to the question."

"I just asked you if you knew you were under oath."

"Exactly," Steve said. "It's a thoroughly objectionable question. I'm a lawyer. I know what it means to be under oath. Your asking that is a snide attempt to imply to the grand jury that you don't believe what I'm saying."

"No, it isn't."

"Then what is it?"

"It's a question."

"Sure, it's a question, but it's not a question designed to elicit any information. It's merely an attempt to belittle my testimony."

"How could that belittle your testimony?"

"I told you. By implying you don't believe what I'm saying."

"I *don't* believe what you're saying," Dirkson blurted.

Steve smiled. "There you are."

Dirkson suddenly realized he was fighting a losing battle. "All

THE ANONYMOUS CLIENT 129

right," he said. "Let's get back to what you did. When you entered Bradshaw's apartment, did you have any money on you?"

"Certainly."

"You did?"

"Of course I did. I always carry money on me. So many taxi drivers don't take checks."

"This is no joking matter."

"I agree. Then ask me a question that makes sense. Everyone carries money."

"You know what I'm getting at," Dirkson said. "When you entered that apartment, did you have a large sum of money on you? To be specific, did you have ten thousand dollars in one thousand dollar bills?"

"No, I did not."

"You deny that you had ten thousand dollars on you when you entered that apartment?"

"Yes, I do."

Dirkson crossed to the prosecutor's table and picked up a piece of paper.

"Mr. Winslow, I hand you a piece of paper and ask you if you have seen it before."

"Yes I have."

"What do you recognize it to be?"

"It is the list of serial numbers off of ten one thousand dollar bills."

"Where did you get that list?"

"You just handed it to me."

Dirkson frowned. "Don't swap words with me. You know what I mean. Last night in my office I asked you to produce a list of the serial numbers of ten one thousand dollar bills. Is that the list you gave me at that time?"

"Yes, it is."

"Where did you get it?"

"Once again, you are inquiring into matters that are privileged and confidential."

"But you admit that you had that list in your possession?"

"Yes, I do."

"And do you admit that you employed Mark Taylor of the Taylor Detective Agency to trace the numbers on that list and find out who withdrew those bills from the bank?"

"Yes, I did."

"And do you know who did withdraw those bills from the bank?"

"Only by hearsay."

"I understand. But the list speaks for itself, and it has been checked. Is it not true that, to the best of your knowledge, those bills were withdrawn from the First National Bank by David C. Bradshaw?"

"That is correct."

"And where did that list come from?"

"There again you are inquiring into things that are privileged and confidential."

"Did you ever have in your possession the ten one thousand dollar bills whose serial numbers are on that list?"

"That is also privileged and confidential."

"I'm not asking you what anyone told you. I'm asking you if you had the bills."

Steve shook his head. "You're asking, in effect, if a client gave me those bills. That's privileged information, as you well know."

"You realize that by invoking your professional privilege you're forcing us to draw our own conclusions."

"Go ahead and draw them. I have nothing to say."

"All right, I'll draw them," Dirkson said. "Is it or is it not a fact that when you went to Bradshaw's apartment, you had ten thousand dollars on you in one thousand dollar bills? Is it not a fact that you searched the body, found another ten thousand dollars in thousand dollar bills on it? And is it not a fact that you then switched bills, placing the ten thousand dollars that you had on the body, and removing the ten thousand dollars that was there?"

"No, that is not a fact."

"And," Dirkson went on, as if Steve had not answered, "is it not a fact that before you could leave the apartment you were trapped by the arrival of the police, and, not wanting to be found with the bills in your possession, you hid them in the upstairs hallway of the apartment building?"

"That is not a fact."

"You deny that you hid any bills in the hallway of Bradshaw's apartment house?"

"Yes, I do."

"And you deny that you removed any bills from Bradshaw's apartment?"

"That's right."

Dirkson abruptly changed his tack. "Is Marilyn Harding your client?"

"No."

"Has Marilyn Harding *ever* been your client?"

"To the best of my knowledge, no."

"What do you mean, to the best of your knowledge?"

"Exactly what I said. As far as I know, Marilyn Harding has never consulted me. Does that answer your question?"

Dirkson frowned. He wasn't sure that it had. But he wasn't sure that it hadn't, either.

"Is it not true that you went to Glen Cove and called on Marilyn Harding last night?"

"Yes, I did."

"And that was after you found the body of David C. Bradshaw?"

"That's right."

"And why did you call on Marilyn Harding?"

"There again, I can't tell you."

"Was the reason connected with the death of David C. Bradshaw?"

"I'm sorry. I can't tell you."

"Did you go to consult with her as your client?"

"I told you. Miss Harding is not my client."

"And never has been?"

"And, to the best of my knowledge, never has been."

Dirkson changed his tack again. "When you called on David C. Bradshaw, did you know that he was dead?"

"No, I did not."

"Had you been *told* that he was dead?"

"No, I had not."

"Or that he might be dead."

"No, I had not."

"Did you *suspect* he was dead?"

"You're grasping at straws, Dirkson."

"Answer the question."

"No, I did not suspect he was dead. There. Now you have my thoughts, knowledge, and even my suspicions in the record. Now, do you have anything else?"

"Do you deny that before you went to Bradshaw's apartment, a client told you that Bradshaw was or might be dead. Or," Dirkson said, sarcastically, "does *that* answer betray a confidential communication?"

"No, it doesn't," Steve said. "The answer is no."

"You deny it?"

"Yes, I do." Steve leaned back in the witness chair. "Now, you've asked your questions and I've answered them. I've told you everything I can without betraying a professional confidence. Now then, do you have anything else?"

Dirkson didn't. He suspected Winslow of lying, evading, holding out, and covering up. But he didn't have a damn thing to back it up. And he didn't know, specifically, what Winslow was trying to keep from him. And he was a smart enough campaigner to realize that his efforts to find out were not only futile, but were making him look bad.

"No," Dirkson said. "That's all."

20.

THE ATMOSPHERE in Steve Winslow's outer office was two degrees below zero. Steve noticed it the moment he came in the door. Tracy Garvin was seated at her desk, as usual, but for once her head wasn't buried in a book. In fact, her book was nowhere to be seen. Tracy's desk was clean. Tracy was sitting up straight in her chair. Her hands were folded in front of her on the desk. Her manner was crisp, efficient, businesslike.

And cold.

Steve didn't understand it. All right, so it was almost ten o'clock. He was late. Surely the boss had a right to be late every now and then.

"Good morning," Steve said.

"Good morning."

"Any calls?"

"No."

"Any mail?"

"On your desk."

Steve Winslow gave her a look, wondering what he'd done wrong. He couldn't figure it out. He shrugged and went into his inner office.

Steve walked around behind his desk, started to sit down,

stopped, and grinned. There on the desk blotter lay a pink, perfumed envelope.

Steve chuckled. Women. You could have a sexual revolution, women's liberation, and the whole bit, but some things never changed. Tracy Garvin was having a jealous snit.

Steve picked up the envelope. It really reeked of perfume. No wonder it set her off.

Well, there was an easy way to fix that. All Steve had to do was call Tracy into the room and let her open the envelope and pull out the two Bradshaw letters.

Except Steve didn't want Tracy to know he had them. No, explanations were out. Tracy was just going to have to sulk. Well, she'd get over it.

The intercom buzzed. There. She was over it already. Steve picked up the phone.

"Yes."

"A Miss Judy Meyers to see you," Tracy said. Her voice could have cut glass.

Steve sighed. No, this just wasn't his day.

Being an actress, Judy Meyers made an entrance. She swept into the room wearing a rather daring evening gown, closed the door behind her, and made an elaborate pantomime of looking around furtively before saying in a stage whisper, "Is the coast clear?"

Steve Winslow cracked up. "I should have known better than to ask an actress. My god, you even dressed for the part,"

Judy looked at him. "What do you mean, dressed for the part? I have an audition in a half hour."

"Oh?"

"And not as a gun moll, either. A woman doctor."

"Oh."

Judy frowned. "You think I look cheap? Too flashy? Overdressed?"

"No, no," Steve said. "I'm just not used to seeing you dressed up in the morning. I didn't know you had an audition."

"I look too slinky, is that it?"

"No, no. Really."

"Cause I value your opinion," Judy said. "I mean, you were an actor, you've always given me good advice about auditions and— Say! Nice mail."

Steve looked down at the letter that was still lying on his desk. In spite of himself, he started giggling.

Judy stared at him. "What's so funny?"

He shook his head, but he couldn't stop giggling. "I'm sorry," he said. "It's just too funny. I have a secretary out there giving me the cold shoulder because of this envelope. This envelope happens to contain a bit of evidence that I mailed to myself because I don't want the cops to get their hands on it. I can't tell her because I don't want her to know about it. The cops have grilled her once about my business, and they may grill her again. That's for starters. What she thinks of you, I wouldn't even want to imagine."

Judy cocked an eyebrow at him. "Whatever have you done to make the poor girl so possessive?"

"Absolutely nothing."

Judy nodded. "Ah, the old indifferent act. Good move. Gets them every time."

"Yeah."

Judy looked at him. "You're really in trouble, aren't you?"

"Why do you say that?"

"Because I'm bantering with you, and you're not bantering back. In fact, you just told me about your secretary giving you a hard time, which is totally out of character for you, and not something you'd ordinarily tell me. Which means you're so preoccupied with something you can't think of anything to say other than the simple truth. So what's wrong?"

Steve sighed. "Yesterday I testified before the grand jury. I'm holding out evidence in a murder case. The D.A. knows it, and if he can prove it he's going to try to get me disbarred."

Judy looked at him. "Oh. Good. I thought it was something serious."

Steve shot her a look.

"Sorry," Judy said. "I can't help myself. Here, let me make your day." She reached down the front of her dress and pulled out a piece of paper. "Ta da!"

"You got it."

"Damn right, I got it. Is this it?"

Steve unfolded the paper. Smiled. "That's it, all right."

"Great. Is there anything else I can do for you?"

"The main thing is to forget you ever saw this."

"Consider it done. Are you sure you can't tell me what this is all about?"

"Not unless you'd like to risk going to jail as an accessory to murder."

"Not today, thanks."

The intercom buzzed.

"Ah," Judy said. "That will be Miss Warmth, telling me my time is up."

Steve grimaced, picked up the phone. "Yes?"

"A Mr. Fitzpatrick to see you."

"Tell him I'll be right with him."

"A client?" Judy asked.

"A lawyer."

"Sounds like my exit cue. Don't worry. I'm in your corner all the way and my lips are sealed."

Steve opened the door for her and smiled. Judy could be a pain in the ass in a lot of ways, but in a lot of others she was a brick.

Steve had just had time to have that charitable thought, when Judy stopped halfway through the outer office, turned back and said—largely for Tracy's benefit, he was sure, "Do call me about dinner."

Steve sighed, turned, gestured to his inner office, and said, "Mr. Fitzpatrick?"

Fitzpatrick's manner was certainly different from when Steve had encountered him at the Harding mansion. The chubby face that had been so flushed and angry looked practically congenial.

He wasted no time with any amenities, however. The minute

the door was closed he turned on Winslow and said, "You testified before the grand jury yesterday."

"That's right."

"I read the transcript. You didn't tell 'em much."

"No."

"Among the things you didn't tell them was the substance of
your conversation with my client."

Steve said nothing.

"Well?"

"Well what?"

"Do you care to comment?"

"Not really. You came to me, Fitzpatrick. You're going to have
to carry the ball."

"I'd like to know what you discussed with my client."

"Why don't you ask her?"

"I'm asking you."

"Yes, you are," Steve said. "From which I gather your client
hasn't told you."

"You can gather what you like. I'm asking you a question."

"Client clammed up on you, eh?"

Fitzpatrick frowned. "My client is reticent upon certain matters.
I'm wondering how much of that reticence I owe to you."

"I'm sure I couldn't tell you."

"Interesting thing about the transcript of your testimony."

"Oh?"

"Dirkson kept asking you if you'd ever been Marilyn's attorney.
Your response in every instance was qualified with the phrase, 'to
the best of my knowledge.'"

"Naturally. Any response I'm going to give can only be to the
best of my knowledge."

"Exactly. That phrase could apply to the answer to any question. Which is why there's no reason to say it. And yet in every
answer you made regarding whether or not Marilyn had ever
employed you, you were careful to include that phrase."

"If you say so. I haven't read the transcript."

"But you gave the testimony. And you knew what you were doing."

"Thank you for your assessment of my testimony. Now look, Fitzpatrick, it's real nice swapping words with you and all that, but would you mind telling me why you're here?"

"I thought we might discuss the case. It occurs to me we might have similar interests. We might be able to help each other."

"Oh?"

"Yes. Look. I don't know what your connection is to my client, but you obviously have some interest in this case. And I have an interest in this case. Those interests are probably similar."

"You think so?"

"Yes, I do. Now let's get down to brass tacks. I got a problem, and a big one. Confidentially, the case against my client is pretty bad. And she's not helping me any. And you obviously know something about her situation. And you know what you and she discussed. If you can give me some information to make her open up and level with me, well, we might just crack this thing."

Steve looked at him. "What sort of information did you have in mind?"

"Anything to crack her shell and start her talking. The fact that she knew she was in trouble before the Bradshaw business happened. Just the fact that she made overtures to you would be enough. Just so I get her talking and can find out what this is all about. And if I had some inkling of what it was, I might learn something that would benefit you, and then I'd be in a position to reciprocate."

Steve considered that a moment. He smiled. "Bullshit," he said.

"I beg your pardon?"

Steve shook his head. "Bullshit. Here you are in the spirit of friendship and cooperation. Mutual interests, indeed. You've just come from the District Attorney's office, haven't you?"

Fitzpatrick looked somewhat taken aback. "Well, I—"

"Sure you have. Now *I'll* tell *you* what's going on here. Yesterday I testified before the grand jury. I didn't give 'em squat, but what I did give 'em, they don't like. Dirkson's pissed off and he's ready to throw the book at me at any given opportunity. And now you come here in the spirit of cooperation. And what do you want to know? If your client ever consulted me. And why? Because I told the grand jury she didn't. Which means if you can just get me to admit she did, that's all Dirkson needs. He'll get me for perjury and obstructing justice, and he'll have me disbarred. He's so eager to get me, I bet he offered to let Marilyn cop a manslaughter plea if you could trap me into an admission. That's what you were talking to Dirkson about, and that's why you're here."

Fitzpatrick's eyes faltered. "Oh now, look here—"

"No. You look here. This interview is over." Steve pointed his finger in Fitzpatrick's face. "So if it wouldn't be presuming too much upon our mutual interests, would you please take your spirit of cooperation and get the fuck out of my office."

21.

THE EXPERT shook his head. "They're not the same."

Steve frowned. "You sure?"

He nodded. "Of course I haven't done a thorough analysis, but just from a preliminary look I can tell. They're very similar—probably both Smith Corona—and both in very poor condition. But the alignment's different. The two letters were both done on the same typewriter, but the note about 'all good men' is different. For one thing, the *t* is broken on the note. It shows up in 'the,' 'time,' 'to' and 'party.' Whereas in the letters it's not broken. That alone is conclusive."

"Couldn't it have been broken after the letters were typed?" Steve asked.

"No. That's just one instance. There are others. Of course, I'm just giving you an off-the-cuff answer. If you want a careful analysis it will take some time. But believe me, it's conclusive."

Steve nodded grimly. "Thanks."

"You want a complete analysis?"

Steve shook his head. "What do I owe you?"

"If that's all you want, fifty bucks."

Steve nodded.

"How you gonna pay?"

"In cash."

"Fine. What name you want on the receipt?"

"No receipt."

Steve walked out of the office building into the din of Broadway. A crew with a jackhammer was tearing up the sidewalk. Steve detoured around them, stood on the corner, and looked around.

Damn. Was it the jackhammer that was giving him the headache?

Or the letters?

Steve took the letters and the note out of his jacket pocket. Well, at least this time he was prepared for it. He took a stamped, self-addressed envelope out of his other pocket. White, business size. No perfume this time. Steve put the letters and the note in the envelope, sealed it, and dropped it in the mailbox on the corner.

Steve sighed and rubbed his head.

What a fucking mess. Bradshaw hadn't sent the letters. Bradshaw wasn't his client. Somewhere out there was a person with a half a dollar bill. A person who held Steve's fate in his hands. A person who could walk up to him at any minute and suddenly turn his world upside down.

Steve shook his head angrily. Damn it. Snap out of it. Think.

Steve realized he hadn't been thinking clearly at all so far. He'd been too caught up in the events, events so bizarre and outlandish they seemed straight out of one of Tracy Garvin's detective thrillers. That was the problem. The whole thing just didn't seem real. I mean, come on. Anonymous letters, ten thousand dollar cash retainers, and mystery clients, for Christ's sake. It just couldn't be.

But it was. That was the thing Steve had to concentrate on. It could happen and it had happened. Someone had sent him ten thousand bucks in the mail.

And there had to be a reason why.

22.

"SHEILA BENTON."

Mark Taylor leaned back in his desk chair, cocked his head at Steve Winslow, and said, "What about her? I thought she was in Europe."

"She is."

"So?"

Steve shifted position in Taylor's overstuffed clients' chair. He rubbed his head. "I want you to dig into her background."

Taylor stared at him. "What?"

"That's right."

"You want me to investigate a client in a case that's been closed for months?"

"I don't want you to investigate the case. Just her."

"Why?"

Steve took a breath. "Let's look at this case objectively, Mark."

"O.K."

"To begin with, someone sent me those letters."

Mark Taylor laughed nervously. "What letters, Steve? I don't know about any letters, remember?"

"Right, right," Steve said impatiently. "You don't know about any letters. It's just you and me talking here, Mark. But if it makes

142

you nervous, we'll have a hypothetical conversation. *Suppose* someone sent me some letters."

Taylor groaned. "Oh Jesus, cut the comedy."

Steve shrugged. "You're hard to please. All right. Either way you want it, start with the letters. Someone sent them to me. And the question is why?"

"And the answer is I don't know. And I bet you don't know either."

"Right. I don't know who and I don't know why. But I do know one thing. They were sent to *me.*"

Taylor frowned. "What do you mean?"

"That's the key to this whole thing. I don't know who this person was. And I don't know what sort of trouble they were in that made them feel they needed an attorney. But I do know that when they did decide they needed an attorney, they thought of me. And that's mighty interesting."

"Why?"

"Figure it out. I've only been an attorney for one year. I've had one case and one client. Sheila Benton. And after the showing I made in court on that case, there was no reason for anyone to assume I was any good.

"And then someone sends me a retainer. Why me? How would they hear of me? How would they know?"

Taylor frowned. "I see."

"Right," Steve said. "It's not as if I were William Kunstler or something. Nobody knows me. The only person in the world who would have any reason to think I'm a good attorney would be Sheila Benton. She's the only person I could think of who could possibly recommend me to someone who was in a jam."

"That makes sense," Taylor said. "So why don't you ask her?"

"Because I don't know where she is. She's in Europe, that's all I know. Her itinerary was deliberately vague. She wanted to travel, forget, and not be reached for anything. I have complete power of attorney to handle her affairs. She trusts me completely. With everything. Except knowing where she is."

"I see."

"So start digging around. See if there's anyone connected with this case that you can link with Sheila Benton."

"Right."

"Start with Marilyn Harding's circle of acquaintances."

Taylor grimaced. "I knew you were going to say that."

"Well," Steve said, "they both come from money. It's a logical assumption."

"That's just it," Taylor said. "Steve, I'm your friend, and I want to help you. And I need the work. I'm not in business for my health. But, Jesus."

"What?"

"Well, if I go sticking my nose around Marilyn Harding's business, the cops are going to get onto it. They're not going to be pleased."

"You're a private investigator. You have every right to investigate, right?"

"Yeah."

"So I'm hiring you to investigate. If the cops give you a hard time, you refer them back to me."

"I know. It's just the whole letter business. I don't want to be interrogated again."

"You and me both," Steve said.

Steve walked back to his office. Tracy Garvin was at the desk. She looked at him when he came in the door. He couldn't make out her mood behind those large-rimmed glasses. The girl, Steve realized, was something of an enigma. How could one girl be so old in so many ways, and so immature in others, so smart in so many ways, and so slow in others. Just what was her story anyway?

For the moment, Steve realized, he didn't care. He had too much on his mind to deal with her. He gave her a noncommittal nod and plodded into his inner office.

He sat at his desk to think things over. Though, he realized, there was nothing much to think about. Just let Mark come up with something. Anything. Something that got him off the hook. A lead. A human being he could go to and say, "Damn it, you're my client, now what the hell is going on?"

And even if they wouldn't tell him, it wouldn't matter. Because just knowing who the client was would be enough. Because, Steve realized, it didn't really matter who the client was. All that mattered was that it *wasn't* Marilyn Harding.

It was three hours later when the phone rang.

"Got it, Steve."

"Yeah, Mark."

"It wasn't hard, really, once you told me what you were looking for. I got men out digging around and—"

"Mark. Please. I don't need a rundown. Who's the client?"

"Whoa. I'm not making any deductions. That's your department. All you said was find someone with a connection with Sheila Benton. So that's what I did."

"Yes? And?"

"And it's a definite. Hell, they went to school together, for Christ's sake."

"Yes, damn it. But who?"

"Oh. Sorry," Mark said. "I thought you knew. It's Marilyn Harding, of course."

23.

JUDY MEYERS watched the waiter depart with their orders, grimaced, and said, "I'm going to have to diet for two weeks to make up for this."

"Then why did you order so much?" Steve said.

Judy smiled. "Are you kidding? Because you're paying for it. I don't get breaks like this that often."

"You gettin' any work?"

Judy shrugged. "A few auditions. I'm making the rounds."

"Any callbacks?"

"Nothing to speak of. Things are slow. Look. Enough chitchat. This is a payback dinner, and, for your information, the payback's gonna take more than food."

Steve raised his eyebrows. "Oh?"

"You have a dirty mind," Judy told him. "I mean the piece of paper. I've never been mixed up in a mystery before. So let's have it."

"Oh," Steve said.

Judy stared at him. "You *are* going to tell me what's going on?"

"Look," Steve said. "I told you. I'm in trouble. Big trouble. I could be charged with something. If I am, anything I tell you could be construed as an admission of guilt. You could be forced to testify. I could—"

"Oh, bullshit," Judy said. "I got that paper for you. If there's anything illegal about it that makes me an accessory. If you think you can make me an accessory to a crime without letting me know what's going on, that makes you a candidate for the Asshole of the Month award."

"You got the paper without knowing what it's all about. At worst, you're an unwitting accomplice. The more you know, the more trouble you're in."

"Spoken like a lawyer. Hey, Steve, look, it's me. It's Judy sitting here. If you want to get all cutesy-poo legal on me, well, fine, tell me a hypothetical story of what might have happened. Then we'll all be protected because we were just saying 'what if.' But let me tell you, if you don't start talking, you are going to wind up with your salad in your lap."

He told her the whole thing. More than he'd told Mark Taylor or Tracy Garvin. He told it from the beginning, from getting the letters, to finding Bradshaw's body and tossing the note out the window, to everything that had happened since.

"So," Judy said. "How true to form. The white knight on the charger. You raced down to the police station and rescued your secretary from the clutches of the law. No wonder the poor girl's so starry eyed."

"Come on," Steve said irritably.

"Well, what girl could resist such a courtship?"

"She happens to have given two weeks' notice."

"Oh? Was that before or after the daring rescue?"

The food had long since arrived and was sitting untouched in front of them. Steve picked up a knife and fork and cut into his steak. After a moment or two, Judy followed suit.

They ate in silence.

"So," Judy said. "What do you do now?"

Steve shook his head. "That's the problem. There's nothing I *can* do."

"Why not?"

"I'm not her lawyer. Fitzpatrick is. The grand jury's indicted her for murder. He's got her out on bail. Dirkson's pushing for a speedy court date, and Fitzpatrick is stalling like crazy. It's the same old shit. Business as usual. But it's not my business."

"If she's out on bail, why can't you talk to her?"

"You don't understand. I'm not her lawyer. But everyone from Dirkson to Fitzpatrick thinks I am, or at least used to be. And if Dirkson can prove it, he's going to have me disbarred. The minute I go sniffing around her Dirkson's gonna go bananas."

"Fuck him."

Steve stared at her. "What?"

"Fuck him. Let him go bananas."

Steve sighed. "Judy, I'm afraid your usual incisive wit is somewhat lost on me. What the hell are you saying?"

Judy took a sip of her drink. "This thing has really got you tied up in knots, hasn't it?"

Steve shook his head. "Yeah."

"Talk to me."

"What?"

"Tell me about it."

"I told you about it."

"No, not the damn case. I know all about the damn case. Tell me about you. Your first trial was over. Sheila Benton got acquitted."

"The charges were dismissed."

"Whatever."

Steve shook his head. "No. Big difference. If she'd been acquitted in court, I'd have got credit for it. I'd have had a law practice."

"Exactly. But she didn't, and the cops grabbed all the credit, and then what?"

"And then nothing. I didn't have a law practice. But I still had Sheila Benton for a client. And she came into a lot of money. Not just her own trust fund, she inherited from her uncle too. And that was a straight inheritance, not bound up in trust. She's worth millions."

Steve shrugged. "And she put me in charge of it. Complete power of attorney. At a substantial annual retainer. I rented an office, set up a practice, began to handle her affairs. Not very taxing work. But after years of driving a cab, not bad.

"But it got boring. Sheila went off to Europe. What little work there was dried up. The job trickled down to about one letter or phone call per day. I hired a secretary to handle that. I stopped coming by the office. I figured I deserved the leisure time. Maybe I'd learn to play golf."

Steve rubbed his head. "What I really wanted, of course, was another case. Something I could sink my teeth into. Hell, just something to do. But I wasn't going to get it because nobody knew about me, and those that did, from my first case, had to figure I was some sort of incredible asshole.

"And then, out of the blue, I get it. But it's not a case. It's some outrageous, improbable, storybook fantasy that makes no sense whatsoever. I have no idea what's going on, and my only immediate prospect is being disbarred."

"Which is great," Judy said.

Steve stared at her. "Huh?"

"Hey, it's just what the doctor ordered. Here you are, the embattled hero, fighting insurmountable odds. It's a thoroughly glamorous position to be in."

"Judy, this is not a play."

"No, but it's theatrical, and that's where you shine. So stop crabbing, fuck Dirkson, and start fighting."

"For whom?" Steve cried in exasperation. "That's the whole fucking problem. Give me someone to fight for, and I'll fight for 'em. Then I can be aggressive. Do things. Right now, I'm on the defensive all the time."

"Oh, is that all?" Judy said. "No client, huh?" She reached under the table and fumbled in her purse.

"What are you doing?" Steve said.

"Just a minute," Judy said. "Ah. Here we are." Judy's hand came up from under the table holding the torn half of a dollar bill. "There you are. I'm the client. Start fighting."

Steve gawked at her. "What the hell!?"

Judy shrugged and shook her head. "Can't take a joke, can you?" Her other hand came up from under the table holding the other half of the dollar bill she had just torn. "Steve, the point is, it doesn't matter who the client is. Fuck Dirkson. Get out there and kick some ass." Judy smiled, cocked her head at him, and held up the two halves of the dollar bill. "Got any scotch tape?"

24.

STEVE WINSLOW scrunched down in the front seat of the rental car as Marilyn Harding's Mercedes pulled out of the front gate
of her mansion in Glen Cove. He gave her a couple hundred
yards and pulled out after her.

If Marilyn had any idea she was being tailed, she didn't show it.
She drove straight to the Long Island Expressway, and headed for
New York City.

He almost lost her at the Queens Midtown Tunnel. He didn't
want to be right behind her in line, so he picked another tollbooth. And, just as it was every time he picked a line in the
supermarket, his line was slow. The guy in front of him didn't
have his money ready. When he got it out, it was apparently a
twenty, because the tollbooth clerk looked at it for some time
before slowly counting out the change, just as Marilyn Harding's
Mercedes disappeared into the tunnel. Then the guy wanted a
receipt.

Steve took a breath, restrained himself from hitting the horn. If
he'd done that, the guy probably would have turned around and
given him the finger, wasting more time. Instead, he pulled away
slowly.

Steve gunned the motor, lurched into the tollbooth, slapped his
two dollars into the tolltaker's hand, gunned the motor again, and

J. P. HAILEY

zoomed off. In the tunnel he weaved in and out, ignoring the double yellow line and the "KEEP IN ONE LANE" sign. He caught the Mercedes just as it emerged from the tunnel into Manhattan.

Marilyn Harding went down Second Avenue, across 34th Street, and pulled into a garage. Steve didn't want to go into the same garage, but there were no others around. He pulled over to the curb and waited. About five minutes later Marilyn emerged, tucking her keys and her claim ticket into her purse. Steve hopped out of his car and tagged along behind.

She walked down the street and went into Macy's. Steve groaned. After hours of sitting in the car, he wasn't up to hours of shopping. And Macy's wasn't really a good place to approach her.

On the other hand, Steve realized, there *was* no good place to approach her. Well, what the hell. He had to take a shot.

Marilyn hopped on the escalator. Steve hopped on behind. As soon as she lights, he told himself.

She lit in lingerie. Just his luck. As if he didn't have enough problems, the saleslady would think he was a masher. Well, the hell with it.

Steve walked up behind her. "Miss Harding?"

Marilyn wheeled around. She was holding a lacy bra. From the expression on her face, one would have thought she'd been caught shoplifting it. Then she recognized him.

"You!"

"Yes. Steve Winslow, in case you've forgotten. I thought it was time we finished our talk."

Marilyn's eyes flashed. "Oh, is that so. I've been indicted for murder. I have a lawyer, and he doesn't happen to be you."

"I sure wish you could convince some other people of that."

"What?"

"Hasn't Fitzpatrick been after you to get you to admit you hired me?"

"Oh, that."

"Yeah. That."

"I don't know why—Wait a minute. I'm not talking to you."

"Yeah. I noticed. Look, I don't want to talk to you about the case. I just thought we could discuss a mutual acquaintance."

"What?"

"Sheila Benton."

Marilyn frowned. "What?"

"Yeah. Old school chum. You went to college together, remember?"

"What are you talking about?"

"Sheila was my first client. My only client, actually. Quite a coincidence, don't you think so?"

Marilyn said nothing, just kept staring at him.

"So I wondered. When was the last time you two talked?"

Marilyn kept her lips clamped tightly together.

"Huh?" Steve persisted.

"I have nothing to say to you," Marilyn said.

"Fine. Understandable," Steve said. "You'd like to be rid of me? Want to see me walk out that door? Then just answer one question and I will. When was the last time you talked to Sheila Benton?"

Marilyn took a breath, looked down at the floor, then looked Steve right in the eye. "I haven't seen Sheila in years," she said.

Steve looked back at her and shook his head. "God, I wish I could believe that."

Steve turned on his heel and walked off. On the escalator down he shook his head again. Yeah, Judy. Great advice. This is really getting me somewhere.

Steve emerged onto 34th Street just in time to see his rental car being towed away.

By the time Steve Winslow, one hundred twenty-five dollars poorer, had retrieved his car from the pier, dropped it off at the rental agency, and hailed a cab back to the office, he was in a foul mood to say the least. He had also decided something. Fuck this. No more chasing will-o'-the-wisps. No more groping in the dark. If his client wanted to come forward, fine, but in the meantime he was through. Marilyn Harding could go hang for all he cared. Dirkson could think what he liked. Steve Winslow, attorney, was not involved in the case, and that was that.

Having made that decision, Steve walked into his outer office fully prepared to face the wrath of Tracy Garvin.

He didn't. Tracy was over her snit. More than that, she was excited. It didn't take him long to learn why.

There was another letter. Typewritten. Unsigned. Just like the first two. And, to the best Steve could determine, written on the same typewriter.

It said: "Sit in on the trial."

25.

DISTRICT ATTORNEY Harry Dirkson bowed, smiled, and said, "Ladies and gentlemen of the jury, this will be a very brief opening statement, because this is a very simple case. We expect to prove that on the ninth day of October, at approximately five thirty in the afternoon, the defendant, Marilyn Harding, did feloniously and with malice of forethought, kill one Donald Blake, alias David C. Bradshaw, by stabbing him with a knife. The events leading up to this murder are simple and straightforward, and we shall lay them out for you.

"We hold no brief for the decedent. He was a blackmailer and an extortionist, and he had a prison record. He made his living preying on people, and his end was probably the inevitable consequence of his existence. But none of that matters, and the judge will instruct you that you must give it no weight. Donald Blake may have been a despicable human being, but he *was* a human being, and every human being's life is sacred, and no person has the right to take it."

Fitzpatrick was on his feet. "Objection, Your Honor. Is this an opening statement or a closing argument?"

Dirkson, nettled, whirled to glare at the defense attorney. "Your Honor—" Dirkson began.

155

Judge Randell Graves banged the gavel. The thin, reedy, elderly judge had a reputation for brooking no nonsense in his courtroom. "Gentlemen," he snapped. "Approach the sidebar."

Graves stepped down from his bench, and the two lawyers and the court reporter joined him at the sidebar. They proceeded to confer in low tones, out of earshot of the jury.

In the back row of the court, Tracy Garvin grabbed Steve Winslow's arm. "What's going on?"

"A sidebar," he told her.

"I know it's a sidebar," Tracy said impatiently. "I've been in court before. What's the point of law?"

"Virtually none," Steve said. "Fitzpatrick's just trying to needle him. Interrupt the opening argument, break the flow, get him pissed off."

"Has he got a point?"

"Technically, yes. Dirkson shouldn't be arguing the case at this time. But all lawyers do, it's really splitting hairs, and Dirkson's pretty pissed off at Fitzpatrick for calling him on it."

"So it's a good move on Fitzpatrick's part?"

Steve shook his head. "No, it's a bad one."

"Why? It throws Dirkson off, doesn't it?"

"A little. But it irritates the judge. It's a hollow tactic, and Judge Graves isn't going to like it. Judges don't like to put up with a lot of overtechnical crap. They like to keep the trial moving along. Fitzpatrick may score a point now, but it's going to cost him later on."

The lawyers had resumed their positions. Judge Graves addressed the jury.

"Ladies and gentlemen of the jury. As I have instructed you, during the course of the trial there will be many occasions upon which we depart to the sidebar to discuss various objections. You should give those discussions no weight, and you should not speculate on what goes on in those discussions.

"Now, I would like to instruct you that we are not arguing the case at this time. The prosecutor is merely outlining what he intends to prove. That is all that should concern you.

"Mr. Dirkson?"

Dirkson rose. "Ladies and gentlemen of the jury. To resume, we expect to prove that Marilyn Harding killed Donald Blake, alias David C. Bradshaw. The motive for this murder is simple and straightforward. We expect to prove that Donald Blake was a blackmailer, that he was blackmailing Marilyn Harding. We expect to prove that Marilyn Harding paid Donald Blake the sum of ten thousand dollars. We expect to prove that Donald Blake had evidence that Marilyn Harding had poisoned her father, Phillip Harding, and—"

Fitzpatrick jumped to his feet. "Objection!" he roared. "Objection, Your Honor! The prosecutor is attempting to prejudice the jury by introducing evidence of a previous crime. I move for a mistrial."

Dirkson smiled. "I offer that evidence only as proof of motive, Your Honor."

"May I have a sidebar, Your Honor?" Fitzpatrick demanded, already heading in that direction.

Graves banged the gavel. "Attorney, stand back. We'll do this in open court. Bailiff, please show the jurors to the jury room. Ladies and gentlemen of the jury, I am going to excuse you while we discuss this motion. Please follow the bailiff to the jury room."

As the jury filed out, Dirkson's grin was smug.

"Big victory for Dirkson," Steve said.

"What?"

"Sidebar denied. I told you it would cost him. Now we're going to hear the argument in open court."

"But the jury won't hear it."

"No, but we will, and so will the media. And the idea that cases aren't tried in the papers is bullshit. And it doesn't even matter which way Graves rules. Phillip Harding's murder is going to make the front page."

When the jurors had filed out, Judge Graves said, "I will now hear arguments on the objection. Mr. Fitzpatrick?"

"Yes, Your Honor. Marilyn Harding is on trial for killing Donald Blake, not for killing her father, Phillip Harding. Any evidence of the fact she killed her father is prejudicial, inadmissible, and grounds for a mistrial."

"Mr. Dirkson?"

"Your Honor, we are not attempting to prove that Marilyn Harding killed her father. As I said, we are introducing this evidence only to show motive. It is our contention only that Donald Blake *claimed* that Marilyn Harding had killed her father, and was therefore blackmailing her. We are not attempting to show that Marilyn Harding killed her father, merely that Donald Blake had reason to believe that she had and was blackmailing her about it. That, therefore, she paid him the ten thousand dollars and, when he demanded more money, she killed him. As evidence of motivation, it's clearly admissible. We introduce it only for that limited purpose."

"Nonsense, Your Honor," Fitzpatrick said. "This talk of limited purpose is absurd. So is the prosecution's statement that they will only be introducing evidence of Donald Blake's *contention* that Marilyn Harding killed her father. They intend to show that Marilyn Harding paid Donald Blake ten thousand dollars. Then they're going to claim Donald Blake demanded that money because he knew she'd killed her father. Now, after they prove she paid him that money, what juror is going to believe she *didn't* kill her father?"

Steve Winslow shook his head and laughed silently. "Jesus, what an asshole. Even if he wins the point, he just managed to convince the whole world his client's guilty."

"Is he going to win the point?" Tracy asked.

"Technically, yes. The judge is going to instruct the jury that the evidence is being introduced for a limited purpose and they must give no weight to the contention that Marilyn Harding killed her father. Which is like telling them, don't think of an elephant. Which is just what I expected of Fitzpatrick, really. He's the type of lawyer who loses when he wins."

After a long and tedious argument, the jurors were brought back in and Judge Graves instructed them just as Steve had predicted.

The jurors listened to the judge's instructions gravely. Some looked at each other. Some nodded. And by the end of the instructions, each and every one of them was looking directly at the defendant, Marilyn Harding.

Dirkson watched this with extreme satisfaction.

Having finished his instructions, Judge Graves turned to the District Attorney and said, "You may proceed, Mr. Dirkson."

Dirkson rose to his feet. "Thank you, Your Honor." He smiled. "We shall prove all this by competent evidence, and we shall expect a verdict of guilty at your hands."

And Dirkson sat down.

Steve Winslow grinned.

"Brilliant," he said. "Give Dirkson credit. I didn't know he was that good."

"What?" Tracy said.

"His opening statement. He didn't have to finish it. He let Fitzpatrick's objection do it for him. He knew Fitzpatrick would object, and he knew how the judge was going to rule, and he knew how the jury would respond. He *planned* it that way."

Judge Graves turned to Fitzpatrick. "Does the defense wish to make an opening statement?"

Fitzpatrick rose. "We will reserve our opening statement until we begin putting on our case."

"Very well. Mr. Dirkson, is the prosecution ready to proceed?"

"Yes, Your Honor."

"Very well. It is approaching the hour for noon recess. I am going to excuse the jury and adjourn for lunch, and we'll resume at two o'clock."

26.

FOR HIS first witness, Dirkson called Police Officer Frank Sullivan, who stated his name and cited his eighteen years of duty on the force.

"Now, Officer Sullivan, were you on duty on the ninth day of October."

"I was."

"And what was your duty on that day?"

"I was on radio patrol."

"In what vehicle?"

"In a marked police car."

"And did you have a partner at that time?"

"Yes I did."

"And who was your partner?"

"Officer Sanford Hill."

"Directing your attention to the address 249 East 3rd Street, did you receive any instructions regarding that address?"

"Yes, I did."

"Could you tell us what happened, please?"

"Yes. We got a call on the police radio reporting an altercation at that address."

"Can you tell us what time you got that call?"

"I do not recall the exact time, but I wrote it in my notebook."

"Would looking at your notebook refresh your recollection on that matter?"

"Yes, it would."

"Would you please do so?"

Officer Sullivan took out his notebook and flipped through the pages. "Yes, sir. The call came in at 5:42 P.M."

"And what did you do?"

"My partner and I proceeded to that address."

"What time did you get there?"

"Approximately five minutes later."

"That would be 5:47?"

"Yes, sir."

"And what did you find when you got there?"

"The downstairs door was open and we went in."

"Did you hear the sounds of an altercation."

"No, sir. We did not."

"What did you do then?"

"We went up the stairs to apartment 2A."

"And what did you find?"

"We found the body of a man lying on the floor. He had been stabbed in the back with a knife."

"What did you do then?"

"We radioed for Emergency Medical Services, and radioed to report a possible homicide."

"Thank you, officer. Your witness."

As Dirkson sat down, Fitzpatrick got ponderously to his feet.

Steve Winslow smiled. This really was going to be a battle of the giants. Steve watched Fitzpatrick with some interest, wondering what tack the attorney was going to take.

Fitzpatrick smiled and approached the witness.

"Officer Sullivan," he said. "I believe you stated that you have been a police officer for eighteen years?"

"That's right."

"During the course of that time, have you ever been called upon to testify in a court of law?"

"Yes, sir. I have."

"On how many occasions?"

"I can't recall, sir."

"Approximately."

"Say fifty to a hundred times."

"I see. Now in this particular case, I notice several glaring gaps in your testimony."

"Objection, Your Honor."

"Sustained."

"Well, let's discuss your testimony. You say you got a radio call, requesting you to proceed to 249 East 3rd Street?"

"That's right."

"The downstairs door was open and you went in?"

"That's right."

"Now, when you got to the door to 2A, the apartment of the deceased, what happeneded?"

"I knocked on the door."

"And what happened?"

"A voice said 'Come in.'"

Fitzpatrick raised his eyebrows. *"A voice?"*

"Yes. A man's voice."

"A man's voice. How interesting? You didn't mention this on direct examination."

"I wasn't asked."

"No, you weren't, were you, Officer Sullivan? So a man's voice said, 'Come in,' and what did you do then?"

"I opened the door and went in."

"The door was unlocked?"

"Yes."

"Well, that's mighty interesting too. And when you got into the apartment, did you by any chance encounter the owner of this voice, the man who said, 'Come in'?"

"Yes, I did."

"And where was he?"

"Seated on the couch."

"The living room couch?"

"Yes."

"That is the same room in which you found the body of the deceased?"

"That's right."

"So, if I understand it correctly, when you entered the apartment, you found two people, a dead man lying on the floor, and a live man, sitting on the couch. Is that right?"

"Yes, sir."

Fitzpatrick shook his head and laughed. "Well, Officer Sullivan, you must forgive me for thinking there might be a few glaring gaps in your story."

"Objection, Your Honor," Dirkson said.

Judge Graves frowned. "Mr. Fitzpatrick. If we could avoid such side remarks."

"Yes, Your Honor," Fitzpatrick said. "Now, Officer Sullivan, you say you found a man sitting in the apartment?"

"That's right."

"Did you by any chance identify the gentleman in question?"

"I did."

"And who was he?"

"His name is Steve Winslow."

"Steve Winslow? I see. And did you have a conversation with this Mr. Winslow?"

"I did."

"Perhaps ask him what he was doing there?"

"That's right."

"And did he make any explanation for his presence?"

"He did not."

Fitzpatrick raised his eyebrows incredulously. "You mean he refused to explain his presence in the apartment of a murdered man?"

"Objection," Dirkson said. "Argumentative, assuming facts not in evidence, and in effect already asked and answered."

"Sustained."

Fitzpatrick smiled broadly and shook his head. "Well, well. And what did you do with this individual?"

"I held him until homicide arrived."

"And turned him over to them?"

"That is correct."

"And who was the officer to whom you turned him over?"

"Sergeant Stams."

"You held this Mr. Winslow in the decedent's apartment until homicide arrived?"

"Not in that apartment, no. My partner stayed there. I held him in custody in the landlady's apartment downstairs."

"Until such time as you turned him over to Sergeant Stams?"

"Actually, until Sergeant Stams was finished with him and he was released."

"Until he was *released?*" Fitzpatrick managed to convey the impression that Sullivan had just confessed to the most heinous of crimes. "You're telling me this man found at the scene of the crime was released?"

"Yes, sir."

"He was not taken to police headquarters?"

"No, sir."

"He was questioned at the scene of the crime?"

"By Sergeant Stams, yes."

"And you were present for the questioning."

"That's right."

"Did you have any other dealings with this gentleman before he was released?"

"Yes, sir."

"And what were those dealings?"

"I searched him."

"You searched him?"

"Yes, sir."

"For what?"

Sullivan shrugged. "For whatever I might find."

"At who's request did you search him?"

Sullivan hesitated.

"Well?"

"Well, actually, I searched him twice."

Fitzpatrick stared at him. "Twice?"

"Yes."

"Why did you search him twice?"

Sullivan shifted his position on the witness stand. "Well, you see, he asked to be searched."

"Who did?"

"Steve Winslow."

"You mean the man himself asked to be searched?"

"That's right."

"And so you accommodated him?"

"Well, it seemed a good idea at the time."

"You wanted to see if he had any evidence on him that might incriminate him in this murder?"

"Objection. Argumentative."

"Sustained."

"This was before Sergeant Stams arrived?"

"That is correct."

"And then you searched him a second time?"

"That's right."

"When was that?"

"After Sergeant Stams arrived."

"And had questioned the suspect?"

"Object to the word 'suspect,' Your Honor," Dirkson snapped.

"Sustained. Rephrase the question."

Fitzpatrick smiled ironically. "And this was after Sergeant Stams had questioned the *gentleman?*"

"That's right."

"And who suggested you search him a second time?"

"Sergeant Stams."

"And on these two occasions when you searched the, uh, gentleman, did you find anything you considered significant?"

"No, I did not."

"And it was after the second search that you let the gentleman go?"

"That's right."

"And, to the best of your knowledge, this gentleman, Steve Winslow, has never been indicted on any charges in this matter?"

"Objection, Your Honor. Assuming facts not in evidence, and calling for a conclusion on the part of the witness."

"It is a simple yes or no question, Your Honor, asking for the witness's personal knowledge."

"Objection overruled."

"No. As far as I know he has not."

"I see," Fitzpatrick said, nodding gravely to the jury. "No further questions."

As he sat down, several of the jurors were looking at each other with puzzled expressions.

In the back of the courtroom, Steve Winslow shifted in his seat. Well, at least that answered his question. Fitzpatrick might not be the best of attorneys. He might not be that bright, and his methods might be slightly heavy-handed. But there was no question what his courtroom strategy was going to be.

Fitzpatrick was going to try to pin the murder on him.

27.

"LET'S LOOK at the case against me."

Mark Taylor's grin seemed rather forced. "You're serious about this?"

They were in Mark Taylor's office. It was eight in the evening. Steve Winslow had just given Taylor a rundown of the day in court. After the testimony of Frank Sullivan, the rest of the day had been rather tame. Sanford Hill, called to the stand, had gone over much of the same ground Sullivan had. The medical examiner had fixed the time of death between five fifteen and five forty-five in the afternoon, and refused to budge, despite a grueling cross-examination by Fitzpatrick. The landlady, Miss Dobson, had testified to identifying the body as that of the man who had rented an apartment from her under the name of David C. Bradshaw. And Sergeant Serota of the FBI had testified to matching the decedent's fingerprints to those of one Donald Blake, a known blackmailer and extortionist.

Which normally would have been pretty interesting stuff. It was only after Officer Sullivan's testimony that it seemed tame.

"I'm kidding," Steve said. "The problem is, Fitzpatrick's serious."

"That's absurd. He has no proof at all."

167

"He doesn't need it. Dirkson has to prove Marilyn guilty beyond all reasonable doubt." Steve shrugged. "I'm his reasonable doubt."

"Yeah."

"So let's consider the case against me. I'm found in Bradshaw's apartment. I can't explain why I went there without betraying the confidence of a client—and don't say what client. Therefore I can't say anything, and therefore I can't defend myself. That puts me in the apartment, so I had the opportunity. Means? No problem there. The knife was there at hand. That leaves only motive. What motive did I have for killing Bradshaw? Just the ten thousand big ones that I admittedly knew about and even had a list of the serial numbers of. From the questions Dirkson asked me before the grand jury, it's a cinch those bills were found in the upstairs hallway of the building. Just where I might have had to ditch them if I were trapped in the apartment by the arrival of the police. Add to that the fact that Tracy Garvin, my secretary, was apprehended attempting to enter that building a couple of hours later. Put that all together and tell me how much of a case Fitzpatrick's going to be able to make."

Taylor thought a moment. "Shit."

"You said it. And I can't do anything about it because I'm not a party to the case. I can't object. I can't cross-examine. I just have to sit there and take it."

"Yeah."

Steve shook his head. "And if that weren't bad enough, I have to sit next to Tracy Garvin, who thinks the whole thing's exciting as hell."

"Nice of you of let her sit in."

"Nothing nice about it. She told me that since I wasn't the attorney in the case I wouldn't be getting transcripts so I'd need her to take shorthand notes of the testimony."

"Do you?"

"No, but if I told her that I'd have a mutiny on my hands, and if I piss her off too much, she knows enough to crucify me."

THE ANONYMOUS CLIENT 169

Mark frowned. "Hey. She wouldn't do that. She's a game kid, you know?"

"Accent on kid. She's really young, you know it."

"I don't think you do her justice."

"I forgot, I forgot. You're in love. Look, Mark, I gotta do something here. Fitzpatrick's out to get me. Dirkson's out to get me. If I'm not careful, one of them will."

"Wait a minute. You said Fitzpatrick brought out all of this stuff. Dirkson didn't even mention you at all."

Steve nodded. "That's right."

"Then I don't get it."

"Dirkson's smart, and he's a politician. He's not going to go after me in court. That would make him look bad. He's a prosecutor, and he's supposed to be prosecuting a woman for murder, not airing some personal grudge. So what does he do? He bends over backwards. He has Officer Sullivan give his testimony and carefully refrain from mentioning me at all. He knows damn well Fitzpatrick's going to bring it out on cross-examination and make a big deal about the fact it wasn't mentioned on direct. He has it both ways. The fact I was found in that apartment makes a bigger stink than if he'd mentioned it to begin with, but he's not the one bringing it out. On the other hand, he's ignoring this extraneous matter that has nothing to do with his contention that Marilyn Harding killed Donald Blake."

"I see."

"Right. And he'll go on along the same lines, letting Fitzpatrick bring out stuff about me all through the trial. Then when it's all over and Fitzpatrick's stirred up enough of a mess, if the bar association should decide I might be guilty of tampering with evidence and obstructing justice, well, hell, it wasn't Dirkson who went after this poor helpless attorney, it was Fitzpatrick. Though, once the bar association cites me, I'm sure Dirkson will feel it his bound duty to prosecute me with great vigor."

Mark thought that over. "Aw, shit. So what you gonna do?"

"I'm going to sit in court." Steve shrugged. "After all, I have to earn my half a dollar."

28.

DIRKSON LED off next morning with Detective Wallace of the Crime Scene Unit, who introduced a series of photographs he had taken of the apartment. Dirkson then called Detective Franciosa, who testified as to having developed and lifted latent fingerprints from the apartment. Referring to the photographs, he pointed out the various places the fingerprints had been found. There were none on the murder weapon.

Dirkson next called Phillip Riker, a fingerprint expert in the police crime lab.

"Mr. Riker," Dirkson said, "directing your attention to People's exhibits 2A—2CC in evidence, the fingerprint lifts taken by Detective Franciosa, I ask you if you have had occasion to compare those prints with the known prints of any person?"

"Yes, sir, I have."

"And could you tell us whose prints that would be?"

"Yes, sir. I compared the prints in question with the known prints taken from the defendant, Marilyn Harding."

"And that were the results of that comparison?"

"I found four instances where the prints matched."

"And could you point them out to us, please?"

"Certainly. If I could refer to my notes."

"Please do."

170

Riker flipped open his notebook, and began to compare the lifts.

"The print on 2D is Marilyn Harding's right thumb. The print of 2L is Marilyn Harding's right index finger. The print on 2P is again Marilyn Harding's right thumb. The print on 2T is Marilyn Harding's right ring finger."

"And where were those prints found?"

"2D was found on the inside doorknow. 2L and 2T were found on the coffee table. 2P was found on the wooden arm of a chair."

"Thank you. No further questions."

Fitzpatrick rose to his feet. "Mr. Riker, you were asked if you compared the prints on those lifts with those of any known person, and you responded, yes, to those of Marilyn Harding, is that correct?"

"That's right."

"Did you compare the prints on those lifts with those of any *other* known person?"

"Yes."

"And who was that?"

"The decedent, Donald Blake."

"And were any of the prints his?"

"Yes. Several."

"Could you be more specific?"

"If I could consult my notes."

"Certainly."

Riker looked in the notebook. "Yes. Seven of the prints matched those of the decedent."

"How many prints were there in all?"

"Twenty-nine."

"And four of them were Marilyn Harding's, and seven of them were Donald Blake's?"

"That's right."

"Aside from the defendant and the decedent, did you compare those prints with those of any other known person?"

"No, I did not."

Fitzpatrick raised his eyebrows. "You did not?"

"No, I did not."

"Mr. Riker, you stated that four prints proved to be those of the defendant, and seven proved to be those of the decedent. Yet there were twenty-nine prints in all. Now, if my elementary school math serves me, that leaves eighteen prints that you *didn't* identify. Is that right?"

"That is correct."

"Mr. Riker, are you prejudiced against the defendant?"

"Certainly not."

"And yet, aside from the decedent, she happens to be the only person in the whole world whose prints you compared with the prints lifted from the apartment."

Riker smiled. "That's hardly a coincidence, counselor. She happens to be the person charged with the murder."

That sally was greeted with an appreciative murmur. Dirkson grinned broadly.

Fitzpatrick frowned. "Tell me this. Had she been charged with the murder when you did your fingerprint comparison?"

"As to that, I'm not sure."

"Oh no? Is it not a fact that Miss Harding was indicted for the murder several days after you did your fingerprint comparison?"

"That may be."

"Well, you testified before the grand jury, didn't you? Is it not a fact that your fingerprint comparison was part of the grounds on which the prosecution *based* the indictment of Marilyn Harding?"

"Yes. It was."

"So when you say flippantly, she's the one charged with the murder, isn't that utter hogwash? Isn't that you trading words with me and making a smart remark that does not answer my question and has no basis in fact, seeing as how Marilyn Harding had *not* been charged with the murder when you did your comparison and, therefore, that was *not* the reason you singled her out as the only person whose prints to compare?"

"Objection, Your Honor," Dirkson said. "Counsel is badgering the witness. It's argumentative. It's also incompetent, irrelevant, and immaterial."

"It shows bias, Your Honor," Fitzpatrick said.

"The objection is sustained as to form. You may rephrase your question if you like."

"I will withdraw it, Your Honor. Then let me ask you this, Mr. Riker: Aside from the decedent, the only person whose finger-prints you compared with those in question was Marilyn Harding?"

"That's right."

"Did you compare the fingerprints found in the apartment with the known prints of a Mr. Steve Winslow?"

"I did not."

"You did not? Even though Steve Winslow was found in the murdered man's apartment?"

"Objection, Your Honor."

"Sustained."

"You found no prints on the murder weapon?"

"That's right."

"The prints you found of Marilyn Harding indicate merely that she was in that apartment?"

"That's right."

"The prints that you made no attempt to identify indicate that at least one other person was in that apartment?"

"That's right."

"And yet you made no attempt to match those prints with those of any other known person?"

"That's right."

"Well, thank you for such a fair and impartial evaluation of the evidence."

"Objection, Your Honor. I characterize that remark as misconduct."

Judge Graves banged the gavel. "Mr. Fitzpatrick," he said, sternly. "Such remarks are uncalled for."

"I apologize, Your Honor."

"Do you have any further questions of the witness?"

"None, Your Honor."

"Call your next witness."

"Call Jason Fisher," Dirkson said.

In the back of the courtroom, Tracy Garvin grabbed Steve's arm. "Look," she said, pointing to the man making his way to the witness stand. "Isn't that one of the detectives?"

Steve looked. It was indeed one of the men they had observed that night on the Binghamton.

"Sure is," Steve said. "This is going to be fun."

After the witness had been sworn in, Dirkson said, "Your name is Jason Fisher?"

"That's right."

"What is your occupation?"

"I'm a private detective."

"For what agency?"

"The Miltner Detective Agency."

"Directing your attention to the ninth of this month, were you employed on that day?"

"Yes, I was."

"What were you employed to do?"

"My instructions were to keep Marilyn Harding under surveillance."

There was a gasp of surprise from the courtroom. Judge Graves banged the gavel.

"What time did your surveillance start?"

"I picked her up at four o'clock that afternoon."

"Were you alone?"

"No. I was with my partner, Michael Reed."

"You picked her up at four o'clock?"

"That's right."

"Why four o'clock?"

"That's when our shift began. We took over from two detectives who'd had her under surveillance earlier in the day."

"I see. And where did you pick her up?"

"At a coffee shop on Lexington Avenue and 46th Street."

"Can you tell us what happened?"

"Yes, sir. We took up positions on the street from which we could watch through the window and observe the defendant in the coffee shop."

"What was she doing?"

"She was sitting at a table having coffee and a roll."

"Was anyone with her?"

"No. She was alone."

"And what did she do?"

"Well, evidently she was waiting for someone, because—"

"Objection, Your Honor."

"Sustained."

"That's a conclusion on your part, Mr. Fisher. Don't tell us what you thought, just tell us what you saw. What did you observe her do?"

"She sat at the table. She sipped her coffee. She seemed—"

Dirkson held up his hand. "Uh uh. Just what she did."

"Yes, sir. She looked at her watch several times. She kept looking at the door. She looked out the window toward the street. I know that particularly, because my partner and I had to keep ducking back out of the way so she wouldn't spot us."

"How long did she remain in the coffee shop?"

"Until five o'clock."

"A whole hour after you took over?"

"That's right."

"Did anyone join her in that time?"

"No, sir."

"And in that whole time, the only thing she did was to consume a cup of coffee and a roll?"

"Yes, sir. Actually, I believe the waiter freshened her coffee once, but that was it."

"She left the restaurant at five o'clock?"

"Yes, sir."

"Where did she go?"

"She went down the street to a garage and got her car."

"You followed her?"

"Yes we did."

"How?"

"In our car."

"There's no parking in that area, is there? So where was your car?"

"In another garage."

"How did you manage to get to your car and still keep the suspect under surveillance?"

"Well, we knew she was parked in a garage, so—"

Dirkson held up his hand again. "Uh uh. Please, Mr. Fisher. You only know that because of what someone else told you, right? The other detectives. And you can't testify to that. Just tell us what you did."

"Yes, sir. When she left the coffee shop, my partner ran to get our car, while I tailed the defendant." Fisher looked at Dirkson. "Am I allowed to say why?"

"As long as you just describe the procedure and don't give us your conclusions and tell us what you suspected."

"Yes, sir. Well, the procedure was I would tail the woman on foot while my partner got the car. That way, in case we had to follow her by car we'd be prepared. In the event she took off by car or taxi before my partner could bring the car around, then I would tail her alone in a taxi, and phone in her location at the first opportunity. My partner, not finding me, would call the office, get the location, and meet me there."

"Did that happen in this case?"

"No sir. The defendant went straight to a garage and handed in her claim ticket. My partner drove up in our car before she went out."

"What happened then?"

"She got in her car and drove downtown."

"To where?"

"East 3rd Street."

"What happened then?"

"She drove around until she found a parking space."

"Did she find one right away?"

"Actually, it took a little time. We went around the block a few times and made a few loops."

"But eventually she found one?"

"Yes, she did."

"And what time was that?"

"Approximately five twenty-five."

"What happened then?"

"She parked the car, got out, walked directly to 249 East 3rd Street, and went inside."

"Did you follow her inside?"

"No, sir, we did not. We set up surveillance outside the building to pick her up again when she came out."

"And did she come out?"

"Yes, she did."

"And when was that?"

"Approximately five minutes later."

"What happened when she came out?"

"She seemed terribly agitated."

"Objection, Your Honor."

"Sustained."

"Never mind what you thought. What did she do?"

"She came out the front door. She looked up and down the street. Very quickly, you know. Then she came down the front steps fast, turned, and headed toward her car."

"At what speed was she walking?"

"Fast. Very fast. She was practically running."

"Did she do anything else?"

"Yes, sir. She kept looking back over her shoulder."

"What did she do then?"

"She got in her car and drove back to her house in Glen Cove."

"What time did she get there?"

"About seven o'clock."

"What did you do then?"

"We stayed and kept the house under surveillance."

"Until what time?"

"A little after nine."

"Was that the end of your shift?"

"No."

"Then why did you break off surveillance at that time?"

"At nine o'clock I called in to report. I was instructed to cease the surveillance and—"

"Objecton to what he was instructed to do," Fitzpatrick said. Then, noting the look on Judge Graves's face, he said, "Never mind. Let's hear it, Your Honor."

"Go ahead," Dirkson said.

"Yes, sir. I was told to break off surveillance and to report directly to the office."

"And prior to that time had you called the office to report that Marilyn Harding had entered the decedent's building at aproximately five thirty that afternoon?"

"Yes, I had."

"What happened when you got back to your office?"

"Charles Miltner was there."

"That's your boss?"

"Yes, sir. He runs the detective agency."

"Was it normal for him to be there at that time of night?"

"No, sir, it wasn't."

"Did he give you any instructions at that time?"

"Yes, sir, he did."

"And after he gave you those instructions, what did you do?"

"I typed up my reports on the surveillance of Marilyn Harding and delivered them to the police."

"Thank you. That's all."

Fitzpatrick stood up and approached the witness. His manner was grim.

"Who hired you?" he demanded.

The witness smiled. "Charles Miltner."

Fitzpatrick frowned. "You know what I mean. Who hired you to shadow Miss Harding?"

"I don't know."

"You don't know?"

"No, sir. I was instructed to place Miss Harding under surveillance. I was not told who the client was in the case."

"Wait a minute. Don't you turn in time sheets to get paid?"

"Yes, I do."

"And when you put in for work, don't you have to designate on your time sheets what case the hours were for?"

"Yes, I do."

"So what name did you designate those hours to on your time sheet?"

"Marilyn Harding."

"Really? I thought the time sheets usually bore the name of the client who was to be billed."

"They usually do."

"But in this case the name on your time sheet was Marilyn Harding?"

"That's right."

Fitzpatrick frowned and thought a moment. "You had Marilyn Harding under surveillance on the afternoon of Wednesday the ninth?"

"That's right."

"Was that the only time you'd had Marilyn Harding under surveillance?"

"No, sir."

"It wasn't?"

"No sir."

"When was the first time?"

"The afternoon of Tuesday the eighth."

"From when till when?"

"From four in the afternoon till midnight."

Fitzpatrick hesitated, wondering if he wanted to open up that can of worms. On reflection, he considered there was nothing the witness could say that could damage his client any more than he already had. So he decided to go for it.

"Could you tell us what happened on that occasion?"

"Yes, sir. We picked up the witness in midtown Manhattan, followed her while she went out to dinner in New Jersey, and then followed her home."

"She didn't go near the decedent's apartment?"

"Not while we were on duty, no."

"You reported this surveillance to the police?"

"That's right."

"Yet there's nothing in the report of that day's surveillance that you considered significant?"

The witness hesitated. "Actually, there was."

"Oh? And what was that?"

"At the time, the defendant, Marilyn Harding, was also being followed by detectives from another agency."

Fitzpatrick stared at him. "What?"

"That's right."

"Do you know who those detectives were?"

"Yes, sir. They were operatives from the Taylor Detective Agency."

"And they tailed Miss Harding for how long?"

"As long as we did."

"All the way back to Glen Cove?"

"That is correct."

"Anything else that you considered significant?"

"Yes, sir."

"What is that?"

"The defendant had dinner on the Binghamton. That's an old ferry boat that's been converted into a restaurant located in New Jersey. She ate dinner with her stepsister and her stepsister's husband. During the course of dinner I also noted the presence of Mark Taylor, the head of the Taylor Detective Agency."

"Is that right? He joined his operatives there?"

"He didn't actually join them. I believe he spoke to one of them at one point. He arrived with another man and had dinner."

"Is that so? And did you learn the identity of the other man?"

"Not at the time."

"But subsequently, you learned it?"

"Yes, I did."

"And who was he?"

"An attorney by the name of Steve Winslow."

A grin slowly spread over Fitzpatrick's face. "Did you say Steve Winslow?"

"That's right."

"That's the man who came to the restaurant in the company of Mark Taylor, the head of the Taylor Detective Agency, the agency whose operatives were keeping my client under surveillance?"

"That's right."

"Taylor and Steve Winslow dined there together at the same time as my client?"

"That's right."

"And is this the same Steve Winslow who was discovered by the police in the apartment of the victim, Donald Blake?"

"Objection," Dirkson said.

"Sustained."

Fitzpatrick was grinning from ear to ear. "Thank you very much," he said. "No further questions."

In the back of the courtroom, Steve Winslow nodded his head. "Yeah," he said. "I knew that was gonna be fun."

29.

THE AFTERNOON session began on much the same theme. Sergeant Stams, called to the stand, testified to finding ten thousand dollars in thousand dollar bills in a money belt on the body of the decedent, and to finding an additional ten thousand dollars in thousand dollar bills secreted in a hollow behind a fire hose in the upstairs hallway.

Fitzpatrick had a field day on cross-examination. He pounced on the fact that Sergeant Stams had interrogated and searched Steve Winslow at the scene of the crime, and he played it for all it was worth. The expression on Fitzpatrick's face when he inquired, "You *released* him?" was a wonder to behold. Sergeant Stams actually squirmed.

Fitzpatrick also had the benefit of the grand jury testimony, so he knew just which questions to ask.

"Well, Sergeant Stams, you claim you found ten thousand dollars in a money belt on the body, and an additional ten thousand dollars in the upstairs hallway, is that right?"

"Yes, sir."

"Referring to the money hidden in the upstairs hallway—that was ten thousand dollars in thousand dollar bills?"

"That's correct."

"Did you attempt to trace those bills to determine where they'd come from?"

"Yes, I did."

"And do you know who withdrew those bills from the bank?"

"Only by hearsay, from the bank teller."

"I understand. Then let me ask you this: did you carry those bills around with you when you went to talk to the various bank tellers?"

"No, I did not."

"Then how did you know which bills you were inquiring about?"

"I made a list of the serial numbers."

"Then let me ask you this: aside from talking to the bank tellers, did you have occasion to compare your list of serial numbers, the numbers taken from the thousand dollar bills found in the upstairs hallway, with any *other* list of serial numbers?"

"Yes, I did."

"And did those serial numbers match?"

"They did."

"Each and every serial number?"

"Yes."

"In other words, the ten serial numbers on your list matched ten serial numbers on another list?"

"That's right."

"And where did you get this other list of serial numbers you compared it with?"

"It was handed to me by the District Attorney, Harry Dirkson."

Fitzpatrick frowned. "And do you know, of your own knowledge, where Harry Dirkson got that list of serial numbers?"

"Yes, I do."

"And where was that?"

"It was given to him by Steve Winslow."

Fitzpatrick smiled. "In your presence?"

"That's right."

"And where did this take place?"

"In Mr. Dirkson's office."

"When?"

"In the early morning hours of the tenth. One or two in the morning is the closest I can recall."

"And is this the same Steve Winslow whom you had interrogated at the scene of the crime?"

"That's right."

"And this was later that same evening? Though technically it was the next day, since it was after midnight, is that right?"

"That's right."

"So," Fitzpatrick said. "You interrogated Steve Winslow at the scene of the crime. And then you saw him several hours later in Harry Dirkson's office, where he produced that list of bills, is that right?"

"That's right."

"Tell me, did you happen to encounter Mr. Winslow at any time between those two times?"

"Yes, I did."

"Could you tell us when and where?"

"Yes, sir. At around ten thirty that evening I went to Glen Cove to interview Marilyn Harding. When I arrived, Steve Winslow was there talking to her."

"Steve Winslow was talking to Marilyn Harding?"

"Yes."

"The defendant in this case?"

"Yes, sir."

"Steve Winslow is an attorney. Did he claim to be her attorney?"

"No, sir."

"Did he make any explanation for what he was doing there talking to my client at ten thirty in the evening?"

"No, he did not."

"So, if I understand your testimony correctly, at around seven o'clock you interview and search Steve Winslow, who was found in the apartment with the deceased. At ten thirty in the evening, you encounter Steve Winslow in Glen Cove, Long Island, talking to the defendant, Marilyn Harding. And at around one o'clock in the morning, in District Attorney Harry Dirkson's office, this same Steve Winslow produces a list containing the serial numbers of the ten one thousand dollar bills that you found hidden in the upstairs hallway near the apartment of the deceased?"

"That's right."

Fitzpatrick chuckled and shook his head. "And yet it is *Marilyn Harding* who has been charged with this crime."

Dirkson lunged to his feet. "Objection, Your Honor.'

Judge Graves banged the gavel. "Sustained. Mr. Fitzpatrick, I have already warned you about such side remarks."

"Yes, Your Honor. No further questions."

Dirkson next called the bank teller who identified Marilyn Harding as the person who had withdrawn the ten thousand dollars found in the money belt on the victim.

Fitzpatrick did not cross-examine.

The last witness of the day was Margaret Millburn, Donald Blake's next door neighbor, who testified to hearing an altercation in Bradshaw's apartment, and calling the police to report it. She was not sure of the exact time, but placed it around five thirty.

As Fitzpatrick rose to cross-examine, Steve Winslow watched the witness with some interest. Margaret Millburn was not an unattractive woman. She was of medium height, full-figured, but not fat. Curly brown hair framed a face that was attractive but hard. Steve put her age about thirty five.

And she was nervous.

Steve Winslow hadn't had a lot of courtroom experience, but he had good instincts, and he could tell. There was something in the witness's manner that was not right. Maybe it was the way she shifted her eyes, maybe it was the way she gripped the witness stand, maybe it was merely the way she sat. Steve Winslow didn't know. But whatever it was, it was something. That, coupled with the fact that Dirkson's direct examination had been very brief, told Steve Winslow that there was something the witness was holding back.

And Steve realized, if he could see it, it was a cinch Fitzpatrick could see it too.

"Miss Millburn," Fitzpatrick said, "you say you heard the sounds of an altercation coming from the victim's apartment?"

"That's right."

"What kind of altercation?"

"What do you mean?"

"You tell me. What did you hear?"

"The sound of things being knocked over. Furniture being smashed."

'Did you hear voices?"

"Voices?"

"Yes. Did you hear voices? Was it also a verbal altercation? Did you hear the sounds of an argument?"

"Yes, I did."

"Really? You didn't mention that on direct examination."

"I wasn't asked."

"No, you weren't, Miss Millburn. Now why do you suppose that was?"

"Objection, Your Honor."

"Sustained."

"Did you *know* you weren't going to be asked about voices on direct examination?"

"Objection"

"Sustained as to form."

"Miss Millburn, when you gave your testimony, was there any intention *in your own mind* not to mention the fact that you heard voices?"

"Objection, Your Honor."

"Overruled. Witness will answer the question."

"Yes, there was."

"And why was that?"

"Because I couldn't hear the voices clearly enough to identify them, and Mr. Dirkson told me—"

"Objection, Your Honor!"

"No, no," Fitzpatrick said, grinning broadly. "Tell us. What did District Attorney Dirkson tell you?"

Judge Graves banged the gavel. "That will do," he snapped.

"Mr. Fitzpatrick, it is not your place to rule on objections, it is mine. Is that clear?"

"Yes, Your Honor."

"In this case, the objection is overruled. The witness is explaining why she refrained from mentioning certain things in her testimony. It is entirely relevant. The witness will answer the question."

"You didn't mention voices because of something District Attorney Dirkson told you?"

"That's right. He said that since I couldn't recognize the voices, there was no reason I should mention them unless specifically asked."

"I see," Fitzpatrick said, grinning. "Now then, you are being specifically asked. The fact is, you heard voices?"

"That's right."

"You say you couldn't recognize them?"

"No."

"Are you familiar with the voice of the decedent, Donald Blake?"

"Not really."

"You were next door neighbors. You had never been to his apartment?"

"No."

"Surely you must have bumped into him in the hall."

"He'd only lived there a couple of months. I'd bumped into him a few times."

"Just to say hello in passing?"

"That's right."

"Then you had heard his voice?"

"Yes. I had."

"Was one of the voices you heard arguing that of Donald Blake?"

"I tell you, I couldn't hear the voices well enough to identify them."

"But one of them *might* have been Donald Blake?"

"Objection."

"Sustained."

"Miss Millburn, although you couldn't identify the voices, could you hear clearly enough to tell that there were two?"

"No, I could not."

Fitzpatrick raised his eyebrows. "You're stating that there were *not* two voices?"

"No, I'm not. There might have been two. I'm merely saying I couldn't identify them."

Fitzpatrick stopped, frowned. "Miss Millburn, have the police or the prosecution at any time asked you to listen to the voice of the defendant, Marilyn Harding?"

"No, they have not."

"They have not?"

"No."

Fitzpatrick frowned again. He stopped, thought for a moment. Suddenly he smiled. He turned back to the witness.

"Miss Millburn, you claim you couldn't distinguish between the voices."

"That's right."

"Miss Millburn, just for the sake of argument, assuming that there were two voices—you will concede it takes two to make an argument—and assuming that one of the voices was that of Donald Blake, let us consider the other voice you heard. You say that you couldn't distinguish between the voices. I ask you, considering all that, is it possible that the second voice you heard was that of a *woman?*"

The witness shifted on the stand, and Fitzpatrick knew he'd scored.

She batted her eyes. "No," she said.

"No?" Fitzpatrick said.

"No," she said. "It was a man."

Fitzpatrick turned from the witness stand with a broad grin. But his eyes were hard. And they moved to the back of the courtroom, where they sought, caught and held those of Steve Winslow.

30.

STEVE WINSLOW leaned back in Mark Taylor's overstuffed clients' chair and rubbed his head.

"So," he said, "what's his game?"

Mark Taylor looked at him. "Fitzpatrick? I thought that was fairly obvious."

Steve shook his head. "Naw. Screw Fitzpatrick. I mean Dirkson."

Mark Taylor frowned. "I don't get it, Steve."

"I don't get it either," Steve said, "and it bothers me."

Mark Taylor took a sip of coffee. "Look, Steve. We're not connecting here. I don't know what you're thinking, and I don't know what you're talking about. If you expect me to contribute to this conversation, you better let me in on what you're trying to say."

"All right," Steve said. "Look. To start off with, Dirkson's not dumb."

"All right. Dirkson's not dumb. So? You told me that yesterday. He's gonna let Fitzpatrick bring out all the shit and then let the bar association go after you. I know that."

"Right. But besides that. Look what he's doing."

"What?"

"All right. Take the witness. Margaret Millburn. He gives her as perfunctory a direct examination as you ever heard. A child of three can see she's not telling the whole story. Naturally, Fitzpatrick rips into her on cross-examination and brings out the fact that the person she heard arguing with the victim was a man."

"So?"

"I was watching Dirkson when it happened. He didn't bat an eye."

"What's wrong with that?"

"Everything."

Steve Winslow got up and started pacing.

"I don't understand, Steve," Taylor said. "We know Dirkson's out to get you. This is exactly what he's been doing all along— letting Fitzpatrick bring out the damaging stuff. So what's the big deal?"

Steve shook his head. "Dirkson wants to get me for obstructing justice and tampering with evidence. He isn't out to get me for murder. Look, Mark. Dirkson's trying Marilyn Harding on a murder rap. Much as he might love to take a few pot shots at me, his prime concern is convicting her. Margaret Millburn's testimony that the person she heard having an altercation with the decedent was a man has to be a serious blow to Dirkson's case. But it doesn't seem to faze him. And the question is why?"

"And the answer is, I don't know."

"Right. And that's what bothers me. Sooner or later, Dirkson's gonna rest his case. As soon as he does, Fitzpatrick's gonna slap a subpoena on me. He'll put me on the stand, get me declared a hostile witness, and rip into me. I'll have to take the position that I can't answer certain questions without betraying the confidence of a client. You know how that's gonna look to the jury. Ten to one, Fitzpatrick will rest his case right there. Then he'll argue that the prosecution's case is all circumstantial, and that I am just as likely to have killed the victim as his client. Add to that the fact that Margaret Millburn claims she heard Bradshaw arguing with a man, and there's no way the jury's going to being back a verdict of guilty."

Taylor frowned. "That's right. So what the hell is Dirkson up to?"

Steve shook his head. "That's the question."

31.

WHEN COURT reconvened the next morning, District Attorney
Harry Dirkson stood up and said, "Call Douglas Kemper."

That announcement drew no reaction from the spectators in
the courtroom. Most of them didn't know who Douglas Kemper
was. But it certainly produced a reaction in Marilyn Harding. She
came half out of her chair, twisted around, and looked toward the
back of the room. Fitzpatrick was immediately on his feet, inter-
posing his bulk between his client and the spectators in the courtroom, but not before Steve Winslow caught the look on her face.

Steve Winslow turned to Tracy Garvin. "This is it. Dirkson's
about to drop a bombshell."

"Like what?"

"I don't know. Probably an admission or confession of some
sort. She must have told Kemper something damaging. Dirkson's
gonna bring it out."

"Can he do that?"

"I don't know. Kemper can lie, evade, even take the Fifth
Amendment. He may simply take the position he knows nothing
at all. Then Dirkson will have to try to impeach him."

"Can he impeach his own witness?"

"On a material point, yes. Not on character. Even then he has
to show surprise."

"What do you mean?"

"That he expected one answer and the witness gave him another. It rarely happens. Here we go."

Kemper took his place on the witness stand.

"Mr. Kemper," Dirkson said. "Are you related to the defendant in this action?"

"That's right. I'm married to her stepsister."

"You've known the defendant for some time?"

"Yes. Six or seven years."

"And you talk to her from time to time?"

"Naturally."

"Have you and the defendant ever had occasion to discuss the decedent, Donald Blake?"

Fitzpatrick was quick, but not that quick. There was a plainly audible gasp from Marilyn Harding before he roared, "Objection, Your Honor!"

"Overruled," Judge Graves said. "The prosecution is asking for an admission against interest. Witness will answer the question."

"I'll repeat the question, Mr. Kemper," Dirkson said. "Have you and the defendant ever had occasion to discuss the deceased, Donald Blake?"

Kemper shifted position on the witness stand. "No, we have not," he said.

"You have not?"

"No."

"You claim that in all the conversations you have had with the defendant, she never once mentioned to you the man Donald Blake, otherwise known as David C. Bradshaw?"

"Objected to as argumentative and already asked and answered."

"Sustained."

"Well now," Dirkson said. "Let me ask you this: have *you* ever had any dealings with the decedent, Donald Blake?"

"No, sir, I have not."

"Never met the man?"

"No, I did not."

"Never been to his apartment?"

"That's right."

"Then if a witness should state that they had seen you in his apartment, that witness would be mistaken, is that right?"

"Objection. Argumentative."

"Sustained."

"Mr. Kemper, have you ever paid any money to Donald Blake?"

"No, sir, I have not."

"Mr. Kemper, an examination of your bank account reveals that on the morning of the seventh of October, you withdrew the sum of twelve thousand dollars in small bills. Did you by any chance give any of that money to Donald Blake?"

The courtroom was abuzz with excitement. The witness blinked twice. "No, sir, I did not."

"No? But it is a fact that you withdrew twelve thousand dollars on the morning of the seventh?"

"Objection, Your Honor," Fitzpatrick said. "What this witness may or may not have done is not binding on my client."

"Sustained."

"Mr. Kemper, is it not true that the decedent was blackmailing you as well as the defendant?"

"No, it is not."

"It is not? Mr. Kemper, you claim that you and the defendant never discussed the decedent, Donald Blake?"

"Objected to as already asked and answered."

"Sustained."

"Directing your attention to the afternoon of the second of October, did you and the defendant not discuss the decedent, Donald Blake, at that time?"

"No, we did not."

"Perhaps I can refresh your memory," Dirkson said, boring in. He raised his voice. "I am referring to the time when you and the defendant checked into the Sand and Surf Motor Inn in Queens, registering as Mr. and Mrs. Sampson. Did you discuss Donald Blake at that time?"

The effect of the question was electric. The courtroom was in an uproar. Fitzpatrick was on his feet, shouting objections, but he could barely be heard above the din.

What created the furor was not so much the question, but the witness's reaction to it. Douglas Kemper looked as if he'd just been shot through the heart.

It was several minutes before Judge Graves managed to restore order. Fitzpatrick, under pressure, seemed capable of finding grounds for objection unheard of before in any court of law. Judge Graves listened to them all, then said calmly, "Objection overruled. It is an impeaching question, directed to a material point of the testimony of the witness. I direct the witness to answer."

Dirkson smiled. "Can you answer that question, Mr. Kemper?"

Douglas Kemper was still visibly shaken. He opened his mouth, closed it, then said, "Could I have a glass of water please?"

"Certainly," Dirkson said. He made a show of being solicitous. He went to the judge's bench and personally poured the water, then handed the glass to the witness. "Here you are. Take all the time you want. Just drink your water, and when you're through, please answer my question."

Kemper gulped the water and took a breath. Some of the color returned to his cheeks. "The answer is, no, I did not."

"You did not discuss the decedent Donald Blake with Marilyn Harding? But you and Marilyn Harding did register at the Sand and Surf Motor Inn as Mr. and Mrs. Sampson?"

"Objection," Fitzpatrick said. "Incompetent, irrelevant, and immaterial."

"Sustained."

"But is it not true," Dirkson persisted, "that you and the defendant were having an affair; that Donald Blake learned of this affair and demanded money for his silence; that Marilyn Harding paid him ten thousand dollars and you paid him an additional twelve?"

"No, it is not."

"And is it not true that after that Donald Blake demanded even more money? Money that you refused to pay? Is it not true that you argued with Donald Blake about that? In fact you argued on the very afternoon that he was killed?"

"No, I did not."

"And didn't that argument take place in Donald Blake's apartment? And wasn't the time of that argument at five thirty in the afternoon of the ninth of October? And wasn't it your voice the witness Margaret Millburn heard when she called and reported an altercation to the police?"

"No."

"It was not?"

"No."

"And you've never been in Donald Blake's apartment?"

"No, sir."

Dirkson picked up the glass from the witness stand. "Then sir, if I were to take this glass that you have been drinking from, and give it to Mr. Riker of the police crime lab, and ask him to compare the prints found on it with the unidentified prints found in the apartment of Donald Blake, are you telling me that there is no chance whatsoever that one of those prints might happen to be yours?"

Douglas Kemper opened his mouth. Closed it again. He blinked twice. He looked around the courtroom, as if looking for a way out. His right hand reached up inside his jacket.

There was a moment's stunned anticipation. Dirkson took a step backward. The bailiff stiffened and reached for his gun.

But it was not a gun Douglas Kemper pulled from his inside jacket pocket.

It was the torn half of a dollar bill.

32.

DOUGLAS KEMPER looked at Steve Winslow with pleading eyes. "You have to understand," he said.

"Oh, do I?"

They were talking through the wire mesh screen in the police lockup. It was approximately two hours since Kemper produced the half of a dollar bill in court. In those two hours a lot had happened. Steve Winslow had come forward and announced that he was Kemper's attorney. Judge Graves then dismissed the jury and refereed a long, brawling argument among Winslow, Dirkson, and Fitzpatrick. In the end, Graves adjourned court for the day and remanded Douglas Kemper to custody.

So now, at long last, Steve Winslow was face to face with his elusive client.

He wished he wasn't.

"You have to see it from my point of view," Kemper said.

"I can barely see it from mine," Steve said. "You wanna talk, talk, but you better start now, cause my patience is wearing thin."

"I know, I know," Kemper said. "Well, look, this thing with Marilyn. It wasn't my fault. Or hers, either. We never planned anything. It just happened."

"It always does."

Kemper's eyes flashed. "No, it doesn't. You're trying to make

197

this sound like something cheap. It wasn't. This is different. This is special. This is—"

"Bullshit. You can save that for someone who wants to hear it. I don't give a fuck if you were Romeo and Juliet. The fact is, you woke up and realized you married the wrong stepsister. Big mistake. You could have had the younger, prettier one with all the money."

Kemper came out of his chair. "You son of a bitch!"

"Right," Steve said. "I'm very brave with the wire mesh screen between us. That's your next line, Kemper. Go on. Say it."

Douglas Kemper glared at him in helpless frustration.

"All right, look, clown," Steve said. "You happen to be in one hell of a mess. Believe it not, it happens to be entirely of your own making. You want to try to get out of it, fine. You want to sit around trying to justify yourself, protesting to high heaven how wronged you've been, I can always come back later. I happen to be in no mood for that shit. So you calm down, get control, and then when you're good and ready, tell me what the fuck happened."

Kemper glared at him for some time. Then he seemed to wilt. He sank down in his chair and rubbed his forehead. "I don't know where to begin."

"Start with Bradshaw," Steve said.

"Yeah. Bradshaw."

"You know him?"

"Yeah. I knew him."

"Been to his apartment?"

"Yeah."

"Well, that's perjury for starters. Tell me about it."

Kemper took a breath, blew it out again. "Well, it's pretty much as he said."

"Who?"

"The prosecutor. That smug son of a bitch—"

"Skip that. What about Bradshaw?"

Kemper shrugged. "He was blackmailing Marilyn."

"Not you?"

"No, just Marilyn."

"About her father's death?"

Kemper shook his head. "No. About me."

"What did he have?"

"Photostat of the motel reservation."

Steve sighed. "You'll pardon me," he said, "I'm just a little too pissed off to have to drag this out of you. Go on and tell me what happened. What was his approach? Did he contact you or Marilyn?"

"That's just it," Kemper said. "He hit on Marilyn. By the time I found out about it, it was too late."

"You need a prompter? Go on. What happened?"

"Well, you understand, this is what Marilyn told me, after the fact. Bradshaw called her up. Cold. Out of the blue. Calls her on the telephone. Calls her by name. Identifies himself as 'a friend.' Says he has something he thinks she should have. Marilyn tries to ask questions but the guy's evasive and mysterious. All he'll tell her is he has something she forgot. She's about to hang up on him when he tells her he has something from the Sand and Surf Motor Inn."

Douglas Kemper grimaced. "And that's where she made a mistake. That's where she should have called me right away. But she didn't. Instead, she agreed to meet the guy. So she goes to his apartment. He told her to go there, and like a damn fool she goes. I mean, in a building like that. It could have been a shakedown, it could have been anything.

"When she gets there Bradshaw whips out a photostat of a registration form from the Sand and Surf Motor Inn. It's the card I signed, registering us as Mr. and Mrs. Sampson. Then he goes through the usual bullshit spiel about how he's a really nice guy but he happens to be hard up and really needs the money, and if she'd just give him ten thousand dollars and—well, you know the rest."

"No, I don't know the rest. Let's go through it. She drew out ten thousand dollars from her bank account and paid him off, right?"

"Right."

"Did you know it?"

"No."

"You hadn't seen her in the meantime?"

"No, I hadn't. We couldn't meet that often. It's kind of awkward, you know, and—"

"Yeah, sure. So you hadn't seen her and she hadn't told you, and she paid off the guy, and then what?"

"I saw her the next day and she told me about it. I couldn't believe it. If she'd only come to me. She'd done everything wrong. Taking ten one thousand dollar bills out of her bank account. On a cash withdrawal of that size, they note the serial numbers. I knew it. She didn't. She didn't realize what she'd done. A blackmailer never quits. Giving Bradshaw that ten thousand dollars was just giving him a stranglehold over her. The motel reservation was nothing. It wasn't even solid evidence. Against me, maybe, but not her. But that ten thousand dollars would fry her.

"That's when I stepped in. I contacted Bradshaw and arranged to buy those bills back."

Steve stared at him. "You're kidding."

"No, I'm not. I contacted Bradshaw and made a deal. It wasn't that hard. Bradshaw was always willing to deal. That was part of his game. He was most agreeable. He would be delighted to return me Marilyn Harding's ten grand in return for small bills. The only catch was, he wanted twelve thousand."

"So you brought Marilyn's bills back?"

Kemper grimaced. "I thought I did."

"And you put them in an envelope and sent them to me. Along with the letter."

"That's right."

"Why?"

"Marilyn was in trouble, big trouble. I wasn't sure I could deal with it alone. I knew she needed help, and a special kind of help. This wasn't something you could take to the cops. Or to any regular lawyer. Then I thought of you."

"Why me?"

"I know Sheila Benton. I met her a long time ago through

Marilyn. Happened to run into her just before she left for Europe. She told me about her case. What you did for her. Not so much in court. She said you did other things. Discreetly. Confidentially. Things no one would ever know about. She said you were a genius. I figured that's what Marilyn needed. So I typed the letter and sent you those bills as a retainer. But I had to be very discreet. Very belowboard. I didn't want to implicate Marilyn by mentioning her by name. I knew if you were as quick as all that, you'd immediately trace the serial numbers of the bills and find out who'd withdrawn them from the bank. You'd find out it was Marilyn, and you'd start protecting her.

"Only I hadn't figured on Bradshaw."

"He switched the bills?"

"Of course. As soon as I offered to buy them back, Bradshaw knew what I was after. So he played me for a sucker. He charged me twelve grand, and instead of Marilyn's ten grand, he sold me ten bills he'd drawn out of the bank himself."

"Which you promptly mailed to me," Steve said. "Making my life a living hell ever since. Tell me something. Did you mention my name?"

"What?"

"To Bradshaw. When you called on Bradshaw. Did you mention me?"

"Yeah. As a matter of fact, I did. I told him you were my lawyer, and if he made any more trouble he'd hear from you."

Steve shook his head. "Jesus Christ."

"What's wrong with that?"

"Little presumptuous, don't you think? You hadn't even consulted me."

"Yeah. At first I was bluffing. But that's when I decided to. Hire you, I mean."

"Great. And when was this?"

"Monday."

"The seventh?"

"Yeah."

"That's when you met Bradshaw and bought back the bills?"

"Right."

"Then why did Marilyn go see him on Tuesday, the eighth?"

"Cause she didn't know I'd got the bills back. I hadn't been able to talk to her."

"You hadn't told her you were going to do it?"

"No. I hadn't figured it out at the time. When I was talking to her, I mean. I only told her she made a mistake giving 'em to him. She was worried about it, and she went to Bradshaw to try to straighten things out herself."

"That's on Tuesday?"

"Yeah."

"What happened?"

"Nothing. Bradshaw was nice as could be. He was sorry she'd upset herself, but there was nothing to worry about. I'd been there the day before and bought the bills back, hadn't I told her? Relax, everything was going to be just fine, and if she didn't believe him, why didn't she talk to me.

"Which it turned out she couldn't do, because when she met me on the boat I was with my wife and we never got a moment alone."

"All right. That's Tuesday. What about Wednesday?"

Kemper grimaced. "Just what you'd expect. Bradshaw made another pass at Marilyn. The son of a bitch. He'd just told her everything was straightened out to let her think she was off the hook. To give her one peaceful day. To let her see just how good that felt, just how wonderful that feeling of relief could be. Before he jerked the rug out from under her."

"What happened?"

"She called me at work. She was hysterical. You gotta remember, that was the same day she found out her father'd been murdered. She'd had cops at the house all morning. She'd just gotten rid of them when she got the phone call. It was Bradshaw at his oiliest best. He was so sorry, but he needed more money, and the whole spiel. He had another photostat of the motel reservation—what a surprise, right?—and he had the bills she withdrew from the bank, proof she paid blackmail. Of course that shocked the hell out of her. She thought I'd bought them back. He told her different. He had her ten grand, he wanted another ten grand, and he'd give her till five thirty that afternoon.

"She called me at work. Just caught me as I was going out the door. I was supposed to show some people some properties. It was a tough moment. The boss was there. I had to act cool on the phone. I couldn't really tell her anything, I had to just listen. And she's telling me what Bradshaw did and what Bradshaw demanded. She wants me to meet her and bring her the ten grand I bought back from Bradshaw. So she could use it to pay him off again.

"Well, I didn't have it, I'd sent it to you, but I can't tell her different with the boss standing there and this young couple at my elbow waiting to go see some properties. So the best I can do is to get the message across that I can't talk now, but I'll meet her at this coffee shop on Lexington Avenue around four o'clock. I figure I'll meet her there and we'll tackle Bradshaw together.

"Only I get hung up. This young couple's picky. They don't know from my problems, they're planning a life together. They want to see this, that and the other thing. And they're do-it-yourselfers. They must spend all their time watching "This Old House" on PBS. They're tapping walls and talking about structural beams and types of molding. They probably don't know shit, but they're talking a lot, you know what I mean. You know the type. So I'm going crazy with 'em. But it's an emergency, and I probably would have just ditched them, except the fucking boss comes along. He does it now and then when he thinks someone's slacking off. What with me sneaking off to meet Marilyn now and then, I know he's been suspicious of me, and what with me getting that phone call and all. So the son of a bitch tagged along.

"So I couldn't get out of there, and the end result's I'm late. I get to the coffee shop at five after five, double park and run in. She's gone."

"So what'd you do?"

"Beat it down to Bradshaw's, to try to head her off. I was too late there too. Or so I think. There's no sign of Marilyn. I double park the car. I run in. I go upstairs. The door's open. I walk in. I find him there on the floor, dead."

"So what do you do?"

"What do you think I do? I'm in a panic. I'm afraid Marilyn got there first and killed him. I look around the apartment real quick, trying to see if she left anything incriminating. Then I beat it out of there.

"I hop in my car and drive off. Just as I'm turning the corner, I look back down the block at Bradshaw's building to see if anything's happening. When I do, I see Marilyn come around the corner and walk in the front door."

Steve's eyes narrowed. "Oh yeah?"

"Yeah. Well, I would have waved to her, but it happened too quick. I'm too far away, and she doesn't see me. She's already gone in. It's a one-way street. I can't turn around and go back. So I zoom around the block. I'm going to double park again, run in and get her.

"But I get caught in traffic. By the time I'm coming down the street again, I see her come tearing out of the building and run around the corner again. I beat it down to the corner just in time to see her hop in her car and pull out.

"But then another car pulls out and tags along behind her. I realize she's being followed. I don't dare contact her then.

"By then it's late. I'm supposed to pick up my wife for dinner. I've stalled her off. But now I've gotta go. I pick her up. We go out to eat. It's a real bitch with all this churning inside of me. But there's nothing I can do about it.

"After dinner we drive up to the house in Glen Cove, and that's where I ran into you. You know what happened. I don't get to talk to Marilyn, the cops pick her up, and I don't get to talk to her until Fitzpatrick gets her released the next day."

Kemper stopped. "There you are. That's it. That's the story."

Steve Winslow looked at him for several moments. Then he shook his head. "No, it isn't," he said.

"What?" Kemper said.

"No, it isn't. It's bullshit. At least part of it. The part about you finding Bradshaw's body. It never happened that way. You made it up."

"No, I didn't."

"Sure you did. And you didn't even do a good job of it. You're so transparent, Kemper. You know what you're doing? I'll tell you what you're doing. You're trying to be some goddamn storybook hero—that gallant, noble, romantic leading man who cheerfully takes the blame to save his ladylove. The problem is, you don't fit the part. Gallant? Noble? Shit, give me a break."

"You son of a bitch."

"No. You sit there and take it, cause you have to. *I'm* going to tell *you* what happened. The bit about you finding Bradshaw's body is all wrong. You made it up from what you heard in court—from the testimony of the detectives who were following Marilyn, and the testimony of the witness who heard a voice in the apartment. You put that together and you say, 'Hey, I'll shade my story a little bit and I'll be the gallant hero and I'll give her an alibi.' So you say you got there first and found him dead. You figure your statement, coupled with the testimony of the detectives who were following Marilyn, will put her in the clear. Bradshaw was dead before she got there. Of course, that puts your ass right on the line, but that's what the romantic hero's supposed to do, right?

"And it doesn't really put your ass on the line, because your story's so bad no one will believe it. You got to the coffee shop after Marilyn left, but you want me to believe you got to Bradshaw's first."

"She had to pick up her car."

"Sure she did, but you got in and out before she even got there? Bullshit. And then you're just turning the corner when you saw her go in. And then you race around the block and you just see her come out. But you miss her both times. And you're about to go after her, but then you spot a car tailing her."

Steve Winslow stopped and shook his head. "Jesus Christ. I mean, here you are, a poor fucking real estate salesman. You just found a dead body. You just had a huge emotional shock, and you're suddenly in the worst mess you've ever been in in your life, and what do you do? In the midst of all this hysteria, in the midst of racing after your girlfriend to warn her about what has happened, in the midst of New York City traffic, you *spot* a detective tailing her in a car." Steve shook his head in mock wonderment. "Wow! What powers of perception! What ice water must run in your veins! This is not just your ordinary romantic hero. This is fucking Superman here."

Kemper merely glared at him.

"No," Steve said. "Here's what happened. You missed Marilyn at the coffee shop just like you said, and then you beat it down to Bradshaw's, went in and found him dead. But you didn't get there before Marilyn, you got there after. You never saw her there at all. You found Bradshaw dead, you figured Marilyn killed him, you were in a total panic, and you got the hell out of there. I don't know if you still think she killed him, but you probably do, even if she's denied it. As far as you're concerned, it's the only thing that makes sense. That's why you're telling this bullshit story, and acting noble like you were willing to take the rap."

Steve leaned back in his chair. "Yeah, that's what happened. The only thing I don't know is whether you were the guy who searched Bradshaw's body, found those bills on it, assumed they were Marilyn's, and hid 'em in the upstairs hallway."

"I didn't do that."

"No, I don't think so. You'd only have done that if you were trapped there by the arrival of the cops. You weren't, cause they didn't get you. But the rest of it's just like I said."

"No, it isn't."

Steve nodded sarcastically. "Right, right, noble to the end. Including holding out on your lawyer. Good move. All right, tell me about the dollar."

Kemper, startled by the change of subject, said, "What?"

"The dollar. The half a dollar. The one you sent me in the mail. Why did you do it?"

Kemper said, "Oh. Well, after I sent you the bills I got back from Bradshaw, I got to worrying."

"About what?"

"Well, Bradshaw'd been too agreeable. Too willing to sell. I got to thinking about it, and it occurred to me maybe he'd pulled a switch."

"On the bills?"

"Yeah."

"You got this thought *after* you bought the bills?"

"Yeah."

"After you sent them to me?"

"Yeah."

"Little slow on the uptake, aren't you?"

"Hey, give me a break."

"Yeah, sure. You deserve all the breaks. So what about the torn dollar?"

"Well, if Bradshaw'd switched the bills, there was no way for Marilyn to prove she was your client. So I sent you the half a dollar as a means of identification."

"So why didn't Marilyn have the other half of a dollar? Why you?"

"She didn't know I'd done it. I hadn't had a chance to talk to her. The only time we'd spoken was when she called me in the real estate office, and I couldn't say anything then. She was telling me to meet her with the ten thousand dollars. She didn't know I'd mailed them to you. Or the half a dollar. And I didn't see her after that. Not until my wife and I walked in on you and her that night. And by that time she'd already called in Fitzpatrick to act as her lawyer. All right, she'd made her decision. She didn't need you. But I did. So I kept the half a dollar."

Steve Winslow looked at him. "What a great way of handling things," he said. "Anonymous letters. A half of a dollar bill. Tell me, where did you get that idea?"

Kemper shifted in his seat. "I read it in a book."

"Yeah," Steve said. "Yeah. I was sure you had." Steve shook his head. "Tell me something, will you? The hero in the book you read, the book about the half a dollar—did you like him?"

Kemper stared at him. "What?"

"Was he sympathetic, a nice guy, someone you'd really root for? I mean, you really wanted him to win, right?"

Kemper frowned. "Yeah. Why?"

"That's what's wrong here. If you were the hero of that book, it never would have gotten published. The editor would have thrown it back in the author's face. Because you're not sympathetic. You're not the romantic hero. You're a self-centered egotistical son of a bitch, who's playing around with a younger, richer woman who happens to be the stepsister of his wife. And then you get involved in a murder, but that doesn't faze you, because you ripped some idea out of a storybook to hire some poor fucking lawyer to get you out of this mess. Well, I've got news for you. There ain't a hell of a lot I can do. Sheila Benton told you I was good, well good for her. She didn't get acquitted in court. She got acquitted cause there was a break in the case and it had nothing to do with what went on in that courtroom. I had something to do with it, yeah, but that was just luck. I wouldn't count on it happening here. The problem is, you're spoiled by books and TV, you think everything has a happy ending. I know what you expect from me. You want a courtroom confession. I'm gonna cross-examine the witnesses, and someone's gonna break down on the witness stand and say, 'I did it,' and you and Marilyn will live happily ever after.

"Well, I got news for you, it doesn't happen that way. I can't get you a courtroom confession. I can't solve this fucking crime. All I can do is make a showing in court and try to make the jury, one, like you and two, believe you. And we got a big problem there. Because I don't like you, and I don't believe you. So how the hell am I gonna make twelve other people do it?"

Kemper started to flare up again, but it just wasn't in him anymore. His face contorted, and he wilted in his chair. He looked as if he were about to cry. For the first time, Steve almost felt sorry for him.

Kemper controlled himself and looked up at Winslow. "You're saying you won't be my attorney?"

Steve Winslow chuckled. "Now there, Mr. Kemper, you bring up an interesting point. Am I your attorney? You're damn right I am. I happen to be withholding evidence from the police on the grounds that I'm protecting the confidence of a client. You're the client. So like it or not, I'm stuck with you. So let's cut out the bullshit, and get down to brass tacks."

33.

FITZPATRICK REGARDED Steve Winslow with superior disdain. "I fail to see what we have to talk about."

"That's because you haven't had time to think things over. When you do, you'll see that we have a lot to talk about. I'm afraid I don't have time for your thought process to catch up with you, so I'm going to fill you in."

"Your arrogance is amazing."

"Isn't it? When I find myself painted into a corner, I see no reason to be polite."

"You threw me out of your office. Can you give me one good reason why I shouldn't throw you out of mine?"

"I can give you plenty of reasons. You haven't thought this over yet, but when you do you're going to find out you're painted into a corner too."

"I fail to see it."

"Only one of your many failings, Fitzpatrick. Remember when you came to my office in the spirit of cooperation?—we have similar interests, we could help each other?—well, it was bullshit then, but it happens to be true now."

"I don't think so."

"I know you don't. So I'm going to spell it out for you. Then

you can throw me out of your office, and we'll be even, and you'll
feel you've had a good day."

"You're trying my patience, Winslow. Why don't you cut the
commercial and get on with it."

"Fine. Here's the situation. You and I have to sit here and figure out which way the cat's gonna jump. The cat is Dirkson. He's
gonna have Douglas Kemper indicted for murder. Now, is he
gonna have him indicted as a codefendant in this action, or is he
gonna try him separately later on?"

"He'll try him separately, of course."

"Of course. I heard Marilyn Harding's indictment. '. . . acting
alone, or in concert with others, did feloniously cause . . ." etc., etc.
Dirkson doesn't need Douglas Kemper as a codefendant. He has
the criminal conspiracy element already in the charge. He can
show Marilyn Harding and Douglas Kemper were acting in concert. That's why he's not concerned that the witness Millburn says
she heard a *man* arguing with Bradshaw. As far as Dirkson's concerned, he couldn't care less whether it was Marilyn Harding or
Douglas Kemper who struck the actual blow. Both of them were
being blackmailed together. He's got criminal conspiracy, he's trying Marilyn on the charge, and some of it's gonna stick.

"And the thing is, Dirkson doesn't even care how much,
because as soon as he nails her on anything, he's gonna turn
around and try her for killing her father. And when he does that,
if he's got any conviction at all in this case, she is gonna have the
chance of the proverbial snowball in hell."

"Tell me something I don't already know."

"All right, I will. Your client hasn't talked. Mine has."

Fitzpatrick seemed interested for the first time. "He's told his
story?"

"Yes, he has."

"And?"

"And it doesn't help us a bit. Kemper would like to make a case
for Marilyn being innocent without actually implicating himself.
Marilyn, if she were willing to talk, would probably do the same
for him." Steve shrugged. "Big deal. In the first place, nobody's

gonna believe either one of them. Which leaves you with the basic toss-up situation. One of them must have done it. Pick a client, any client. She's your client, and he's mine. You could probably make a fairly strong argument for the fact he must have done it, and I could probably make a fairly strong argument for the fact she must have done it. But the thing is, we'd be slitting our own throats. Because of the criminal conspiracy bit."

"That's elemental. So you're saying because of that we should work together. Well, I don't buy it."

Steve grinned. "I know you don't. That because that's not your plan. You don't want to push it on Kemper. You want to prove some third party committed the crime. And I happen to be the third party. The problem is, it won't work."

"Is that so?" Fitzpatrick grinned. "You're an attorney, Winslow. Think about it. I don't have to prove you killed Bradshaw. All I have to do is raise reasonable doubt. You've been in court. You heard what happened. You tell me. Do I have reasonable doubt?"

Steve shook his head. "You did, but you don't now. I told you, you haven't thought it over, Fitzpatrick. You may be a good attorney, but you're a bit of a slow take. I'm Douglas Kemper's attorney. Anything I've done reflects on him. I was acting for my client. You want to put me at the scene of the crime, it doesn't implicate me anymore, it implicates him. And if he and Marilyn were acting in concert, it implicates her. So all this good work you've done creating reasonable doubt just went down the tubes. Worse than that, it's all backfiring in your face, cause the mud you throw at me sticks to her."

Fitzpatrick frowned.

"Now look," Steve said. "We are in a mess. I say we, and I mean we. It's you and me, kid. Semper fidelis. Now if you still wanna throw me out of your office, feel free. But if not, let's sit down, put our heads together, and see what we can do to get out of this mess."

34.

MARILYN HARDING had been crying. This time, she had done nothing to conceal the fact, not that it would have done her any good. Her eyes were red, and her cheeks were caked with tears.

She was sitting in a chair in Fitzpatrick's office. Fitzpatrick had lead her in and sat her down. She had come docilely, mechanically, without life or spirit. Now she sat, staring blankly ahead of her, as if she'd lost all will of her own, as if she were an automaton, just waiting to be told what to do next.

"Marilyn," Fitzpatrick said. "This is Steve Winslow. Douglas Kemper's lawyer. The lawyer who spoke with you at your house. I've just had a long talk with him, and I think he can help us. Frankly, we need help."

Marilyn gave no sign of comprehension.

Fitzpatrick leaned forward. "Do you hear what I'm saying? Do you understand?"

Marilyn's head nodded slightly. She said, softly, "Yes."

"Good," Fitzpatrick said. "Mr. Winslow has just had a talk with Douglas Kemper. Now he needs to have a talk with you. I'm going to leave the two of you alone now. I want you to listen to him carefully and hear what he has to say."

Fitzpatrick didn't push it by waiting for another response. He just nodded to Steve Winslow and eased himself out the door.

Steve stood looking down at Marilyn Harding. This was it. This was his shot. He had to get her talking now, if he was going to do any good at all.

The prospects didn't look good. Despite Marilyn's outward appearance of defeat, her jawline was still set firmly, her face was still hard, stubborn, defiant. Steve Winslow read it all in that set jaw. How could he get her talking? What could he say?

Steve Winslow pulled up a chair, sat down, stretched, yawned, crossed his legs, leaned back, and said, "Douglas Kemper's a jerk."

Marilyn Harding's head snapped up. She stared at him, defiantly.

"Yeah, I know," Steve said. "I shouldn't be saying things like that about my own client. But what the hell. You gotta call a spade a spade. The man's a complete jerk. You know what he's done?"

Marilyn Harding just glared at him.

Steve Winslow sat calmly and waited.

Finally, Marilyn said, "What?"

Bingo, Steve thought. He'd done it. He got her to say one word. Not a particularly illuminating one by any stretch of the imagination, but still a word. The next ones would come easier.

"He's talked," Steve said. "He's told his story. Don't worry. Not to the press, not to the public. Just to me. Believe me, it's going no further. I promise you that. There isn't a lawyer alive that would let that story go any further."

There was another pause, then Marilyn said, "Why?"

"If you heard it, you'd know. But you haven't heard it, have you? No. Douglas hasn't had a chance to lay that one on you. No, he's had his own problems. Right now he's facing a charge of perjury, but that's the least of it. When I left him a little while ago, back in the lockup, his wife Phyllis was there posting his bail. Some woman, huh? Cold, practical, determined. Gonna get her husband out of the cooler. Stand by her man." Winslow shook his head. "Poor Douglas. If I were him, I'd rather stay in jail. The talk I had with him was nothing. Imagine the interrogation he's going through now."

Marilyn's lower lip trembled. She controlled it.

Steve Winslow sat, said nothing.

Marilyn looked at him. "His story."

"What?" Steve said.

"His story. He told you his story."

Steve shook his head. "Yeah. Bad news."

Marilyn glared at him. "Damn it, what's his story?"

"Oh," Steve said. "Well, first of all, you have to remind yourself none of this is getting out. I've said it before, but it's worth saying again, because I don't want to have to scrape you off the ceiling. None of this is getting out. This is just what the young man has admitted to me, his lawyer, in a confidential communication. All right?"

"Yes, yes," Marilyn said, impatiently. "What is it?"

"Well, he admits the affair. Blames no one, has no regrets. You two were victims of fate, etc., etc. Says Bradshaw made a blackmail approach to you, you paid him off, he found out, was horrified, and bought the bills back for twelve grand. Only Bradshaw switched bills on him, which is why the bills found on the body turned out to be yours." Winslow shrugged. "No big deal. You knew all that. The cops don't, but they can make a lot of inferences. Fortunately, inferences don't stand up in court.

"Now, here's the bad part. Day of the murder. You called Kemper at work, hysterical, cause Bradshaw made another blackmail demand. He's to meet you at the coffee shop at four o'clock. He doesn't show. You leave without him.

"Now, what he *claims*, and I stress the word *claims*, is he got to the coffee shop just after five and missed you, so he beat it down to Bradshaw's, double parked, ran in, and found Bradshaw dead on the floor."

Marilyn looked at him. She was a poker player, betraying nothing. "That's it?"

"No, it's worse. He came out the front door, got in his car, started to pull out, and just as he was turning the corner he saw you come down the street and enter the building. He beat it around the block to catch up with you, but got caught in traffic and got back just in time to see you leave the building, hop in a car and pull out. At which point he would have stopped you, had he not noticed you were being followed by detectives."

Marilyn said nothing. She sat looking at him. Her face was white.

"You see why I can't let him tell that story," Steve said. "In the first place, no one on God's green earth is going to believe it. It's a lie, and a clumsy lie at that. He's trying to protect you by proving that when you got to Bradshaw's apartment, Bradshaw was already dead. Nice try, but it won't work. It may be inadmissible in court, but the fact is, in the eyes of the jury, you and Douglas Kemper were lovers. That means any alibi he tries to give you isn't worth a damn. He claims he got to Bradshaw's first. Out of twelve jurors, we'd be damn lucky if half of them believed that. Of the few that did, none of them are going to believe that Bradshaw was already dead. Not with the next door neighbor testifying to an altercation. One doesn't have an altercation with a dead man. Anyone who believes Kemper got there first is gonna believe he had a fight with Bradshaw and killed him. Which doesn't help you in the least. Because of the theory that you and Douglas Kemper were lovers, you're a coconspirator, which makes you equally guilty."

Marilyn bit her lip.

"That's the story, and I'm not going to let him tell it, and I guess you can see why."

Marilyn said nothing.

"Now," Steve said, "no one's gonna let you tell your story either, Fitzpatrick or I, but we need to hear it."

She still said nothing.

"Look," Steve said. "There's no reason for you not to talk now. The cat's out of the bag. At least as far as we're concerned. You can't hurt Douglas, and you can't hurt yourself. There's no reason to sit on your hands. There are some things we gotta know. I happen to know Douglas Kemper's story is bullshit. Now let's talk about what really happened. You got there first, didn't you?"

Marilyn set her jaw.

"Didn't you?" Steve persisted.

"I'm not going to talk about it," Marilyn said.

"All right, then I will," Steve said. "If you got there first, there are only two possibilities: Bradshaw was already dead, or you killed him. I know that for a fact. How do I know that for a fact? I know that because Douglas Kemper arrived right after you, not before you like he said, but after. And he went in there and he found Bradshaw dead. And that's why he's in such a panic, and that's why he's telling this bullshit story. It's a story no second grader would believe, but he has to say something, and you'll forgive me but he's not that bright.

"No, the way I see it, you got there first and Bradshaw was already dead. And the ironic thing is you. *You* buy Kemper's story. You're probably the only person in the world who'd buy it, but you do. The reason is, you got there and found Bradshaw dead, and you immediately figured Kemper killed him. That's what you thought, and that's what you still think, and that's why you're refusing to talk. You buy Kemper's story that he got there first. You don't buy the part that he found him dead. If you did there'd be no reason for you not to talk. You figure Kemper got there first and killed him. You're taking the rap to protect him, just like he's taking the rap to protect you. Very noble, very romantic, and very stupid. Kemper didn't get there first. Unless you killed Bradshaw, there's no reason for you to keep quiet."

Marilyn still said nothing.

Steve sighed. Yeah. He'd really got her to open up, hadn't he? "All right," he said. "Here's the situation. I'm joining the defense team. The only way for me to get Kemper out is to get the two of you out. So I'm hoppin' on board. Fitzpatrick isn't too happy about it, but he realizes he has little choice.

"You don't have much choice either, but it's still your decision. You have any objections to me working on your behalf?"

Marilyn looked at him a few moments. "No," she said.

Steve nodded and stood up. "Fine," he said. "See you in court."

35.

JUDGE GRAVES was attempting to maintain his air of judicial impartiality. Even so, he couldn't help betraying his skepticism as he peered down from his bench at the defense table.

"I'm sorry, Mr. Fitzpatrick," he said. "Would you mind repeating that again?"

"Yes, Your Honor," Fitzpatrick said. "I merely wanted to inform the court that Miss Harding has secured additional representation. Mr. Winslow here has joined the defense as associate counsel."

Judge Graves frowned. He looked again at the defense table, where Steve Winslow, in a white shirt, blue tie, corduroy jacket and jeans, made such a incongruous picture standing next to Fitzpatrick in his three-piece suit. "That is Mr. *Steve* Winslow?" he said.

"That's right."

"The same Steve Winslow who came forward yesterday as counsel for Douglas Kemper?"

"Yes, Your Honor."

"The same Steve Winslow who has been referred to in these court proceedings as the gentleman discovered by the police in the apartment of the deceased?"

"That's right."

Judge Graves picked up a document from his bench. "The same Steve Winslow who filed a motion with me this morning, charging Harry Dirkson with prosecutorial misconduct, to wit, violating the rights of one Douglas Kemper by calling him as a prosecution witness, and tricking him into waiving his constitutional rights by forcing him to testify against himself, when in point of fact Dirkson had every intention of proceeding against him as a codefendant?"

Dirkson was on his feet. "With regard to that, Your Honor, I—"

"Mr. Dirkson, sit down," Judge Graves snapped. "You'll get your chance." Graves turned back to Fitzpatrick. "Is that right?"

"Yes, Your Honor."

"The same Steve Winslow who has filed a motion for a mistrial in this case, demanding that the defendant be retried, and that she and Douglas Kemper be tried jointly?"

"Actually," Fitzpatrick said, "Mr. Winslow and I filed that motion jointly, Your Honor."

"I see that you did," Graves said. "I must ask you, Mr. Fitzpatrick, if you are also appearing as attorney for Douglas Kemper?"

"Not at this time, Your Honor. Circumstances, however, may dictate the necessity."

"I see," Judge Graves said. "Now then, Mr. Winslow. You are now here appearing for Marilyn Harding in concert with Mr. Fitzpatrick?"

"That's right."

"You see no conceivable conflict of interest between that and your duties to your client, Douglas Kemper?"

"I do not, Your Honor. If you will read my motion, you will find that my contention is that the opposite is true."

Judge Graves held up his hand. "I have read your motion. I understand your contentions. I am asking these questions because I want the answers in the record. Now, do you see no possible conflict of interest?"

"None, Your Honor."

"Mr. Fitzpatrick, you see no conflict of interest?"

"None, Your Honor."

"Miss Harding?"

"Yes, Your Honor."

"You have heard what Mr. Fitzpatrick has said?"

"Yes, Your Honor."

"And what Mr. Winslow has said?"

"Yes, Your Honor."

"You have no objection to Mr. Winslow representing you as associate counsel?"

"No, Your Honor."

"You understand that he is also representing Douglas Kemper?"

"Yes, Your Honor."

"You have no problem with that arrangement?"

"No, Your Honor."

Judge Graves frowned. "Very well. Now then, Mr. Dirkson."

Dirkson was on his feet before Judge Graves even got the words out of his mouth. "Yes, Your Honor," he said. "With regard to the charge of prosecutorial misconduct in the case of Douglas Kemper, I must say that the charge is completely unfounded and absolutely without merit. Your Honor need look no further than the transcript of yesterday's testimony to see that this is true. Mr. Winslow contends that we violated Mr. Kemper's rights by calling him as a witness when he himself was a possible codefendant. That is utter nonsense. Mr. Kemper's own testimony clearly shows that we had not one scintilla of evidence against him prior to his appearance on the stand. It was only during his direct examination that it became clear that he was actively involved in the matter. We had never compared his fingerprints with those found in the apartment. That comparison was done only after yesterday's session in court."

"That is exactly the basis for my charge, Your Honor," Steve Winslow said. "The prosecution suspected Douglas Kemper of being the person who left those fingerprints, but deliberately refrained from making a comparison until after they had got him to commit himself on the stand."

Judge Graves banged the gavel. "That will do, Mr. Winslow.

This is not a debate. Mr. Dirkson is replying to the allegations in your motion. You may proceed, Mr. Dirkson."

"Thank you, Your Honor. As you can see, the charge of prosecutorial misconduct is absolutely without merit. With regard to the motion for a mistrial, I naturally oppose it. Likewise, the demand that Marilyn Harding and Douglas Kemper be tried jointly. In the event that we should proceed against Douglas Kemper, we shall do so separately and at a later time. Hence, there are no grounds whatsoever for making these motions, and they should be denied."

Dirkson pointed to a stack of books on the prosecution table. "I have some precedents, Your Honor. If I could just have a moment."

"Very well," Graves said.

As Dirkson began citing cases into the record, Fitzpatrick turned to Steve Winslow. "We're going to lose."

"I know," Steve said. "We're just laying the groundwork for an appeal."

"I know. But I hate to lose."

"Stick with me. You'll get good at it."

When the arguments were finally over, Judge Graves took a thirty minute recess. When court reconvened, he said, "I have considered the motions carefully. They are denied. These proceedings will continue.

"Now then, with regard to procedure, the witness Kemper was on the stand. I understand he's been charged with perjury, and is out on bail. Is that right?"

"Yes, Your Honor," Dirkson said.

"I understand he has not been charged as a coconspirator or as an accessory to this crime?"

"That's correct, Your Honor. It is possible that he will be, but he has not been so charged at the present time."

"Very well," Graves said. "Mr. Winslow. Is it your intention to advise the witness not to answer questions?"

"Your Honor, it is my contention that he should not be on the stand to begin with."

"I understand that. I have already ruled. I am attempting to expedite this trial without embarrassing your client or infringing upon his rights. After all this time, I would hate to call the jury in and immediately send them out again. But we're not going to argue this in front of them, so I'm attempting to determine if we can resolve this matter now."

"If I might interpose, Your Honor," Dirkson said. "The point is moot. I have no further questions for the witness, Kemper."

"You have concluded your direct examination?"

"I have."

"Mr. Fitzpatrick. Do you intend to cross-examine the witness?"

"No, I do not."

Judge Graves nodded. "That simplifies things. We'll bring back the jury and call the witness to the stand. You can both announce that you have no questions and the witness will be excused. Bring in the jury."

Fitzpatrick was on his feet. "I assume Your Honor will explain to the jury the presence of Steve Winslow?"

A trace of a smile crossed the judge's lips. "I will *try,*" he said dryly.

That sally produced a roar of laughter that Judge Graves made no attempt to quiet. After all, the jury was not present.

After the jurors had filed in and been seated, Judge Graves addressed the jury. "Ladies and gentlemen of the jury. I would like to apologize for the delay. As I explained at the outset of the trial, there are numerous occasions when we have matters to discuss outside your presence. Sometmes they relate to this trial, sometimes they are matters relating to other trials. In some instances, it is merely because one of the parties is indisposed and cannot be present in court. As I told you, it is not your place to speculate as to what goes on in the courtroom during the time you are in the jury room.

"At any rate, we are ready to resume the trial. Before we do so, I call your attention to the presence of another attorney in the courtroom. Mr. Steve Winslow has joined the defense as associate counsel for Marilyn Harding. He is seated at the defense table and will be taking part in the trial."

The jurors looked at each other. Steve Winslow grinned. He knew that despite Judge Graves admonition, each and every juror was wondering just what the hell had gone on since court had adjourned yesterday afternoon.

While this was going on, Douglas Kemper entered the courtroom and took the stand. He did not make a good impression. His manner was furtive and sheepish. He carefully avoided looking at Marilyn Harding.

Judge Graves, though aware that Kemper's examination was through, still went through the charade. "Mr. Kemper, I must remind you that you are still under oath. Mr. Dirkson, you may proceed."

Dirkson stood up. "Thank you, Your Honor. I have no further questions of the witness."

Graves nodded. "Very well. Mr. Fitzpatrick?"

Fitzpatrick stood up. "No questions, Your Honor."

Graves nodded. "The witness is excused."

Kemper got up and left the stand.

The jurors, who had waited all day to see only that, found it funny. Some began to giggle.

Judge Graves gave them a few minutes to blow off steam, then banged the gavel. When the court was quiet, he said, "Mr. Dirkson. Call your next witness."

Dirkson stood up. He looked at the jury. Then at the defense table. Then back up at the judge. His smile was rather smug. "The People rest, Your Honor."

36.

FITZPATRICK HEAVED his bulk around the small conference room in the courthouse like an angry whale.

"Son of a bitch!" he said. "Son of a fucking bitch!" He poured himself a glass of water and gulped it down. "I don't need this," he said. "My specialty is corporate law. I've got myself some juicy plum clients. Chief among them, Phillip Harding. He dies, and I inherit his daughter. She inherits a murder. Suddenly I'm in court. But even then I'm all right, because I've got a genuine, first-class, made-to-order red herring, scapegoat, fall guy, to take the rap. Only he turns out to be the attorney for my client's lover, and suddenly I'm fucked. Suddenly I'm in court with a smug-ass district attorney who just wants to play games with me. 'Your Honor, I rest my case.' Jesus Christ, he hasn't *made* a case. What the hell's he doing resting now?"

"It's good move," Steve said. "If we don't put on a case, he's given the jury enough to convict. If we do put on a case, he's still got a whole bunch of witnesses left for rebuttal."

Fitzpatrick threw up his hands. "What case? We have no case. You talked to Marilyn Harding. You know what she's like. We don't dare put her on the stand."

"No argument there."

"It's a no-win situation. If we don't put her on the stand, she's a

224

dead duck. If we do put her on the stand, Dirkson will tear her apart."

"All right," Steve said. "What's your plan?"

Fitzpatrick stared at him. "Plan? What plan?"

"All right. What's Dirkson plan?"

"What you just said. It depends what we do. If we don't put on any defense, we've lost. If we put Marilyn on the stand, he'll tear her apart." Fitzpatrick shrugged. "If we try to make a case *without* putting her on the stand, it's like you said. He's got a whole bunch of witnesses saved up for rebuttal."

"Right. And what's he gonna hit us with?"

"Everything."

"Yeah, but pick one. What's he gonna hit us with?"

Fitzpatrick pursed his lips. "Best guess, the Phillip Harding murder. He alluded to it in his opening statement, hasn't mentioned it since. I'd imagine if we make any showing at all, if we manage to swing the sympathy of the jury in the least, he'll come back at us with that. He'll bring in the Phillip Harding murder and try to poison the minds of the jurors with the thought that Marilyn is a habitual killer."

"Yeah," Steve said. "That's what I think too. And if he does, what are you going to do?"

Fitzpatrick looked at him in surprise. "Fight it, of course. Try to keep it out of the record. Once Dirkson gets that in the minds of the jurors, we're sunk."

"Right," Steve said. "And what do you think Dirkson expects you to do?"

Fitzpatrick frowned. "What is this, twenty fucking questions? You wanna make a point, make it. Frankly, your Socratic method's getting to be a pain in the ass."

"All right. Sorry. Look, we agree Dirkson's going to try to bring in the Phillip Harding murder. You plan to fight it. You think Dirkson doesn't know that? Of course he does. And if he knows it, he's prepared for it. You saw how many precedents he cited in opposition to my motion? Well I'll bet you a nickel he's got twice as many to cite to back up his contention that evidence of a prior crime may be introduced to show motivation. And you know what, I think he's probably right."

"So," Fitzpatrick said, "you're telling me we're fucked before we start."

"No, I'm not," Steve said. "I'm telling you what Dirkson has in mind. The way I see it, Dirkson has certain expectations. If we fulfill those expectations, we're playing right into his hands."

"So?"

"So, we can't do that. We can't play this conservative and conventional. This is a situation that calls for heroic measures. We gotta throw the game plan away. We've got to get off the defensive and on the attack. The hell with what Dirkson expects. Let's rock the son of a bitch in his sockets. Hit him where he least expects it, get the jury interested, and then give 'em a show."

Fitzpatrick frowned. "I don't know how to do that."

"I do."

37.

JUDGE GRAVES said, "Is the defense ready?"

Fitzpatrick rose. "We are, Your Honor."

"Does the defense wish to make an opening statement?"

"We do."

"Very well. Proceed."

Fitzpatrick glanced dubiously down at Steve Winslow who was seated beside him at the defense table.

Steve gave him the thumbs up sign and grinned. "Give 'em hell," he murmured.

Fitzpatrick managed a twisted smile. He straightened up, set his jaw, and strode out into the center of the courtroom.

"Your Honor," Fitzpatrick said. "Ladies and gentlemen of the jury. We expect to prove that the defendant, Marilyn Harding, is the victim of a conspiracy. An insidious conspiracy by person or persons unknown. Or I should say, by persons unknown at the present time. We expect to prove that this conspiracy against Marilyn Harding is based only upon the accident of her birth. Marilyn Harding was born into a wealthy family. She is a wealthy woman. As such, she is a target for certain unscrupulous individuals. And she has been used as a target in this case.

"Moreover, we expect to prove that this conspiracy is not

limited to Marilyn Harding, but extends to the entire Harding family."

Fitzpatrick raised his voice. "We expect to show by competent evidence, that Phillip Harding, father of Marilyn Harding, was murdered on the thirteenth of last month!"

There were gasps from the spectators in the courtroom.

Dirkson, startled, rose to his feet. His mouth was open, so great was his surprise. He blinked twice, and slowly sat down again.

"We shall prove this," Fitzpatrick went on, "not by inference or innuendo, but by the autopsy report prepared by the medical examiner himself. We shall prove beyond a shadow of a doubt that Marilyn Harding's father, Phillip Harding, was cold-bloodedly and ruthlessly murdered.

"After proving that, we shall then show how the conspiracy against the Harding family shifted from Phillip Harding to Marilyn Harding, his principal heir. You have heard, from the lips of the prosecution's own witnesses, how Marilyn Harding was being followed by private detectives. Now, has the prosecution attempted to show you who hired those private detectives? Or to show why those private detectives were hired? You know the answer. And the answer is, no they have not.

"But the defense expects to answer those questions. The defense expects to show that those private detectives were hired to follow Marilyn Harding as part of an ongoing conspiracy against the Harding family in general and against Marilyn Harding in partic-ular. We expect to show that Marilyn Harding was cleverly and insidiously manipulated into the position in which she finds her-self today. That she was systematically framed for a murder. That she has been tricked into a position that would seem on the sur-face, indefensible.

"Well, ladies and gentlemen. The defense intends to dig beneath the surface. We intend to fill in the gaps in the story left by the prosecution. We intend to show how a web of lies and deceit has framed this defendant for a crime that she did not commit.

"We shall show all of this by competent evidence and we shall expect a verdict of not guilty at your hands."

As Fitzpatrick bowed to the jury and sat down, the courtroom burst into an uproar. Judge Graves banged the gavel furiously, but nothing he could do was going to stop the stampede of reporters who were running for the exit.

38.

IT MADE the front page of every paper in the city, even the New York *Times*. Fitzpatrick's opening statement was a smash, a stunning reversal, a dramatic bit of courtroom strategy, boldly conceding the very point the prosecution had sought to establish. It was fresh, new, and exciting, and it raised great expectations.

It was all downhill from there.

Dirkson played it smart. He didn't make the big mistake of fighting Fitzpatrick, of objecting to what he was trying to do. That would have put Dirkson in the embarrassing position of arguing against the stance he himself had taken at the opening of the trial. Instead, he sat on his hands and raised no objection when Fitzpatrick called the Nassau County medical examiner to the stand to testify that Phillip Harding died from arsenic poisoning. Dirkson neither objected nor cross-examined. He merely sat at the prosecution table looking slightly bored. His attitude seemed to say that the defense was bringing out points with which the prosecution was well familiar, and unless Fitzpatrick came up with something to connect those points with his wild, fanciful theories of a conspiracy, Dirkson couldn't be bothered. And since Fitzpatrick had no such connection to make, the Phillip Harding bombshell fizzled. Dirkson's attitude prevailed. That attitude was, "So what?"

The next witness was a little better.

"Your name is Charles Miltner?" Fitzpatrick asked.

"That's right."

"You're the head of the Miltner Detective Agency?"

"I am."

"How many people do you employ?"

"It varies. I would say from twelve to fifteen."

"And is one of those a Mr. Jason Fisher?"

"Yes, he is."

"Then let me ask you this. Has your agency ever been employed in any case involving the defendant, Marilyn Harding?"

"Yes, sir."

"What were you employed to do?"

"Place Marilyn Harding under surveilance."

"Were you given any specific instructions regarding that surveillance?"

"No, sir."

"Nothing in particular you were supposed to watch for?"

"No, sir."

"What were your instructions?"

"Merely to place her under surveillance and report what she did."

"And when did the surveillance begin?"

"On Tuesday, the eighth."

"At what time?"

"At 8:00 A.M."

"And when did it end?"

"Wednesday evening around 9:00 P.M."

"You had Marilyn Harding under surveillance from Tuesday, the eighth, at 8:00 A.M. until Wednesday, the ninth, at 9:00 P.M.?"

"No, sir."

"No? I thought you said you did?"

"No, sir. The surveillance was not continuous. We had her under surveillance during part of that time."

"Which part?"

"From 8:00 A.M. till midnight on Tuesday, and from 8:00 A.M. till 9:00 P.M. on Wednesday."

"Was that in accordance with your instructions?"

"Yes, sir."

"Could you elaborate?"

"Yes, sir. The surveillance on Marilyn Harding was to be sixteen hours a day. Two eight hour shifts. The first shift from 8:00 A.M. till 4:00 P.M., the second shift from 4:00 P.M. till midnight. From midnight till 8:00 A.M. she was on her own."

"You contracted to do two eight hour shifts?"

"That's right."

"How many men per shift?"

"Two."

"And Jason Fisher, in your employ, was assigned to one of those shifts?"

"Yes, sir."

"Which one?"

"The 4:00 P.M. till midnight shift."

"On both days?"

"Yes, sir."

"You said two men per shift. Who was his partner?"

"Michael Reed."

"And the 8:00 A.M. till 4:00 P.M. shift? Who was assigned to that?"

"Saul Burroughs and Fred Grimes."

"On both days?"

"Yes, sir."

"These two eight hour shifts were specified in the work that you were contracted to do?"

"Yes, sir."

"And," Fitzpatrick said, raising his voice, "who made those specifications? Who requested two eight hour shifts per day of surveillance on Marilyn Harding? Who hired you, Mr. Miltner?"

Miltner shook his head. "I don't know."

Fitzpatrick stared at him. "You don't *know?*"

"No, sir."

"How is that possible, Mr. Miltner? You're a businessman. You want to get paid for your services. Who did you bill?"

"I didn't bill anyone. I was paid in advance and in cash."

"How?"

"By messenger."

"By messenger?"

"Yes, sir. An envelope came to my office by messenger. It had a thousand dollars cash in it."

Fitzpatrick raised his eyebrows. "A thousand dollars cash? In what denominations?"

"Ten one hundred dollar bills."

"Is that right? Was there a letter with them?"

"No, sir."

"Nothing at all?"

"No, sir."

"Then how did you know what the money was for?"

"I was contacted by phone."

"By phone? Then you spoke to the person who hired you?"

"Objected to as calling for a conclusion on the part of the witness."

"Sustained."

"You spoke with *a* person on the phone who gave you instructions regarding the money you received from the messenger?"

"That's right."

"And this person instructed you to place Marilyn Harding under surveillance?"

"That's right."

"It was this person who requested the two eight hour shifts?"

"Yes."

"When was this phone conversation?"

"On Monday, the seventh of this month."

"And when did the money arrive?"

"That same day."

"Before the phone conversation or after?"

"I believe it was right after."

"This person on the phone—they didn't identify themselves? They didn't give you a name?"

"No, sir."

"Did you ask?"

"Yes, I did."

"And what were you told?"

"I was told to mind my own business."

"Which you did?"

"I beg your pardon?"

"You did. You minded your own business. You accepted the employment?"

"Yes, I did."

"Is it your policy to accept employment from people who refuse to identify themselves?"

"It's my policy to accept employment, period. If it's legal, I'll do it."

"Very virtuous of you, Mr. Miltner. And what can you tell us about this mysterious person, this person who contacted you on the phone?"

Miltner shrugged. "Nothing."

"Nothing? And yet you spoke to them for several minutes."

"About instructions, yes. I learned only what the person wanted done and the fact that they didn't want to be identified."

"Surely you must have learned more than that. For instance, I notice you keep using the word *person* to describe the caller, rather than the pronoun he or she. Which leads me to ask, was the caller a man or a woman?"

"I don't know."

"You don't know? How is that possible?"

"The caller disguised his voice. Or her voice. It was muffled and distorted. It could have been a man affecting a high voice, or a woman affecting a low one. There was no way to tell."

"And you made no attempt to find out to whom this voice belonged?"

"No, I did not."

"You made no attempt to trace the call?"

"No, I did not."

"And the money that was sent to you. The ten one hundred bills. Did you make any attempt to trace them?"

"No, I did not."

"What did you do with them?"

"Put them in the bank."

"And the person who called you. How were you supposed to contact them?"

"I wasn't. They were to contact me."

"How?"

"By phone."

"And did that happen?"

"Yes."

"When?"

"On Wednesday morning the person called in for a report."

"Did you speak to them at that time?"

"Yes, I did."

"And did you give them a report?"

"Yes, I did."

"You reported on Tuesday's surveillance?"

"Yes, sir."

"Accurately?"

"Yes, sir."

"And did the person call back again?"

"No, sir."

"They didn't call Thursday, to ask about Wednesday's surveillance?"

"No, sir."

Fitzpatrick frowned and thought a moment. "On Wednesday night you contacted the police?"

"Yes, sir."

"And told them everything you knew about the Marilyn Harding surveillance?"

"That's right."

"Then let me ask you this: if the person who called you had called back on Thursday, would *that* call have been traced?"

"It sure would. The police had a tap on the phone ready to record the call, and officers standing by ready to run the trace." Miltner shrugged. "The call never came."

Fitzpatrick thought that over. "That's all," he announced.

Dirkson didn't even stand up. He waved his hand. "No questions, Your Honor."

Miltner left the stand.

"Call your next witness," Judge Graves said.

"Call Fred Grimes."

As the witness took the stand and was sworn in, Fitzpatrick leaned down to Steve Winslow. "What can I do with him?" he said. "This guy's gonna do us more harm than good."

"Depends on how we play it," Steve said.

"What do you mean?"

"How would you feel about getting admonished for prejudicial misconduct?"

"I wouldn't like it."

"Then why don't you let me take this one?"

Fitzpatrick sat down. Steve Winslow stood up and approached the witness.

"Your name is Fred Grimes?"

"Yes, it is."

"And you are employed by the Miltner Detective Agency?"

"That's right."

"Directing your attention to Tuesday, the eighth of this month, were you employed to shadow the defendant, Marilyn Harding?"

"Yes, I was."

"Were you alone at the time?"

"No, I was not."

"Who was with you?"

"My partner, Saul Burroughs."

"Where did you pick up the defendant?"

"We staked out her house in Glen Cove."

"At 8:00 A.M.?"

"That's right."

"When did you first spot the defendant?"

"She drove out the front gate about 1:15 P.M."

"You followed her?"

"Yes, we did."

"Where to?"

"We followed her into Manhattan, to 249 East 3rd Street."

"And what happened then?"

"She went into the building at that address."

"Did you follow her in?"

"No, we didn't."

"So what did you do?"

"When she parked near the building, my partner stayed with the car and I got out and followed her on foot. When she went into the building, I tried to get close enough to see where she was going. I couldn't risk following her in, but I wanted to learn all I could. I got close enough to look into the foyer. There was a row of buttons there and a call box. She pressed one of the buttons, waited, then the door buzzed and she went in. The minute she disappeared up the stairs, I went into the foyer and looked at the row of buttons. The one that she had pushed was labeled David C. Bradshaw."

"Nice work," Steve said. "So, to the best of your knowledge, on Tuesday the eighth, the defendant, Marilyn Harding, called on David C. Bradshaw at approximately 2:30 P.M.?"

"That's right."

"When did she come out?"

"About ten minutes later."

"What did she do?"

"She got in her car and drove off."

"So what did you do?"

"We followed her."

"Where did she go?"

The witness shrugged. "She went to Bloomingdale's. Shopping. We followed her through the store."

"Then what?"

"She was still there at 4:00 P.M. when the relief arrived."

"So," Steve Winslow said, "if I understand your testimony correctly, when the crime lab expert, Mr. Riker, states that he found

J. P. HAILEY

Marilyn Harding's fingerprints in the apartment, there is every reason to believe that those fingerprints were made the day before the murder, on Tuesday the eighth."

Dirkson lunged to his feet. "Objection, Your Honor! Argumentative, assuming facts not in evidence, calling for a conclusion on the part of the witness. It's not a question, it's an argument. Counsel is attempting to prejudice the jury by making an argument in the guise of a question. I assign that statement as prejudicial misconduct."

"Objection sustained," Graves snapped. "Mr. Winslow. I am not admonishing you for prejudicial misconduct at this time. I am taking the matter under advisement. However, I would caution you to use a certain amount of prudence in phrasing your questions."

"Yes, Your Honor. No further questions."

"No questions," Dirkson said.

As the witness left the stand, Steve Winslow huddled with Fitzpatrick.

"Well, that wasn't so bad," Steve said.

"No. Or so good, either. As a bombshell, that was a bit of a fizzle. Now we've shot our wad, what the hell do we do now?"

Steve sighed. "First we asked for a continuance until tomorrow. Then I'm afraid it's time for me to do my Faust impression."

Fitzpatrick frowned. "What the hell does that mean?"

Steve smiled grimly. "I'm going to sell my soul to the devil."

39.

DIRKSON PUT his elbows on his desk, tapped his fingers together, and surveyed Steve Winslow.

"I should tell you before we start," Dirkson said, "I am not particularly inclined to plea bargain."

"Neither am I," Steve said.

"Then why are you here?"

"I thought we might talk over the case."

"I'm afraid I have nothing to talk about."

"Then I'll talk and you listen."

"Why should I listen to you?"

"You listened to me once, Dirkson. You didn't come out of that one so bad."

"Neither did you. You got your client released."

"Which she would have been anyway, Dirkson. You know that."

"Yes, but not as quickly. You got her out a day or two earlier than it would have taken with all due process. I don't know why those two days were important to you, but they were."

"I was looking after my client's best interests."

Dirkson snorted. "Sure. You gained some advantage, but you're not going to let me know what it was. So stop talking cooperation and what a good turn you did me when I listened to you before.

239

We're dealing at arms length here, and that's the best you're going to get."

"Don't I know it," Steve said. "I heard your opening remark, Dirkson. You're not inclined to plea bargain. What a crock of shit. You know damn well I'm not here to plea bargain. But you know and I know if I were, you'd jump at it. Because you don't really care what charge you convict Marilyn on in this case as long as you convict her. Cause as soon as you do, you're going to turn around and try her for murdering her father. And if you get a conviction here, you're damn sure to get a conviction there. So let's cut the shit about who's diddling who. Let's get down to brass tacks here."

"Such as what? You going to tell me who killed Donald Blake?"

Steve shook his head. "No. I don't want to talk about the murder of Donald Blake."

"You don't?"

"No. I want to talk about the murder of Phillip Harding."

"You're kidding."

"Not at all."

"O.K., talk."

Steve leaned back in his chair and crossed his legs. "I notice you haven't indicted Marilyn for the murder of her father."

"No," Dirkson said.

"But as soon as you get a conviction in the Bradshaw case, you will."

Dirkson said nothing.

Steve looked at him. "Will you concede the possibility?"

Dirkson shrugged. "It's your party, Winslow."

"Fine," Steve said. "It's my party. Let's concede for the sake of argument that you intend to charge Marilyn Harding with that crime. Now let's look at the evidence. Phillip Harding dies. The doctor pronounces the cause of death to be coronary thrombosis. Phillip Harding is buried. His will is sent in for probate. All well and good.

"Then what happens? A month later the police exhume the body and find out he died from arsenic poisoning. Suddenly it's a murder case, and his daughter, the principal heir, is the prime murder suspect."

Winslow stopped and looked at Dirkson.

"So," Dirkson said.

"So," Steve said, "a little too pat, don't you think?"

"No, I don't," Dirkson said. "That's your argument? Marilyn's the most likely person to have done it, so therefore she must be innocent? Little convoluted, wouldn't you say? This is not some paperback thriller. In real life the most likely person usually did it."

"Yeah, but is she the most likely?" Steve said. "You see, the facts have to make sense. And what are the facts here? Phillip Harding dies, no one suspects anything, and a month later the body's exhumed and arsenic's found. The question is, why did the cops exhume the body?"

Dirkson said nothing.

"I know, I know," Steve said. "You're not going to tell me. So I'll tell you. There's only one reason that makes sense. The cops got a tip. I know you don't want to admit that, but we're talking informally here, so say the cops got a tip. They dig up the body and, sure enough, there's the arsenic." Steve shook his head. "Well, we got a big problem there. And the problem is, where did the cops get the tip? I know you're not going to tell me, cause you're not even going to concede that the cops got a tip. But ten to one it was an anonymous tip. The way I figure it, it would have to be. The question is, who gave 'em the tip? If Marilyn Harding killed her father, it sure wasn't her. And if she killed her father, who else would have known?"

Steve looked at Dirkson. "Any comments?"

Dirkson shrugged. "You're talking, Winslow. I'm listening. That's all."

"Fine," Steve said. "You listen. The way I see it, if Marilyn Harding killed him, it doesn't make any sense. She had the most to gain, she had the opportunity, she fed him the lunch that killed him. For Christ's sake, if you want a suspect, she's it.

"Now, let's assume she didn't kill him. In that case, she's been beautifully framed. The murderer set her up. Arsenic's introduced into the sugar, Marilyn is the one to serve it to him, she's the one who gained. All well and good.

"Except for one thing. The doctor botches the diagnosis. He puts the cause of death down as coronary thrombosis. A natural death. Bad luck for the murderer. Here's a perfect frame-up, only no one knows it's murder.

"So, what happens? The murderer sweats it out, hoping the cops will get wise. When they don't, as a last resort, we get the anonymous tip."

Steve paused. Dirkson still said nothing.

"Now," Steve said, "you're not going to tell me anything. But assuming we got so far as to go to court—on the Phillip Harding murder, I mean—well, I'm going to be calling witnesses and cross-examining yours. And the thing I'm going to be bearing down on is that anonymous tip. And if there was one, I'm going to bring it out. And when I do, if it was a phone tip, the first thing I'm going to bring out is whether the tip was from a man or a woman. And when I do, I'll bet you a nickel it was from a woman. That's assuming, of course, it wasn't a disguised voice.

"Then I'll bring out my theory of the case. Wanna hear it? Well, I'll tell you anyway. It's an old story, really. An old fairly tale. Perhaps you'll recognize it. Once upon a time, there was this sweet, beautiful, young girl. But she had this wicked stepsister. Recognize the story? Now the stepsister wasn't as pretty, or as rich, or as young, or anything. Basically, she had only one thing going for her. And you know what that was? Prince Charming. Slight variation on the old theme. The wicked stepsister had Prince Charming. But then she started to lose him too. And to her worst rival, her beautiful stepsister. So this cold, repressed, unhappy woman plotted her revenge. She'd kill her stepfather, and set it up so her dear stepsister took the blame."

Dirkson made his first comment. "Bullshit."

"Oh is it?" Steve said. "Who do you think hired Miltner? Who do you think was keeping tabs on Marilyn Harding? I mean, come on. If she and Kemper were having an affair, who the hell do you think was keeping tabs on them?"

"You can't prove that."

"No, I can't. We're playing what-if here. And the what-if is, what if Marilyn Harding gets acquitted of killing Donald Blake?"

"That's highly unlikely."

"Is it? All right, let's look at the Donald Blake case for a bit."

Dirkson smiled. "I was wondering when you'd get around to that."

"For the purpose of our discussion it's somewhat incidental, but let's look at it. Say Phyllis Kemper hired Miltner. She's framed Marilyn for one murder, but it hasn't come off. Now she tries to go for two."

"Now you're really stretching," Dirkson said.

"Maybe, but let's play with it a bit. Phyllis Kemper puts a tail on Marilyn. What she's hoping to come up with is some hard evidence of the affair."

"Stop right there," Dirkson said. "If that was the objective, why not tail her husband."

Steve shrugged. "We're playing with theories here. I can give you two reasons, though. One, she didn't want the detectives to know who was hiring them. If the detectives put a tail on her husband, the obvious person to be doing it would be the wife. She went to great lengths to disguise her voice, so it's clear she didn't want to be known. So she put a tail on Marilyn instead, which would work just as well, since all she's interested in is her husband's rendezvous with her. Second reason. Douglas Kemper's a real estate salesman. It would be a large pain in the ass to have detectives tail him around all day as he drove clients from one property to another. With that many trips, and having to stake out the real estate office all the time, there'd be a good chance the detectives would be spotted. She also wouldn't be too keen on having private detectives following her and her husband when the two of them went out for dinner. Under those circumstances, even the coolest person couldn't help looking around a bit wondering where the detectives were."

"That's pretty thin,' Dirkson said.

"As I said, they're just theories. I don't really want to argue. We're playing what-if. What if Phyllis Kemper put a tail on

Marilyn? Well, she's expecting to have Marilyn rendezvous with her husband. But it doesn't happen. Something else does. What? Marilyn calls on someone at a not too affluent address, not the type of place Marilyn would normally go. Very interesting. When Phyllis gets the report from the detective agency the next day, she investigates. Finds Marilyn has called on a David C. Bradshaw. Now things are popping real nice for Phyllis. She's already called in a tip to the cops on Phillip Harding being poisoned, and that morning they act on it. The body's exhumed, arsenic's found. Marilyn has a tough morning with the cops. When they finally leave, Marilyn gets a phone call. Phyllis, thinking it's a rendezvous call from Doug, listens in. But it's not Doug, it's Bradshaw. With a blackmail demand. Jackpot! Phyllis keeps listening. Better and better. Marilyn had *already* paid blackmail money. The detectives can swear Marilyn called upon Bradshaw. And Marilyn makes another appointment to see him. And Phyllis knows detectives will follow Marilyn there again.

"Well, no reason for Phyllis to tag along too. If she tried to, the detectives might spot her. But she knows where Marilyn's going. She gets out of there fast, goes to Manhattan, stakes out Bradshaw's apartment from across the street. Waits for the scenario to unfold.

"What happens? Marilyn arrives, slightly late, since she was held up waiting for Doug. Of course, Phyllis doesn't know Marilyn was going to meet Doug, since she split right after the Bradshaw call. Had she known that, it might have altered her plans. But she doesn't know.

"So Marilyn arrives, goes in, and comes out five minutes later. The detectives are trailing along behind. Great. The stage is set. Phyllis goes up, rings the doorbell, gets buzzed into the apartment, talks to Bradshaw. I don't know what line she pulled on Bradshaw, but knowing he was a blackmailer, thinking up one couldn't have been that hard. At any rate, she kids him along, picks up a knife, and zaps him in the back. Voila! Perfect frame."

Dirkson shook his head. "Full of holes."

"Such as?"

"What about the ten thousand bucks hidden in the hallway?"

"Phyllis does that. She knows Marilyn came to pay him off. She searches the body for the ten grand. Finds it. She doesn't want to leave that money on the body, because why would Marilyn pay him off and then kill him? On the other hand, she wants the money discovered cause it will point to Marilyn. So she takes it and hides it in the upstairs hallway. The theory: Marilyn killed Bradshaw, then, trapped in the apartment and afraid she would be discovered with the money on her, hid it and got out. Not a great theory, but the best she could do. The bills have to be discovered to point to Marilyn, and hiding them is slightly more credible than leaving them on the body.

"Only, what Phyllis doesn't know is the bills she removed from the body aren't Marilyn's, they're Bradshaw's, and Marilyn's ten grand is still left in the money belt. But Phyllis had no reason to suspect there was another ten grand involved.

"And," Steve said, "if you want to talk about weak theories, you're the one dealing with the contention that Marilyn would have paid Bradshaw off, killed him, and then left the money on the body. Frankly, I find that hard to swallow."

Dirkson smiled. "I don't think I'll have a problem. You're forgetting the time of death, Winslow. The altercation? The witness? The phone call to the cops? If Phyllis Kemper did what you describe—and I'm not saying she didn't—by the time she got up the stairs, Donald Blake was dead."

"You're splitting hairs, Dirkson. You're talking minutes here. No medical examiner can be that exact."

"There's the witness and the phone call."

"Sure there is. But how exact is exact? Those detectives who logged the times Marilyn went in and out. You think they got it to the minute?"

"That's their job."

"Yeah. That's their job, and I bet they're aces at it. They probably log everything the instant it happens. Probably set their watches by Greenwich mean time every morning. Totally infallible, I'm sure."

Dirkson waved his hand impatiently. "I don't want to quibble. You save your arguments for the jury. I'm just telling you I don't think they're going to pull very much weight."

"I don't want to argue either. I told you, I didn't come here to discuss the case."

"You could have fooled me. I happen to be rather busy, Winslow. You got a point, make it. Otherwise, I got work to do."

"All right, I'll make it. If Marilyn's found guilty on any count of the Bradshaw murder you're going to turn around and try her for the murder of her father."

"You keep saying me. Phillip Harding was killed in Nassau County. That's outside my jurisdiction."

"Yeah, sure," Steve said. "But you know damn well you've got your hand in. If they haven't indicted her for it, it's cause they're just waiting for your say so."

Dirkson frowned. Said nothing.

"But that's neither here nor there. The point I'm making is this. If she's convicted of this crime, she'll be charged with that one. You know it and I know it. But consider this. If she's acquitted of this crime—the Bradshaw murder—then someone better take a long hard look before they charge her with the murder of Phillip Harding. Cause then you got no prior conviction to throw in her face. And when you think about it, that was really going to be the key evidence against her. Sure, you can show she had an opportunity to tamper with the sugar bowl. But so did her stepsister. And if Marilyn had poisoned her father, do you really think she'd be stupid enough to leave the sugar bowl full of arsenic around for a whole month until the cops thought to look for it? I'd like to see you try to argue that one. And *if* Phillip Harding's body was exhumed because of an anonymous tip, think of the argument I'll be able to make. Think of the doctrine of reasonable doubt. And then ask yourself what chance you'd have of getting a conviction."

Dirkson met Steve's eyes steadily. A good poker player, giving nothing away. "Is that it?" he asked.

Steve sighed. "Yeah, that's it." He got up, smiled. "See you in court."

40.

FITZPATRICK WAS animated.

"I like it," he said. "I really like it. Oh sure, I've known Phyllis Kemper for years, I'm upset about all that. But damn it, she's not my client. I really like it."

"Well, don't get too excited," Steve said. "It may sound good, but it happens to be a bunch of bullshit. It's one thing to try to sell a D.A. a bill of goods, but you don't have to start swallowing it yourself."

"But damn it," Fitzpatrick said, "it all makes sense."

"That Phyllis hired the detectives, yes. I think that's a good bet. That she killed Bradshaw happens to be a hell of a stretch."

"Maybe not. The way you spelled it out for Dirkson sounds logical."

"A lawyer's job is to make things sound logical. It doesn't mean they are. It's just a theory, Fitzpatrick. Let's not go off the deep end over it. Remember this. We have the benefit of Douglas Kemper's story. The police don't. Of course, I didn't bring that up with Dirkson. But if Douglas Kemper's story is true—or rather, if my interpretation of how Douglas Kemper lied to me is true—he was in the apartment right on the heels of Marilyn Harding. Of course, if he's not lying, he was in there right before Marilyn

247

Harding. That means he either found Bradshaw dead or killed
him. And the same goes for Marilyn.

"The problem is, we got two clients here, and despite whatever
finespun theories I might try to lay on Dirkson, the fact is one of
them probably killed him. The best I can see with this Phyllis
Kemper thing is, we got a red herring to play with."

Fitzpatrick frowned. "Well, at least that's something."

Steve stood up, stretched, yawned. "Well, just wanted to fill you
in."

Steve glanced around the sumptuously furnished Wall Street
office of the law firm of Fitzpatrick, Blackburn, and Weed. "Nice
place you got here, Fitzpatrick. Suppose you'll miss it if I get you
disbarred."

Fitzpatrick's grin was somewhat forced.

Steve took a cab back to his office. On the ride uptown he got
to thinking about what he'd just said, about what he'd told Fitzpatrick. "One of the two of them probably did it." Yeah, that was
true. And now they were both his clients. He was charged with
getting both of them off. Regardless of who did it. Regardless of
who actually committed the crime.

That bothered him. That bothered him a lot. Shit. What had
he come to? When he'd defended Sheila Benton, she'd asked him
point blank if he'd defend her if he thought she was guilty. And
he'd told her no. And he'd believed it. Just as he'd believed what
he'd told her about the case he'd handled for Wilson and Doyle,
the case that had got him fired, the case where he'd tricked the
hit-and-run accident victim into identifying someone other than
his client, and then it had turned out his client was actually
guilty. Sheila had asked him if he'd have done it if he'd known,
and he'd said no. And he'd believed that too.

So what the hell was he doing? Here he was defending two
clients, one of whom was almost certainly guilty. How could he
justify that? Why was he doing it?

Well, he knew why. He was doing it because some idiotic,
romantic fool had sent him an anonymous retainer from some
plot ripped off from a storybook, and he'd been placed in a posi-

tion where he had to either defend him or risk being disbarred. That was why.

Or was it?

He'd risked disbarment before. He wasn't a squeamish guy. If he thought he was right, he'd wade right in and let the chips fall where they may. So he wasn't in this just to cover his ass. That was too easy an explanation. Too easy a way out. Too pat an answer to a moral dilemma. If he was in this, he was in it by choice. He'd chosen to defend these two people. To try to get them off.

Well, why not? Everyone's entitled to representation. A lawyer isn't a judge and jury. It isn't a lawyer's place to try to decide if a client's innocent or guilty. Legally, ethically, morally, Steve had every right to do what he was doing.

So why did he feel like shit?

Steve paid off the cab and took the elevator up to his office. Tracy Garvin would be manning desk. Steve felt a twinge of resentment. She'd want to pump him for information, and he just didn't feel like dragging through the whole story again.

Steve realized he was being unkind. Tracy Garvin might be a young, silly, twit of a girl, but why *shouldn't* she be interested.

Steve Winslow pushed open the office door and knew at once that he'd been reprieved. Tracy Garvin's face was animated.

"I tried to reach you at Fitzpatrick's. Mark Taylor called. Said it was urgent."

"Get him," Steve said.

Steve walked into his office, flopped down at his desk. One light on the phone was on, so Steve picked it up and pushed that button. He heard Tracy Garvin's voice asking for Mark Taylor, and seconds later Taylor came on the line.

"Taylor."

"It's Tracy. Hold on for Steve."

"I'm on," Steve said. "What is it, Mark?"

"I got something hot I'd rather not talk about on the phone. You in your office?"

"Yeah."

"I'll be right down."

Steve Winslow hung up the phone. Thank god, he thought. Let it be a break. Something. Anything. Get me off the hook.

Minutes later, Tracy Garvin opened the door.

"Mark Taylor's here."

Taylor pushed by her into the room. Tracy trailed in behind him with a steno pad.

"You'll be wanting notes?" she said.

Steve was about to say yes, largely due to the uncharitable thoughts he'd had toward her earlier, when Mark Taylor said, "No. I'm sorry, Tracy, but this is something I've got to talk to Steve about alone."

Tracy bit her lip, pouted, and went out, closing the door.

"I think you just blew your love life," Steve said. "What's so important?"

Mark Taylor took a breath and blew it out again. He shook his head. He did not look happy. "Steve, look. I'm working for you. You're my client. I gotta protect you. But I got a moral dilemma here."

"Well, let's have it."

"Look, Steve. You know I got a pipeline into police headquarters. Well, that man is very important to me. So important, I don't want to use his name, if you know what I mean. Well, he gave me some information and it's hot. The thing is, it's too hot. It's burning. And because of that, no one's supposed to know about it."

Steve looked at Mark impatiently. "So?"

"So, if I tell you, you'll know. And if you use it, people will know you know. And they'll want to know how you found out. And the thing is, this information is so protected, there are only a few sources it could have come from. You see what I mean? There's a good chance my man's cover could be blown."

Steve frowned. "I see."

"Look," Mark said. "I know you're a lawyer. You can't make any promises. You gotta do what's best for your clients. But I'm begging you. If I tell you this, if there's any way you can, don't use it."

Steve shook his head. "Jesus, Mark."

"I know, I know," Mark said. "It's a bitch. So?"

Steve shook his head. "You said it yourself. I can't make any promises. You wanna tell me or not?"

Mark sighed. "I can't hold it out. It's a murder case. If I didn't tell you, and your client was convicted, I couldn't live with myself."

"All right, Mark, you understand the situation. You got the information. You wanna shoot, shoot."

"O.K.," Mark said. "Pauline Keeling."

Steve stared at him. "Who?"

"Pauline Keeling," Mark said. "She's the best kept secret in this whole case. Well, Pauline Keeling happens to be—or perhaps I should say, *claims* to be—Bradshaw's common-law wife."

"What?"

"That's right."

"How'd the cops find her?"

"They didn't. She went to them."

"You're kidding."

"No. Here's how I got the story. After the murder, after Marilyn had been arrested and charged, a woman named Pauline Keeling shows up at headquarters claiming to be Bradshaw's common-law wife. She read there was money found on the body. She wants the money. She claims she was his common-law wife, and if Bradshaw left no will, the money should go to her."

Steve was excited. "When did she show up? How long has she been in town? Has she been to his apartment?"

"That's the whole thing," Mark said. "The way I got it, she hit town two weeks before the murder. She didn't move in with Bradshaw, she was living somewhere else. Naturally, that weakens her claim. But as I understand it, she *had* called on Bradshaw at his apartment."

"Then her fingerprints would be there."

Taylor nodded gloomily. "Yeah."

"And might even be the unidentified ones currently on display in court."

"That's right."

"Jesus Christ. Where is she now?"

"Same place she's been staying since she hit town. In a furnished room in Queens. Astoria."

"She under police guard?"

"Not that I know."

"Got the address?"

"Yeah." Taylor sighed. "Look, Steve, that's everything I know. How are you gonna play it?"

Steve gave him a look. "How do you think I'm going to play it, Mark?"

Steve pressed the intercom. "Tracy."

Tracy's voice showed she was still angry about being excluded from the interview. "Yes."

"Grab your steno pad and get in here." Steve looked at Mark, then back to the intercom. "We're going to make out a subpoena."

41.

IT WAS a second floor walk-up on Astoria Boulevard. The foyer door was open. Steve stopped Mark Taylor on the stairs.

"Now look. We don't *say* we're cops. We just walk in and start talking."

"You don't look like a cop," Taylor said.

"How would she know? I'm an undercover detective, for Christ's sake. If we can make her think we're cops, that's fine. Otherwise, we just play it the best we can."

"Right."

"Keep the subpoena in your pocket. Don't show it. Don't serve it until I give the signal."

"Right."

"You go first. You're big and beefy, you look more like a cop."

"Thanks a lot. What should I say?"

"I don't know. We're here to talk to her about the trial. Just wing it."

"Great."

They went up the stairs, found the door, and knocked. There was the sound of footsteps and then a woman opened the door. She had dark, teased hair. She was about forty, but had sought to disguise the fact by the use of too much makeup. The end result, Steve thought, was to make her look closer to fifty.

"Yes?" she said.

"Miss Keeling," Taylor said. "We're sorry to disturb you, but it's about the trial."

Pauline Keeling frowned. "What about it?"

Steve pushed forward. "That's just it. We want to keep you out of it if that's at all possible. It may not be possible."

The woman's face fell. "But . . . but the District Attorney said—"

"Yeah, I know what he said. Look, we shouldn't be discussing this in the hall."

"Oh. Yes. I'm sorry. Won't you come in?"

Mark Taylor and Steve Winslow stepped into a small, poorly furnished room, which appeared to have no kitchen facilities. All in all, Steve figured, it must be a depressing place to live.

Pauline Keeling looked around helplessly, feeling impelled to ask her visitors to sit down, but not knowing where to suggest.

"Well, what's this all about?" she said.

Mark looked at Steve to take the initiative.

He did. "I'm sorry, Miss Keeling, but we have to go over your story one more time. I know Mr. Dirkson doesn't want you to appear in court, but it may be unavoidable. What it boils down to is, can you answer our questions well enough here, or do we have to put you on the stand?"

"No, no," she said, quickly. "I don't want to go on the stand."

"I know," Steve said. "And I realize this is going to be a hardship for you, but we have to take it from the beginning."

"The beginning?"

"Yeah," Taylor said. "You come to town and looked up Bradshaw?"

She looked at him. "Blake," she said. "Donald Blake."

"Sorry," Taylor said. "Yes. Donald Blake."

She smiled sadly. "Yeah. That was the whole problem. Bradshaw. I looked for Donald Blake, and he was David C. Bradshaw. The man never learned, you know. Some men are like that. They just never learn."

"Go on," Steve said.

She fixed him with a hard eye. "Look, I know what you're thinking. I didn't come with him. He came out here, I came and found him. But that doesn't make any difference. I lived with him for eight years as his wife. Whether he left me or not, that still makes me his common-law wife, and I'm entitled to what he had."

"No one's trying to prove you're not," Taylor said.

She fixed him with that look again. "That's not the way Dirkson was talking."

"Of course not," Steve said. "You can't expect him to hand over the money to the first person who comes and asks for it. You have a claim, and it would appear to be a legitimate claim. But it has to be checked out, and the final determination isn't up to us. You just have to be patient."

She exhaled heavily. "Yeah. Patient."

"So let's get on with it. You came out here and you looked up Donald Blake. How long ago was that?"

"About two weeks ago."

"And what happened?"

"The usual. He was glad to see me, but he wasn't glad to see me. At least, he wasn't glad to see me right then. The timing was bad, that's the way he put it." She shook her head. "The big jerk. I was all set to move in with him, but he wouldn't have it. Said he was on to something. My being around would mess it up."

"Did he tell you what it was?"

"No, he never did. Secretive, that was him, you know? Always concocting the wild schemes, never letting me in on them.

"Unless they paid off, of course. If they paid off, he'd strut around like a rooster, crowing about how smart he was. But not this time. I mean, I come all the way out from Chicago, and it's 'Hi, hello, good to see you, now get out of here.' He fixed me up with this room." She looked around. Shrugged. "Great, huh?"

"This conversation you're talking about," Taylor said. "When you looked him up—that was in his apartment, right?"

She looked at him. "Of course it was in his apartment. Where else would it be? Not that we were there long. He got me out of there fast. Stashed me here."

"He come to see you?" Steve asked.

"Oh, sure. Whenever he had the time. Big, busy man. Once or twice a week, if I was lucky."

"But you never went back there?"

"No. Not with this big, heavy scheme he was setting up."

"You didn't know it was blackmail?" Steve said.

Now she gave him the cold stare. "Blackmail? Who said anything about blackmail? That D.A. can have any damn theories he wants, but nobody's proven any blackmail. No charge has even been brought. As far as I'm concerned, that money was Donald Blake's, and now that money is rightfully mine."

"I understand your contention," Steve said. "Personally, I'm not challenging it. I'm just trying to discuss what happened. Now, as I understand it, after that first time, when you looked Donald Blake up, you've never been back to his apartment?"

"That's right. But I tell you, that's got nothing to do with whether or not I was his common-law wife, and—"

"I'm sure it doesn't," Steve said. "And I'm not trying to contest your claim. Now, those times Donald Blake called on you—did he ever say anything about what he was doing?"

She shook her head. "No. I told you. Not a word."

"Never mentioned Marilyn Harding?"

"No."

"Or Douglas Kemper?"

"No."

"Or the Harding family at all?"

"No."

Steve frowned. "O.K. Let's get to the day of the murder. If the defense should put you on the stand and try to make a case for the fact that *you* killed Donald Blake, what would happen then?"

"They'd have a hard time," she said. "At five o'clock that afternoon, I had an appointment with my hairdresser."

"Where?"

She jerked her thumb. "Here. Right down the street." She frowned. "You guys checked this all out already."

"I know," Steve said. "But I told you. We have to go over it one more time."

"Why?" she said. "I'm telling the truth. You think I can't tell the same story straight twice?"

"Not at all," Steve said. "And I think that will do it."

Mark Taylor looked at Steve inquiringly. Steve shook his head. "Sorry we bothered you, Miss Keeling. But that's our job."

She ushered them to the door. "But you'll keep in touch,' she said.

"Don't worry."

"And no one else touches that money?"

"You can bank on it."

They came out the front door onto the street.

Taylor stopped, said, "Thanks, Steve."

Steve sighed. "Don't thank me. She's got an unimpeachable alibi. If she was in Queens getting her hair done at five o'clock, there's no way she gets to Bradshaw's in time."

"We could have got the name of the place and checked it out."

"She says the cops have checked it out, and I'll bet they have, too. There's no way she could have done it.

"But don't be too hasty with your thanks. Even so, she's a beautiful red herring, and if worst comes to worst, I just might have to use her. But for the time being, we let her go."

"Fine by me," Taylor said. "So what do we do now?"

Steve rubbed his head. "God, I'm tired," he said. "I'll tell you. Now we beat it back to the office, put our heads together and try to figure what the fuck all this means."

42.

"ASK ME questions."

Steve Winslow was sprawled out in Mark Taylor's overstuffed clients' chair.

"What kind of questions?" Taylor said.

Taylor was seated at his desk.

Tracy Garvin was seated in a straight chair and was holding her shorthand notebook.

Steve Winslow had just finished going over the entire facts of the case as he knew them. He figured just talking it out would do some good. Mark and Tracy had listened without interruption while Steve rambled on. It was a confused stream of consciousness jumble of facts and theories, and when he finished, Steve Winslow was exhausted.

"Any questions. Anything you can think of. Anything you'd like to know, no matter how trivial. Just ask 'em."

"Me too?" Tracy said.

"Damn right," Steve said. "You think of something, fire away."

"O.K.," Tracy said. "Why didn't Bradshaw want Pauline Keeling around?"

Steve chuckled. "Too easy. You didn't meet the woman. You wouldn't want her around, either."

"Who killed Bradshaw?" Taylor said.

"Come on, Mark," Steve said. "If we could answer that, we wouldn't be doing this."

"All right, then," Taylor said, "who got there first, Marilyn or Kemper?"

"Gotta be Marilyn," Steve said. "That's the only way it makes any sense. Kemper missed her at the coffee shop. By the time he got downtown, Marilyn had been in and out."

"But if that's true," Tracy said, "when Kemper got there he found Bradshaw dead."

"Right," Steve said.

"Then who was the man the witness heard arguing with Bradshaw?"

"That's the key question," Steve said. "Everything points to Kemper. Except he had to come second. Marilyn had already been in and out. Bradshaw was already dead. You can't argue with a dead man."

"What if there were two men?" Tracy said.

Steve frowned. "What?"

"Well, you say Bradshaw was already dead. The witness heard an argument. She couldn't identify the voices. Everyone's assuming one of them was Bradshaw, but what if it wasn't? What if he's already dead and the argument is between two other men?"

"One of whom is Kemper?"

"Not necessarily," Tracy said.

Taylor grinned. "You pull this out of one of those mysteries you read?"

Tracy gave him a dirty look.

"No, no. Go on," Steve said. "I like this. This is just what I need. Tell me about the two men."

Tracy warmed right up to it. "The two men killed Bradshaw. I don't know who, I don't know why, but say they do. They just killed him, and they're about to leave when Marilyn Harding arrives. They're trapped in the apartment. They hide in the bedroom. The door is open. Marilyn Harding walks in and finds Bradshaw dead. As you say, she immediately assumes Kemper did it. She's in an absolute panic, and she gets out of there.

"The two men come out of the bedroom and they have an argument. About what, I don't know. Maybe one of them thought the girl saw them and he wanted to kill her too. The other one didn't. Whatever. Anyway, they fight. At any rate, the witness hears the argument and calls the cops. While she's calling them, the two men leave. Douglas Kemper arrives right on their heels, finds the dead body, assumes Marilyn killed him, and makes up the bullshit story he told you."

Steve leaned back in the chair and frowned. "I like it. It takes everything into account and gets our clients off the hook—that's mainly why I like it. But Jesus Christ."

"What?" Tracy said.

"Well, look at the schedule. You got two unidentified men, Marilyn Harding, Douglas Kemper, me, and the cops all arriving at Bradshaw's apartment in the space of about a half hour. I mean, hell, the schedule was damn tight without throwing in two unidentified men."

"It's damn tight, but it happened," Tracy said.

"It did for a fact," Steve said. He leaned back in the chair. "Go on. Ask me more questions."

"What happened to the twelve grand?" Taylor said.

"Now there is a damn good question," Steve said. "Ten grand found in the hallway. Ten grand found on the body. Twelve grand disappeared. So where the hell did it go? Obviously, someone took it. The question is who?"

"The two men who killed Bradshaw," Tracy said, excitedly. "They killed him and took the money."

"Then they're mighty selective," Steve said, "if they took that twelve grand and left the other twenty grand there."

"Ten grand was in a money belt. They wouldn't know he had it."

"And the other ten grand. Who took it and hid it in the upstairs hallway? If you're telling me they did that, then the question is why?"

"Yeah, but maybe they didn't," Tracy said. "Maybe someone else put the money there."

"Who?"

Tracy shrugged. "Bradshaw."

"Bradshaw?"

"Sure," Tracy said. "He knew they were coming and he didn't want to have the money on him."

"But he didn't care about the other money?" Steve said. "You see, it just doesn't make sense."

"Maybe it does," Mark Taylor said. "The ten grand hidden in the hallway was the ten grand stolen from you. Bradshaw had to know you had the numbers on those bills. He didn't want to be found with them in his possession. So he hid 'em outside his apartment. The other ten grand's in his money belt. He's got it, and he doesn't care who knows it. He particularly *wants* Marilyn to know it."

"And Kemper's twelve grand?"

"That was in small bills, wasn't going to do Bradshaw any good, except as cash. So maybe he put it in the bank."

Steve shook his head. "You checked out his bank account with the teller. If there'd been a twelve grand deposit, wouldn't he have told you?"

"That's right, he would," Taylor said. "But that might not be his only account, Or he might have a safe deposit box somewhere."

"That's an idea," Steve said. "And we can check into it. Make a note to see if David C. Bradshaw or Donald Blake had any other bank accounts or safe deposit boxes. O.K. More questions."

"O.K.," Tracy said. "Why did Bradshaw come to your office?"

"What?"

"Why did Bradshaw come to your office? That was the original question, right? Way back when we started. That was why you thought he had to be your client. Because as soon as he realized he was being followed, he came right to your office. You said the only way that made sense was if he'd sent the money.

"But he wasn't your client. Douglas Kemper is. Douglas Kemper sent the money. So why did Bradshaw come to your office?"

"I know the answer," Steve said. "Kemper told me. When he

paid off Bradshaw, he threatened him with me. Told him I was his lawyer. That's how Bradshaw knew."

Tracy shook her head. "Not good enough."

"Why not?"

"Come on," Tracy said. "Bradshaw was a blackmailer. You know damn well Marilyn Harding wasn't the only person in the world he was putting the bite on. Or Douglas Kemper for that matter. He was bound to have had lots of irons in the fire.

"So what happens? He walks out of his apartment. He sees he's being followed. He immediately says, 'Steve Winslow,' and comes right to your office just because Kemper told him you're his lawyer. I don't care how smart Bradshaw is, that was a hell of a leap of logic, don't you think?"

"It was, but it happened. The guy came here."

"Yeah, but I still say why? I mean, look what happened. Marilyn Harding calls on Bradshaw. She leaves. Bradshaw leaves. He makes a phone call. He walks a block. He makes another phone call. Next thing you know, he's ditched his shadows and he's in your office demanding to know why you're having him followed."

Steve Winslow sat up straight in his chair. "Son of a bitch!" he said. "Son of a fucking bitch! Mark!"

"Yeah?"

"The phone calls."

Mark Taylor looked at Steve in dismay. "Jesus, Steve, I can't trace those calls. If I were the F.B.I., maybe, but you're talking quarter calls from a public pay phone, and—"

"No, no," Steve said. "I don't expect you to trace them. But you got your operative's notes there? I want to know where the calls were from."

"From? They're from pay phones. One was a pay phone on the corner, and one was in a drug store."

"Right," Steve said. "Where?"

"Hang on a minute. Let me dig it out," Mark said. He went over to a cabinet, wrestled through some files, and pulled out a folder. "O.K., here we go. The first call was from a drug store on the corner of 3rd Street and Avenue C. The other call was from a pay phone on the corner of 3rd Street and Avenue B."

"Those are the corners on Bradshaw's block, right?"

"Right."

"O.K. Good. Tracy, got your steno pad?"

"Yeah."

"Fine. We're going to make a list."

"What's up, Steve?" Mark said.

"I'm not sure," Steve said. "I want to try a little experiment."

"To prove what?"

"That remains to be seen. I won't know unless it happens. I haven't figured it all out yet. But I just want to try something."

Tracy had opened the steno pad. "All set," she said.

"Good," Steve said. "Now I want you to make a list."

"A list of what?"

"Names. Names of people involved in the case. Start with David C. Bradshaw and Donald Blake."

Tracy's pencil flew over the pad. "Yeah?"

"Let's see. Marilyn Harding, Douglas Kemper, and Phyllis Kemper."

"You want them as a group?"

"No. It's a list. One name to a line."

"O.K."

"Harry Dirkson."

"What?" Taylor said.

"Sure," Steve said. "Harry Dirkson. He's involved in the case, isn't he?"

Taylor shook his head. "I wish I knew what you were getting at."

"Probably better you don't," Steve said. "Put down Dirkson."

"Got him. Who's next?"

"Mark Taylor."

"What?" Taylor said.

"Sure," Steve said. "You're involved in the case, aren't you?"

"Steve, I don't want my name on a list."

"Relax. You feel picked on? O.K. After Mark Taylor, put down Steve Winslow and Tracy Garvin."

Taylor stared at him. "Steve, what the hell are you doing?"

"I'm having fun. It happens to be the first time in this damn case I've had a chance to have fun, and you're not going to spoil it for me. How many names is that?"

Tracy counted up. "That's nine."

"We need a few more. All right, Charles Miltner. And you got the names of his men in your notes?"

"Yeah."

"O.K. Copy 'em in. There are four of 'em, right?"

"Right."

Tracy looked up the names and copied them in.

"O.K.," Steve said. "Read me back the list."

"David C. Bradshaw. Donald Blake. Marilyn Harding. Douglas Kemper. Phyllis Kemper. Harry Dirkson. Mark Taylor. Steve Winslow. Tracy Garvin. Charles Miltner. Jason Fisher. Saul Burroughs. Fred Grimes. Michael Reed."

"Fine," Steve said. "And last but not least, Pauline Keeling."

"Steve," Mark said. "Please. Don't blow that for me."

"Relax," Steve said. "All right, Tracy, look. I want you to type up that list. One name to a line, with a space between 'em so they stand out. That should just about fill a page, right?"

"Yeah," Tracy said. "Should be fine."

"Good. Now, I want you to type the list twice. The second time you type it, leave off the name, Pauline Keeling. Got a typewriter she can use, Mark?"

"By the reception desk."

"O.K. Come on. Let's type 'em up."

They went out to the reception area and Tracy typed the lists. Steve took them and looked at them. He nodded.

"O.K. Now you got a metal clipboard? One that looks official?"

"Yeah."

Taylor rummaged in the desk and came out with a clipboard. Steve took the first list, the one with Pauline Keeling's name on it, and clipped it on. He held it up and inspected it.

"Fine," he said. "Now look, Mark, you got a female operative? One you can really trust?"

"I can scare one up, Steve, but it's gonna take some time."

"We don't have time. Tracy, how'd you like to do a little detective work?"

Tracy looked at him. "You're kidding?"

"Not at all."

"You're on. What have I got to do?"

"O.K. Look, Mark. Here's what I want you to do. Take Tracy down to Bradshaw's. Then I want you to get her in the foyer door. You won't have any trouble, a credit card will do."

"Are we gonna get into trouble over this?" Taylor said.

"We're in trouble already. I'm trying to get us out. Now, the witness across the hall. What's her name again?"

"Margaret Millburn."

"Fine. You go in, you have Tracy knock on her door. It's gotta be Tracy, cause she probably wouldn't open it for you. You keep in the background. But when the door's open, you're there. See what I mean?"

"Yeah."

Steve looked at Tracy. "All right. This is important. You don't *say* you're cops. Got it?"

"Right. What *do* we say?"

"Sorry to inconvenience you, it's about the trial, you've been asked to verify the names on that list. That's all you say. Don't give her a chance to think about it, just hand her the list.

"And that's where you play detective. You watch her carefully when she reads the names. See if there's any reaction."

Taylor's eyebrows raised. "Oh, shit, Steve, I get it. You mean Pauline Keeling may have been lying. She may have been there more than once. You know this may fry my source."

"Come on, Mark," Steve said. "If Pauline Keeling killed him, you can't expect me to hush it up. Short of that, I'm going to protect you any way I can. That's why there are two lists."

Steve turned to Tracy Garvin. "Look, Tracy. I know you're going to love playing detective, and you're going to want to make a big score. But some things work and some don't. You can't push it. You just do the best you can. The main thing is, get her to take the list. Put it in her hands, first thing. If you can get her to look at it, great, but if she refuses and hands it back, well, it's not your fault, there's nothing we can do about it, and you shouldn't go kicking yourself in the head about it all night."

Tracy looked disappointed. "And that's all we do?" she said.

"Believe me, that's a lot," Steve said. "But, no, that's not all. Mark, after Tracy's done her stuff, no matter how it goes, slap a subpoena on her."

Mark looked at him. "On a prosecution witness?"

"That's right," Steve said. "Only don't play it too soon. Give Tracy every chance to do her stuff first. But make sure you get it served."

"You're going to put Margaret Millburn on the stand?" Taylor said. "What the hell are you going to have her testify to?"

Steve shrugged. "Anything she knows."

43.

STEVE WINSLOW was late getting to court. That was because he'd had his first good night's sleep in a week. He'd left Mark Taylor and Tracy Garvin at the office making out the subpoena, told them not to call him to report anything short of Margaret Millburn positively identifying Pauline Keeling as the murderer, gone home, flopped on his bed, and gone out like a light.

He'd slept long and late, got up, showered, shaved, had breakfast, and caught a cab to the court.

Mark Taylor and Tracy Garvin were waiting for him outside the courtoom.

"Jesus Christ," Taylor said. "I thought you weren't going to make it."

"Never fear," Steve said. "So, how'd it go?"

"Like a charm," Taylor said. "Tracy wanted to call you and tell you, but I wouldn't let her."

"My appreciation will be reflected in your check," Steve said.

Tracy looked ready to explode.

"O.K.," Steve said. "Let's have it. She took the clipboard?"

"She sure did."

"She read the list?"

"Yes, and that's why I wanted to call you. We got a reaction. I'm sure of it. It hit her, and it hit her hard."

"Well, that's what I was looking for," Steve said. "Mark did right. I said not to call, even if you got a reaction."

"Yeah," Tracy said. "But it wasn't what you wanted. I'm sure of it."

"Oh?"

"Tracy has this theory—" Mark said.

"It's not a theory, damn it," Tracy said. "I know what I saw."

"I was there too," Mark said, "and—"

Steve held up his hands. "Hey kids, let's not bicker. I gotta go to court. One at a time. Tracy, what did you see?"

Tracy gave Mark Taylor a look, then turned to Steve. "I saw her react. Just like you wanted. Only thing was, it wasn't to the name Pauline Keeling."

"Oh?"

"Mark thinks I'm crazy. But I was watching her carefully. Pauline Keeling was the last name on the list. I swear to you, she wasn't halfway down the list when she reacted."

"Really?"

"Yeah," Taylor said. "That's her theory, and you're not going to shake it. Phyllis Kemper happens to be the fifth name on the list. Tracy thinks it's a good shot."

"And you don't?"

Taylor shrugged. "Personally I'd love it to be true. But I just can't see it. I mean, I'd give anything for it not to be Pauline Keeling. But Phyllis Kemper? The witness knows all about Phyllis Kemper. Why would that name cause a reaction? Whereas, Pauline Keeling's never been mentioned, and finding that name on that list would have to be a shock."

"I know what I saw," Tracy said.

"Fine," Steve said. "You serve the subpoena?"

"Yeah. No problem."

"The witness here in court?"

"She's here."

"Fine. Now, Tracy, I want you to sit where you've always sat. Will that be a problem?"

"No. I already saved the seat."

"Fine. Now, be ready. I may ask you to stand up in court. If I do, don't worry. You won't have to do anything."

"I wouldn't mind that."

"I know. I'm just telling you. Mark, you got the clipboard?"

Taylor tapped his briefcase. "Got it right here."

"Is it in anything?"

"It's in a paper bag."

"Fine. And you switched the lists?"

"You bet I did. Just as quick as I could. The list on the clipboard does *not* have the name Pauline Keeling."

"Good. Let me have it."

Taylor opened the briefcase and took out the paper bag. Steve took it, nodded to the two of them, and pushed through the doors into the courtroom.

Fitzpatrick was pacing up and down by the defense table.

"There you are," he said. "I didn't think you were going to make it."

"Never miss a court date," Steve said.

Fitzpatrick pointed to a copy of the New York *Post* lying on the defense table. "HARDING MURDERED, DEFENSE CHARGES," the headline read. "You see the paper?"

"I saw the headline," Steve said.

"Not that," Fitzpatrick said. "I mean this."

Fitzpatrick took the paper and flipped it open. Steve looked. It was a cartoon, a caricature of the two of them, standing in court side by side like some singing duo, Fitzpatrick in a three-piece suit, and Winslow in close to rags. A word balloon coming out of both of their mouths said, "Your Honor, we object." The caption beneath the cartoon read: "THE ODD COUPLE."

"I missed that," Steve said.

"Oh, did you?" Fitzpatrick grumbled. "Well I'll bet you none of the partners in my firm did. I'm a senior partner, for Christ's sake, and I'm going to be lucky to get out of this with my job."

Fitzpatrick tossed the paper back onto the table. He pointed to the paper bag. "What the hell is that?"

"That's our defense," Steve said. "Don't open it. I don't want anyone to see what's inside."

Fitzpatrick looked at him. "What the hell are you up to? What's going on? I understand you served a subpoena."

"That's right."

"On Margaret Millburn. A prosecution witness."

"Yeah. Is she here?"

"She's here all right, but she's hopping mad. So is Dirkson, for that matter."

"Is he charging us with abuse of process?"

"Not yet, but he isn't happy, and he wants to know what the hell is going on."

"I hope you didn't tell him."

"How could I tell him? *I* don't know what the hell's going on." Fitzpatrick mopped his brow. "Tell me, do you do this deliberately, or does it just happen that the people you work with wind up having nervous breakdowns?"

"Relax, Fitzpatrick. I'll handle the questioning."

"Yeah. That's fine. But if you don't come up with some good questions, and if she doesn't come up with some good answers—if you can't show a definite purpose for calling this witness—then Dirkson *is* going to hit us with abuse of process. And from what I know of Judge Graves, that charge is going to stick."

Harry Dirkson lumbered over. "You subpoenaed Margaret Millburn."

"That I did," Steve said.

"Why?"

"Because I want her to testify."

"She's already testified. She was a prosecution witness."

"And now she's a defense witness."

Dirkson shook his head. "You can't do that. She was a prosecution witness. You had a chance to cross-examine her. You can't call her as your witness just to cross-examine her some more. Unless you have new evidence, unless you have a definite plan in mind, that's abuse of process."

"I'm familiar with the law," Steve said. "You want anything else?"

"I just wanted to warn you," Dirkson said.

Steve smiled. "Thanks for your concern."

Dirkson bit his lip, turned, and stalked back to the prosecution table.

Judge Graves entered and the bailiff called court to order.

"Call your next witness," Judge Graves said.

Steve rose. "Your Honor, we call Margaret Millburn."

Judge Graves frowned, but said nothing.

Margaret Millburn entered the courtroom from the back. She looked angry and tight-lipped. She strode down the aisle and took her place on the stand.

"Now, Miss Millburn," Judge Graves said. "You have already been sworn. I remind you that you are still under oath. Mr. Winslow, you may proceed."

"Thank you, Your Honor. Miss Millburn, you have already testified in this case, as to hearing an altercation in the decedent's apartment?"

"Objected to," Dirkson said, "as already asked and answered. I submit, Your Honor, that Miss Millburn has already given her testimony in this case, and unless counselor has some definite purpose in mind, his calling this witness to the stand borders on abuse of process."

"I have a definite purpose in mind, Your Honor," Steve said. "But this is a prosecution witness, and I see no reason to disclose the purpose to her. Some of the questions I am asking are necessarily preliminary, and may in essence already have been asked and answered, but I do have a point, and if allowed to proceed, I intend to connect the matter up."

Judge Graves frowned. "You may proceed, Mr. Winslow. But before you do so, let me add my caution to that of Mr. Dirkson. In the event that you do *not* connect the matter up, I trust you are aware of what the consequences might be."

"Yes, Your Honor. Thank you, Your Honor. Now. Miss Millburn, you testified as to an altercation in the decedent's apartment, is that right?"

"That's right."

"You also testified that you knew the decedent only slightly. As his next door neighbor, you had seen him a couple of times in the hall. But you'd never spoken to him other than to say hello. Is that right?"

"Yes it is." Margaret Millburn drew herself up. "And I know nothing about this case other than what I have already testified to in court, and I object to being dragged through it again."

Harry Dirkson grinned.

"I'm sure you do, Miss Millburn," Steve said. "And I'm sorry to inconvenience you. I'll try to make this as brief as possible."

Steve Winslow walked to the defense table. He reached into the paper bag and detached the list of names from the metal clipboard. "Your Honor, I ask that this piece of paper be marked for identification as Defense exhibit A."

Harry Dirkson stood up. "May I see that?"

"Certainly," Steve said, and passed the paper over to him.

Dirkson took it, frowned, and said, "No objection, Your Honor."

The court reporter took the paper and marked it. Steve took it back from him and approached the witness.

"Now, Miss Millburn, I hand you this paper marked for identification as Defense exhibit A, and ask if you have ever seen it before."

The witness took the paper, looked at it, then glared at Steve Winslow.

"Well?" Steve said.

"Yes, I have."

"I want to be sure of this," Steve said. "Will you look at the list again? And read it over to yourself?"

The witness glared at him. Then looked down at the list. A few moments later she looked up. "Yes," she said.

"You've read the list over?"

"Yes, I have."

"And to the best of your recollection, you have seen this list before?"

"Yes."

"Fine," Steve said. He crossed back to the defense table, and took the metal clipboard out of the paper bag. "Your Honor, I ask that this clipboard be marked for identification as Defense exhibit B."

"Any objection?" Judge Graves said.

"None, Your Honor," Dirkson said.

"So ordered."

The reporter marked the clipboard. Steve took it back from him.

"Now," Steve said, "I am going to take the paper, Defense exhibit A, and attach it to the clipboard, Defense exhibit B, and hand it to you and ask you if this is not the way the paper was presented to you when you saw it before."

The witness took the clipboard. "Yes. That's right. It was."

"Fine," Steve said. He looked around the courtroom. "Tracy Garvin. Please stand up."

Tracy got to her feet.

"Now," Steve said. "I ask you to look at the young woman standing in the back of the courtroom, and ask you if you have ever seen her before."

"Objection, Your Honor. Incompetent, irrelevant, and immaterial."

"I'll connect it up in a moment, Your Honor," Steve said.

"I think the connection should come first," Dirkson said.

"Very well," Steve said. "In that case, I will withdraw that question and ask you this: is it not true that the person standing in the back of the courtroom, Tracy Garvin, is the person who handed you the clipboard which you now hold?"

"Objection. Same grounds."

"I can connect it up, Your Honor."

"I still maintain the connection should come first," Dirkson said.

"Very well," Steve said. "Then let me ask you this: did you know that that person standing there is a private detective in my employ? Did you know that the clipboard you are holding in your hand is a highly polished metal clipboard used by private detectives for the purpose of obtaining clear latent prints of suspects?

Did you know that Tracy Garvin, on my instructions, got you to handle that clipboard just as you are holding it now, specifically for the purpose of obtaining your latent prints for comparison? And did you know that when we compared your prints, two of them matched absolutely with the latent prints taken from the decedent's apartment and introduced in evidence here in court?"

Dirkson lunged to his feet. "Objection!" he thundered. "Your Honor—"

Judge Graves' gavel cut him off. "That will do," he snapped. "Court is still in session. Jurors will remain seated. Witness will remain on the stand." Judge Graves paused, took a breath, and then glowered at the defense table. "Attorneys," he said grimly. "In my chambers."

44.

DIRKSON ANGRILY paced up and down in the judge's chambers while he waited for the court reporter to set up his stand.

When everyone was ready, Judge Graves said, "Now, Mr. Dirkson."

"Yes, Your Honor," Dirkson said. He glowered at Winslow and Fitzpatrick. "I charge the asking of that question as misconduct. It is a barefaced lie. Counsel may have obtained the fingerprints of the witness, but he's never compared them to the prints in evidence in court. He doesn't have them. It couldn't have been done. It is a trick. A theatrical grandstand. I charge the asking of that question as misconduct."

Judge Graves turned to Steve. "Mr. Winslow?"

Steve smiled. "I wish the prosecutor would make up his mind. A few minutes ago he was threatening to charge me with abuse of process for having no definite purpose in mind. As I understand it now, his charge is that I *have* a definite purpose in mind, but he doesn't like it."

"Mr. Winslow, the charge is that you are making a false statement in court. That you are claiming to have compared the fingerprints of the witness to those introduced in court, when you have in fact, not. What do you say to that?"

275

"I say it's none of his business," Steve said.

Judge Graves' face darkened. "Mr. Winslow, this is not to be taken lightly."

"If he *did* compare those prints," Dirkson put in, "I charge him with tampering with a prosecution exhibit."

"You see, Your Honor," Steve said. "As far as Dirkson's concerned, I'm damned if I did, and damned if I didn't. I still maintain it's none of his business. And whether I compared those prints or not is totally irrelevant. And I beg to correct the District Attorney—I did *not* make the statement in court that I had compared those prints. I merely asked the witness if she *knew* that I did. I am asking her for her own knowledge, which is what I have every right to do.

"And I maintain that however objectionable the prosecution may feel the form of that question to be, the answer to it is entirely relevant. This witness has testified that she was never in Bradshaw's apartment. If her testimony is true, she will answer by saying, 'no, you must be mistaken, those couldn't be my fingerprints, because I was never there.' If she *can't* answer that way, it means that her testimony was false. That means she's guilty of perjury. And if she's guilty of perjury, she's certainly a biased witness. And that bias is something I have a legal right to establish. The witness has given testimony on a very material point, i.e., the altercation in Bradshaw's apartment at the time of the murder. Therefore, if there is the slightest chance that she committed perjury, I have every right to bring it out."

"Only by legitimate means, Your Honor," Dirkson said. "Counsel's question is entirely irregular."

Judge Graves took a breath. "Mr. Dirkson. On the surface, it might appear to be. However, as counsel has said, he is merely asking the witness whether she knew certain things to be true. But I think you're missing the point here. A young woman is on trial for murder. If there is a chance that one of the prosecution's witnesses is committing perjury, I want to know it. And I think you should want to know it too.

"However," Judge Graves went on, turning to Fitzpatrick and

Winslow. "Once that charge is brought up, if she is *not* committing perjury, I want to know that too.

"I am now going to rule. To begin with, the objection is overruled. I want the question answered. And I want it answered without any sparring between counsel. And I am referring to that particular *line* of questioning, Mr. Dirkson. I don't want you jumping up on the follow-up question, unless a new point is raised. As far as this line of questioning goes, I'm going to allow Mr. Winslow to pursue it to its conclusion. But—"

Judge Graves turned to Steve Winslow. His face was dark. "I'm allowing this on your assurance that you have a definite purpose in mind. In the event that you do not, in the event that it should turn out that you called this witness merely to harass her, to make her a red herring—in the event that it turns out you had no foundation whatever for asking the question that you did, that in fact you had *no* definite purpose in mind, then Mr. Winslow, you and Mr. Fitzpatrick will find that you have laid yourselves wide open for an abuse of process charge. And believe me, this is no idle threat. So, before we resume, I would like to give you one last opportunity to consider: would you care to withdraw your question?"

Fitzpatrick looked as if he were going to be ill. He looked at Steve Winslow with pleading eyes.

Steve looked at him. It could be Fitzpatrick's career. It could be his too, what little career he had. And he had so little to go on. Such a thin thread.

For a second he hesitated.

But only for a second.

"We do not, Your Honor," Steve said. "The question stands."

45.

JUDGE GRAVES looked down from the bench. "Ladies and gentlemen of the jury. I am sorry for the interruption. We are ready to proceed. The objection has been overruled. The witness will answer. The court reporter will read back the question."

There was a delay while the court reporter shuffled through the tapes. The question was way back, since he'd had to record the entire session in chambers. Finally he found it, and droned it out in an expressionless voice, ending with, "And did you know that when we compared your prints, two of them matched absolutely with the latent prints taken from the decedent's apartment and introduced in evidence here in court."

"Do you understand the question?" Steve said.

The witness took a breath. "Yes. I do."

"Then answer it."

She hesitated. "I don't know. I can't explain it."

"You don't know?"

"No."

"You don't know how your fingerprints could have got in Bradshaw's apartment?"

"No, I don't."

"You were never in there on any occasion?"

"I—"

"Think. It's important. You're under oath. How could your fingerprints have gotten there?"

The witness's eyes flicked around the courtroom. "I . . . I . . ."

"Yes," Steve said. "Go on."

"I remember now. I was in there once."

Steve tried hard to keep his face from looking like he had just gotten a death row reprieve. A glance at the defense table told him Fitzpatrick was not doing quite that good a job. He looked positively ecstatic.

But Dirkson looked positively murderous.

"Oh, were you now?" Steve said. "And when was that?"

"Silly of me. It was a long time ago. Right after he moved in. I remember now. I met him in the hall. He called me in, asked me something about the previous tenant. I don't remember what it was. Something about the apartment. Was some shelf in the kitchen permanent, or had the previous tenant put it in."

"So you were in the kitchen of that apartment?"

"Yes. I guess that's right."

"And this was when Donald Blake, the man you knew as Bradshaw, first moved in?"

"That's right."

"You were in his apartment that one time?"

"Yes."

"And you hadn't been back in since? And you hadn't spoken to him since, except to say hello in passing?"

"That's right."

"But you were in his apartment that one time?"

"Yes. I just said I was."

"So when you said in your previous testimony that you had never been in his apartment, you were mistaken, is that right?"

"Yes. I was mistaken."

"I see. And were you perhaps mistaken about any other part of your testimony?"

"No. I wasn't."

"The rest of your testimony is accurate?"

"Yes, it is."

"You were mistaken about that one particular fact?"

"That's right."

"You simply didn't remember, but you remember now?"

"Yes. That's exactly right."

"Before we proceed, I would like to give you a chance to think. Is there anything else that you didn't remember, that you remember now?"

"No, there isn't."

"You remember now that you'd been in Bradshaw's apartment on that one occasion?"

"That's right."

"And if you were in his apartment, you of course spoke to him at that time. I mean, more than just to say hello in passing?"

"I guess so."

"Do you recall what you talked about on that occasion, the occasion when you were in Bradshaw's apartment?"

"No, I don't. Only what I just told you. It was something about the apartment. A shelf or counter or something. I didn't even remember the incident until you reminded me of it."

"You didn't talk about anything else? Anything about his personal life? Or yours?"

"No. Absolutely not."

"And that, to the best of your recollection, is the only time you ever talked to Bradshaw other than to say hello in passing in the hall?"

"That's right."

"And you've never been in his apartment again?"

"No."

"You've never talked to him again, other than the hello in passing we've just mentioned?"

"That's right."

"Did you ever talk to him on the phone?"

"No. Of course not."

"You didn't?"

"No, I didn't."

"You never called him on his phone?"

"No."

"He never called you on yours?"

"No."

"Never?"

"Never."

"Is that so?" Steve said. "I hand you back the clipboard marked Defense exhibit B, and ask you to look at the list."

Steve extended the clipboard, but Margaret Millburn made no move to take it. "Go ahead. You can touch it. You've already admitted being in the apartment. Your fingerprints don't matter now."

Reluctantly, the witness took the list.

"Fine," Steve said. "Now, referring to the paper attached to the clipboard, the paper marked Defense exhibit A, what do you recognize it to be?"

"It's a list of names."

"That's right. A list of names. Now, would you please read the names out loud?"

"I beg your pardon?"

"The names on the list. Read them out loud, please."

Margaret Millburn hesitated. Then she looked down and read off the names in a slow, steady voice, placing no emphasis on any particular name.

"Thank you," Steve said. He took the clipboard, walked back and set it on the defense table. As he did so, Fitzpatrick flashed him a glance of inquiry. Under his breath Steve said, "Hold on to your hat, Fitzpatrick. We're goin' for the gold."

Steve straightened and turned back to the witness. "Miss Millburn. Last night, when you were shown that list of names, the list you've just read into the record, did any name strike you as significant?"

"No."

"No?" Steve said. "That's odd. Suppose I were to tell you that Tracy Garvin, the young woman who showed you that list, noted a definite reaction on your part to one of the names—would that jar your memory any?"

"No, it would not. I don't know what that list is, I don't know where it came from, I don't know what it means. That list has no significance to me."

"And none of the names on that list has any particular significance?"

"No. The names appear to be people involved in this trial. Why that should be important, I couldn't begin to tell you."

"There are many people involved in this trial," Steve said. "But it is my contention that there is one whose name has a special significance to you. Would it change your testimony any to know that the investigator, Tracy Garvin, was convinced that you showed a definite reaction to the name, Phyllis Kemper?"

The witness stared at him. "It most certainly would not."

"It would not?"

"No."

"The name Phyllis Kemper means nothing to you?"

"No, it doesn't."

"Has no special significance?"

"None whatsoever."

"And it is not true that last night when you were handed the clipboard, you reacted to seeing the name Phyllis Kemper?"

"No. It is not true."

There was a pause.

Steve nodded. "You're right, Miss Millburn. I don't think that's true either."

The witness blinked. Stared at him.

Steve shook his head. "No. I think the name you reacted to was the name Mark Taylor."

There was a pause. A time lag in the court, while people caught up with that statement. Mark Taylor? It was clear that most of the people in the court couldn't even place the name.

Most of the people.

On the stand, the witness blinked. Once. Twice. She wet her lips.

"That's true, isn't it, Miss Millburn?" Steve said. "It was the name Mark Taylor that you reacted to, wasn't it?"

"No. No," she said. "It wasn't."

"No?" Steve said. He raised his voice and picked up the pace. "Then perhaps I can refresh your recollection. You have testified, have you not, that you never spoke to the decedent on the phone—that you never called him on his phone and he never called you on yours. Is that right?"

"Yes, that's right."

"Is it, Miss Millburn? I ask you, is it not a fact that on the afternoon of Tuesday the eighth, the man you knew as David C. Bradshaw called you on your telephone in your apartment, and said to you words to this effect: 'I have just left the building and I'm being followed by detectives. I don't want them to know I've spotted them. Here's what I want you to do. I'm going to leave here and walk down the block in front of our building. I want you to look out your window at the car that's tailing me and get the license number. Then I want you to call so-and-so at this phone number and ask him to trace the plate. Tell him it's urgent and to do it right now. Just get the information, and I'll call you right back.'

"And is it not a fact, Miss Millburn, that you did as you were instructed? Is it not a fact that you got the information, and when Bradshaw called you back minutes later, you passed it on to him? Is it not a fact that what you told Bradshaw, when he called you back from a pay phone on the corner, was that the car that was following him was registered to a detective agency? And wasn't the name of the detective who had registered the car, the name that you passed on to David C. Bradshaw—wasn't that name Mark Taylor? Isn't that why the name Mark Taylor has a special significance to you, and isn't that why you reacted so visibly to seeing his name on that list?"

The witness's eyes darted around the courtroom. "No. No," she said. "It's not true."

"It isn't? You deny receiving either of those phone calls?"

"Yes, I do."

"And if the records of the telephone company should show that calls were made from those pay phones to your apartment on the day in question, those records would be in error, is that right?"

"Objection. Argumentative."

"Sustained."

"Do you deny receiving those calls?" Steve persisted.

The witness hesitated. Looked around. "I . . . I . . . "

"It's a simple question," Steve said. "Do you or do you not deny receiving those calls?"

"It's not a simple question," she said. "You ask me if I deny receiving any calls from David C. Bradshaw. I may have received calls from someone else."

Steve shook his head. "Nice try, Miss Millburn, but it's no good. You forget. Bradshaw was being followed by detectives. Those detectives were in Mark Taylor's employ and reported back to him. And those detectives reported the times and places of Bradshaw's phone calls. If you received those calls, they could *only* have been from him."

Margaret Millburn bit her lip.

Steve gave her time to think. He bored right in. "You see, Miss Millburn, it's no use. We can prove you got those calls. Through the phone company, and the testimony of Mark Taylor's men. If you want to try to deny what was said on those calls, that's entirely up to you, but we can prove you got them all right. If we give you enough time, I'm sure you can come up with some plausible explanation for what was said during those calls, but you know and I know what was said, and it's just what I told you. Bradshaw called you, told you he was being followed, and asked you to find who was doing it. Which you did.

"And if you did, it means you and Bradshaw were no casual strangers, as you would like to make it seem. You knew Bradshaw. You knew him well. You knew him before he even moved out here. When the apartment across the hall was about to be vacated, you called him and he snapped it up.

"Now, you've done a good job of keeping your relationship a secret. I happen to know that that was at his insistence, and I happen to know why.

"The fact is, you knew Bradshaw very well, you were in fact intimate with Bradshaw, and you've been in his apartment many times. Is that not a fact?"

"No. No, it's not."

"And is it not a fact that you knew all about the blackmail of Marilyn Harding? That you were in fact Bradshaw's partner in the blackmail of Marilyn Harding?"

Margaret Millburn's face was ashen white. "No. No, it's not."

"Oh isn't it? I think it is. I'm going to tell you what happened, and then you can deny it if you like. You and Bradshaw were close. Damn close. You were his partner. You helped him out. Like tracing the license plate for him. You worked with him. You were a team.

"But no one knew it. Bradshaw insisted on that. Here he moved in across the hall from you and you thought everything would be hunky-dory. Except he didn't want to be seen with you. He wanted your relationship to be a secret. You accepted it. You bought the reason he gave you—that if your relationship was known it would ruin some scam or other.

"But after a while that wore thin. You demanded to know the real reason. And after a while you found out why.

"He was two-timing you, wasn't he? He has another woman on the side. And that wasn't all. He was also cutting you out. He was two-timing you as a woman, and cutting you out as a partner. He was raking in money he wasn't telling you about, and spending it on another woman. When you found out you were furious, and for good reason."

Steve broke off the attack. He stood there looking at the witness for a moment. Then he shrugged his shoulders and said gently, "And that's why you killed him."

Margaret Millburn sat stunned. Steve's casual, flat statement was harder to deal with than a shouted accusation would have been. Then she could have shouted her denial back. But what he'd said wasn't even a question. It was just a simple statement of an assumed fact. She was like a batter expecting a fast ball and getting a change-up. Suddenly off-stride, she had to supply all the power, put all the force into her denial. "No!" she said. "I didn't!"

Steve immediately jumped back on the attack. "Yes, you did, and I can prove it. I'll tell you how you did it.

"You knew he was shaking down Marilyn Harding. That was

one of the things you managed to find out, but you didn't know for how much. But you knew she was calling on him. And you knew she was being followed by detectives—Bradshaw had spotted them when she came to his apartment, and he'd told you that much, probably as another reason why you shouldn't be seen with him. So you knew Bradshaw had the goods on her, and you knew he was still shaking her down, and so you waited for your chance.

"Which brings us to the day of the murder. From the window of your apartment you saw Marilyn Harding enter the building. You even spotted the detectives she had on her tail. You listened at your door while she called on Bradshaw. You heard her go in. And you heard her go out. And that's when you knew you had the perfect frame. Marilyn Harding was being blackmailed—she called on the blackmailer and she killed him.

"It was too good to pass up. As soon as Marilyn Harding left, you knocked on Bradshaw's door. He let you in, of course. You made some excuse about wanting a drink, went in the kitchen, got the knife, and killed him.

"Then you searched the body. You knew he'd been shaking Marilyn down, and you knew he'd been holding out on your. You wanted your share.

"You found ten thousand dollars in one thousand dollar bills. You wanted that money, but you were scared. You knew the cops would be coming. And you knew the numbers on those bills could be traced. You didn't dare keep those bills on you.

"So you took a chance. You hid them in the upstairs hallway, hoping they wouldn't be found. If the cops didn't find them, you were going to retrieve them later. If they did, well it was just too bad, but at least the bills could be traced to Marilyn, and that would clinch the case.

"And that's when you pulled your masterstroke. That's when you did the one thing you thought would frame Marilyn Harding and exonerate you of the crime.

"You called the police. You called up and reported an altercation in Bradshaw's apartment. That would get the police there right away and fix the time of death as just about the time the detectives would have to testify Marilyn Harding had gone to the apartment. And you, having reported the altercation, would be the last person the police would suspect. It was brilliant.

"But then things started going wrong. First, the police found the ten grand you'd hidden in the hallway. All right, it cost you the money, but it would crucify her. Only it didn't. Bradshaw had pulled a fiddle, and that money wasn't Marilyn Harding's ten grand at all. Marilyn Harding's ten grand was found in a money belt on the body. The money found in the hallway was money Bradshaw had withdrawn from the bank himself.

"Of course, that didn't make any sense. Not in terms of your frame-up. Marilyn might have killed Bradshaw, then panicked and ditched the bills in the hallway because she was afraid to have them on her. But why would she have paid Bradshaw, killed him, and then left her ten grand in his money belt? And if she had, who left the ten grand in the hall? It didn't add up, despite what the cops might think.

"It was getting complicated. You'd thought the case against Marilyn Harding would be open and shut. Suddenly it wasn't. Nonetheless, the police took the evidence at face value and arrested Marilyn Harding for the crime.

"That's when you started getting cold feet. You didn't want to go on the stand. You didn't want to submit to the cross-examination you're submitting to now. You knew you couldn't stand up to it, just as you're not standing up to it now.

"And that's when you did a smart thing. Or so you thought. You wanted the prosecution to play down your testimony. In fact, if possible, you wanted them not to call you at all. You knew they were trying to make a case against Marilyn Harding. So when they asked you about the altercation, you told them it was a *man's* voice you heard in the apartment. You figured if you said you heard a man, it would damage the prosecution's case, so they'd try to keep you out of it.

"And it might have worked, except for one thing—Douglas Kemper. The police theory, as it turned out, was that Marilyn Harding and Douglas Kemper were acting in concert. Therefore, your hearing a man's voice didn't bother them at all. And therefore they put you on the stand.

"But you didn't hear a man's voice, did you? You didn't hear any voice at all. You testified to a totally spurious altercation. It never happened. You made it up. You killed Bradshaw, and then you tipped over some furniture so it would look like there'd been an altercation. Then you dashed back to your apartment and you called the police. That's what you did, isn't it, Miss Millburn?"

"No. It's a lie. I didn't."

"Yes you did, and I can prove it. Miss Millburn, do you have a safe deposit box?"

The change of subject was so abrupt the witness said, "What?"

"A safe deposit box. Do you have one? Perhaps one you rented within the last month?"

Margaret Millburn looked at him. Her eyes were wide.

Dirkson came to her rescue. "Objection, Your Honor. Incompetent, irrelevant, and immaterial."

Judge Graves, observing the witness's manner, rather reluctantly said, "Objection sustained."

"Miss Millburn," Steve said, "I can lay the foundation and ask that question again. But I don't have to. I'm just going to tell you how I can prove you killed Donald Blake. You see, when you killed him, you searched the body, and you found the ten thousand dollars, but you found something else too. Bradshaw had a lot of irons in the fire, and he'd pulled another scam. You didn't know about it, and the police *still* don't know about it, but *I* know about it. And I can prove it.

"You know what you found? You found twelve thousand dollars in small bills."

Margaret Millburn reacted.

"That's right, Miss Millburn. You found it, and you took it, and you kept it. You didn't dare keep the ten grand. That was in big bills that could be traced. But the twelve grand was in small bills. You figured no one would have the numbers. So you took a chance. You hid it in your apartment. It was right there in your apartment when you called the cops. You figured they wouldn't search your apartment, and you figured right.

"But you didn't want to leave it there, not after the case broke open, not after things started going wrong. See why I asked about a safe deposit box? Either your bank account will show a twelve thousand dollar cash deposit, or you've got a safe deposit box somewhere with twelve thousand dollars in it. And if you do, after the showing I'm going to be able to make, a court order will open that box."

Margaret Millburn's mouth moved, but no words came out. She swayed slightly.

Steve bored in.

"You killed Bradshaw. You killed him and you took the money. It wasn't in self-defense. It wasn't in the heat of passion. It was a cold-blooded, premeditated crime. It was murder for profit. You set up Marilyn Harding, and you killed Donald Blake. You coldly, ruthlessly, intentionally—"

Margaret Millburn struggled to her feet. "No, No!" she cried. "I swear! I didn't! It was an accident! . . ."

Time stood still.

Margaret Millburn froze, petrified by what she had just said.

No one moved. No one spoke.

An electric silence hung in the air.

No one in the courtroom could quite believe what had just happened.

Steve Winslow could hardly believe it either.

"Son of a bitch," he murmured. "A courtroom confession."

46.

STEVE WINSLOW looked like a prizefighter after the big fight. He was slumped back in his desk chair, totally drained, a can of beer in his hand. He looked as if he didn't have the strength to raise it to his lips.

On the other hand, Mark Taylor and Tracy Garvin were animated. They were sitting there, drinking beer and whooping it up.

"I couldn't believe it," Taylor was saying. "I just couldn't believe it. I'm sitting there in court, and you got the witness on the run, and I'm really digging it cause you'd been off in chambers and things looked pretty sticky and then when you came back she caved in on the fingerprints, and I'm just like everybody else in the courtroom—by that time I figured the list was just a red herring, just a ploy to get her to touch the clipboard and get her to leave her fingerprints. And I know you haven't compared any prints, but she doesn't, and she caves in, and I'm thinking, 'Holy cow, score one for our side!' And the next minute you're back to the clipboard and the list and Phyllis Kemper, and I'm thinking, 'Holy shit, Tracy was right after all!' Suddenly you come out with, 'No, the name you reacted to was Mark Taylor.'"

Taylor shook his head. "I'm telling you, I almost went through the floor. It was like someone changed the channel on me. It was like someone was gonna tap me on the shoulder and say, 'Smile, you're on Candid Camera.'" Taylor shook his head again. "I tell you, I never saw anything like it."

"But you knew it all along," Tracy said. "Last night, when you had us make up the list. Didn't you?"

Steve sighed. He hefted the beer and took a swig. "I had it in mind. But you're the one who gave it to me. With that question about why did Bradshaw come to the office. And then mentioning the phone calls. That was the key, of course. He didn't come to *my* office, he came to Mark Taylor's office."

"What?" Taylor said.

"Well, he didn't, but that's where he was headed. He had Margaret Millburn trace the license number, he looked up the Taylor Detective Agency, and he was on his way to get you."

"Then why didn't he?"

"Callboard in the lobby. He looked at the callboard to get your room number, and right under Mark Taylor, on the bottom of the callboard was Steve Winslow. Kemper had already told him I was his lawyer. He knew private detectives don't work on their own, somebody hires them, so he figured it was me. That was the leap of logic, and it was one that Bradshaw could easily make. And that's why he came to me."

"And on the strength of that, you figured Margaret Millburn killed him?" Tracy said.

"I figured it was a good shot. See, her story didn't fit in with anyone's version of what happened. Or rather, my interpretation of their stories. Or lack of them, in Marilyn Harding's case. I knew something was wrong, but I couldn't figure it out. The reason I couldn't figure it out was I'd made a mistake in logic."

"Really?" Taylor said. "What was that?"

"Douglas Kemper's story was that he got there before Marilyn Harding and found Bradshaw dead. I knew that was a lie. I knew he'd made that up to protect Marilyn. I figured he'd got there second. And, of course, he had.

"It was Marilyn Harding's silence I misread. I figured Marilyn

Harding was keeping quiet because *she* believed Douglas Kemper had got there first. In other words, because she walked in and found Bradshaw dead.

"But I was wrong. I had it backwards. What was making her hysterical was that she found Bradshaw *alive.* She called on him, told him she didn't have the money, he was abusive, threatened her, and she got out. Bradshaw was *alive* when she left. That's the thing Marilyn was trying to conceal.

"You can see how it looked to her. As soon as she heard Bradshaw was dead, she figured Douglas Kemper arrived right after she left, had an argument with Bradshaw, and killed him. See, the cops had the time of death pinned down so well that if Bradshaw was alive when she left, then Douglas Kemper must have killed him. Marilyn figured her statement that Bradshaw was alive when she left would crucify Kemper. And that's why she kept quiet."

"You lost me," Tracy said. "How does all of that point to Margaret Milburn?"

Steve took another sip of beer. "I had the benefit of hearing Douglas Kemper's story. And most of it was bullshit, but some of it wasn't. Some of it I believed. And the part that I believed was the fact that he walked in there and found Bradshaw dead. Cause that's the way it made sense from his point of view. He came second, he walked in there and found Bradshaw dead, and therefore he thought Marilyn had killed him, and that's why he was claiming he came first.

"Now, if that was true, Margaret Millburn's story didn't fit at all. And once you answer the key question, why did Bradshaw come to my office, the answer is Margaret Millburn. Which means Margaret Millburn knew Bradshaw well and is lying up and down the board. Once you realize that and stop taking her phone call to the police at face value, the whole thing is obvious."

"So Phyllis Kemper had nothing to do with it," Mark said. "She was just a red herring to throw the witness off the track."

"She had nothing to do with the Bradshaw murder," Steve said. "I'm sure she's the one who hired Miltner. And the one who killed Phillip Harding too.

"You can see what happened. Here's Phyllis Kemper, a cold, mousy, repressed woman, living in her stepsister's shadow. The only thing she'd got going for her is Douglas Kemper. And then she starts to lose him too. To her stepsister. So she snaps. She cracks up. She frames Marilyn for the murder of her father. But it doesn't come off. The doctor blows the diagnosis and calls it a natural death. She waits for something to happen, but nothing does. So she forces the game. She hires private detectives, hoping to get the dirt on Marilyn and her husband. I don't know what she expected to do with it, whether she was going to throw it in Marilyn's face, or throw it in her husband's, or what. I suspect by that time *she* wasn't that clear on what she wanted to do.

"But she doesn't catch Marilyn and hubby going to a hotel. She gets something else. She finds Marilyn is calling on a mysterious gentleman named David C. Bradshaw under circumstances that can only be shady. Jackpot. She phones an anonymous tip to the cops to get Phillip Harding's body exhumed. Arsenic is found. Now, if Bradshaw hadn't been murdered, I'm sure there would have been another anonymous tip to the cops telling them to check with Miltner's Detective Agency concerning Marilyn's movements. They would have found out that Marilyn had been calling on Bradshaw, and then jumped to the conclusion that Bradshaw was blackmailing her. That would have put Marilyn in the embarrassing position of having to prove that Bradshaw wasn't blackmailing her over the murder of her father—as the police actually figured—but over something else.

"But that didn't happen, because something better did—from Phyllis's point of view, anyway. Bradshaw got killed, and Marilyn got the blame. It was beautiful. She didn't have to do anything. Just sit back and let nature take its course. Which would have happened if we hadn't got lucky."

There was a knock on the door. Tracy got up and opened it. Fitzpatrick came in, grinning from ear to ear and carrying a bottle of champagne and a folded newspaper.

"So," he said. "Beer. I might have known. Suppose it would hurt your amateur standing to join me in some champagne?"

"Well, Fitzpatrick," Steve said. "You're feeling a little better, I see."

"I'll say. You seen the paper? The *Daily News* got out an extra."

Fitzpatrick flipped the paper open and held it up. The headline read: "COURTROOM CONFESSION: LAWYER TRAPS WITNESS."

"And not a quote from you in it," Fitzpatrick said. "It's all, 'Fitzpatrick, speaking for the defense team, stated . . . .' I tell you, I never saw an attorney leave court so fast after a trial. What's the matter, you camera shy?"

"I've never been much good with the press," Steve said. "I figured public relations was a little more in your line. So what did you tell 'em?"

"Whatever they wanted to hear. Of course, I didn't know the answers, so I made 'em up. I figured it didn't matter, right?"

"Right. What did they ask you?"

"Did you really compare Margaret Millburn's fingerprints, or was that just a trick? I told 'em, hell no, you were bluffing. You were weren't you?"

"Yeah. What else?"

"Did you have any hard evidence that Bradshaw and Millburn were partners? Was he really playing around with another woman? I told 'em, hell no, it was all bullshit off the top of your head."

"They like that answer?"

"They ate it up." Fitzpatrick chuckled. "Christ, I feel good. This morning I didn't want to talk to anybody, I just wanted to disappear. This afternoon I'm ready to have 'Odd Couple' T-shirts made up and wear 'em to the office. I mean, what a relief."

"That's fine," Steve said. "But we've still got the murder of Phillip Harding to contend with if they decide to push the charge."

Fitzpatrick shook his head. "Not any more."

"What?"

"You ran out so fast you missed all the action. Phyllis Kemper broke. I don't mean she admitted anything. She just cracked up. Snapped. Went off the deep end. Right after you left. They're taking Margaret Millburn into custody and releasing Marilyn Harding. And Phyllis Kemper stands up and says, 'No, no, you can't do that! She didn't do it! She didn't kill him! Marilyn did it! Marilyn's the one! Marilyn! Marilyn!' Then she gets louder and louder and more and more hysterical, screaming and crying about how it was Marilyn and how it wasn't fair."

Fitzpatrick shrugged. "Now it's not an admission, it's not a confession, it's not really anything. It certainly doesn't prove Phyllis killed Phillip Harding. But after all that, and after what you told Dirkson, there's not a snowball's chance in hell they're gonna prosecute Marilyn on the charge."

"That might well be, Fitzpatrick, but it still might be a good idea to get Marilyn to give you a substantial retainer to defend her in the event the situation should arise."

"Me?" Fitzpatrick said. "What about you?"

"She's your client now," Steve said. "As far as I'm concerned, my services to Marilyn Harding are finished. Now, I'll settle up with Douglas Kemper myself. But you might tell Marilyn my fee for my services to her is a hundred thousand dollars. In case she thinks that's excessive, you might explain to her why it's actually dirt cheap."

"I'm sure there'll be no problem," Fitzpatrick said. "But why are you cutting yourself off now? You suggested I get a provisional retainer. I'm sure you could get one too."

"I don't want it."

Fitzpatrick frowned. "Why?"

Steve sighed. "Because life isn't a storybook and you don't get happy endings. Oh you try. I mean, you're in here with your champagne, and you're so happy because we got our clients off. Well, I'm happy too. They didn't do it, so they should have got off, and everyone likes to win. But happy endings?" Steve grimaced and shook his head. "You see, I don't like our clients much. They're spoiled, rich kids. Self-centered, egotistical, playing their little games. Sure, they're cleared and Phyllis is discredited, and now Doug can divorce her and he and Marilyn can live happily ever after. And am I really supposed to care?

"No, the only one I really feel sorry for is Phyllis Kemper, and she's probably a murderer. But think about her. Her mother marries into money, dies, and leaves her there, a poor relation in a rich man's home. Then Douglas Kemper marries her, probably for her money. And there she is, the ugly duckling that failed to become a swan, in over her head and playing in the fast lane with people who are out of her league. Yeah, she probably killed Phillip Harding, but if so, it was her husband and stepsister that drove her to it.

"But, you know, I'll bet she can't be convicted of it. Even if they should get enough evidence against her—which they may—after her post-trial performance this afternoon, I'll bet there isn't an attorney in the world who couldn't get her off—not guilty by reason of insanity.

"Which kind of mucks up your happy ending. I don't know the law, Fitzpatrick. In New York State can you divorce a woman who's been declared legally insane?"

"I don't know," Fitzpatrick said, "I'd have to look it up."

"It's an interesting idea," Steve said. "Wouldn't it be the crowning irony if Phyllis Kemper got tried for killing Phillip Harding, was proven to be legally insane and then Marilyn and Dougie could live happily ever after, except for the fact that it screwed him out of his divorce?"

Fitzpatrick chuckled and shook his head. "You're a cockeyed moralist, you know it? You'll pardon me if I don't see it that way."

"Hey," Steve said, "it's difference of opinion that makes horse races. And that makes us the 'Odd Couple,' Fitzpatrick."

"Right," Fitzpatrick said. "Though I doubt if we'll be handling another case together again soon." He grinned. "Don't take that the wrong way. It certainly was an experience. Well, I just stopped by to fill you in. I got another shindig down at my office to get to. I have a feeling I'm a bit of a celebrity down there now."

Fitzpatrick shook Steve's hand, grinned and bowed himself out.

"There goes a happy man," Steve said.

"Well, can you blame him?" Taylor said. "Yesterday he was thinking about misconduct charges, public ridicule and disbarment. Today he just won a murder case."

"So did we," Steve said. He grinned. "Don't let me bring you down, folks. I don't care for my clients much, but it sure feels good to win."

Steve heaved himself up out of his chair. "Well gang, it's been nice talking to you, but I'm getting out of here before some enterprising reporter figures out this is where we hang out."

Steve nodded to Mark Taylor. "Mark, I'll see you tomorrow."

He turned to Tracy Garvin. "Tracy, it's been real nice working with you. I wish you the best of luck. Do keep in touch."

Tracy stared at him. "What?"

"Yeah," Steve said. "You probably thought I was too busy to notice, but I don't mean to be an inconsiderate employer, and I realize your two weeks are up."

Tracy's face fell. "Oh."

"You got another job lined up yet?" Steve said. "No one's called yet for a reference."

"Steve . . ."

"Of course, I haven't found a replacement yet either. I've been rather busy. But I'm sure I can get someone from a temporary agency."

Tracy took off her glasses, folded them, and looked at him in exasperation. "Damn it," she said.

Steve grinned. "Of course, on the other hand, if you should change your mind and want to stick around." He chuckled and jerked his thumb at the newspaper Fitzpatrick had left lying on his desk. "It looks like I just might have a law practice after all."